# The Strap

by

## William Blackwell

I0561314

Cover Designed by Telemachus Press, LLC
Published by Telemachus Press, LLC
Paperback ISBN: 978-1-997835-02-8
Version 2016.12.19

## Acknowledgements

Heartfelt thanks to my loyal and supportive readers, friends and family, the hardworking staff at Telemachus Press, and my editor. Special thanks to the Government of Prince Edward Island for it financial support.

*To all the victims of the strap*

*We are visitors on this planet. We are here for ninety or one hundred years at the very most. During that period, we must try to do something good, something useful with our lives. If you contribute to other people's happiness, you will find the true goal, the true meaning of life.*

–The Dalai Lama

# The Strap

# PROLOGUE

The first time Gray Eagleson got the strap was the worst. He remembered it as if it had happened yesterday—the pain, the humiliation, the tears.

He was in third grade.

Art teacher Reginald Butterworth had told students to mold the Plasticine into whatever form they fancied. They had a half hour to create something. Gray went to work, molding his favorite reptile—the snake. He didn't know why he liked the snake so much—his friends said it was a disgusting image.

But he didn't care. He wanted to create a ferocious anaconda—the king of the boa-constrictors.

Reginald, a military-style disciplinarian, insisted on obedience. When he rang the little bell on his desk, everyone had to stop what they were doing and be silent.

But Gray got so lost in his creation he didn't hear the bell. He was still molding the red eye of the snake when he realized the class had grown quiet and all eyes were staring at him.

He cast a frightened gaze at Reginald, a stalky man with neatly-cropped black hair. Reginald was red-faced, his eyes narrowed to slits.

"When I ring this bell, it means stop," Reginald said. "You know that. And I know what you're doing. You're trying to undermine my authority."

Feeling his face redden, Gray said: "I'm sorry. I didn't hear the bell."

But it was too late.

The teacher stomped to Gray's desk, grabbed him roughly by the arm, and dragged him to the front of the class. He bent Gray over the side of his desk and said: "I'll teach you respect for authority. One day you'll thank me."

He opened a desk drawer, produced a black leather steel-tipped strap and commenced the punishment. Tears streaming down his flushed and contorted face, Gray shrieked in pain as Reginald lashed him one, two, three, four, five, six times in the ass.

Young and impressionable eyes stared in shock.

To this day, Gray thought he would never forget the strap ... could never forget it.

# Chapter One

"Forget Ecuador. Why the hell would you want to go there? All I hear about Ecuador is human rights violations, drugs, kidnapping and murder."

"Have you ever been to Ecuador?" Gray asked.

"No," Derrick Richmond said, stroking a two-day facial scruff and eyeballing an attractive waitress.

"Well, how the hell would you know? Do you know International Living rates Ecuador the number one retirement destination in the world?"

"No, I didn't. What is International Living, anyway?"

"It's a web-based magazine that helps people live and retire overseas. They say Ecuador is one of the cheapest retirement countries in the world. The infrastructure is good, education standards are high, politics stable, good healthcare, government incentives for older retirees—all kinds of things. Not to mention the biodiversity. Did you know Ecuador has more plant and animal life per square mile than any other country in the world?"

"No," Derrick said, sounding unconvinced. "Did you hear the story of Sandra Chase?"

Gray wondered where this was going. He wanted this vacation, needed it badly, and he didn't want to listen to any more negativity raining on his parade; he would likely see his fair share of downpours when he arrived in the Amazon jungle. "Who's that?"

"A woman accused of smuggling cocaine who was wrongfully imprisoned in Quito. She lived in awful conditions for twenty-two months before her daughter was finally able to get a US politician to pressure Ecuadorian officials and have her released on humanitarian grounds. She was robbed and beaten while in jail. She claimed she never smuggled drugs—hates drugs."

"Humanitarian grounds?"

"Apparently she suffered from a skin and organ disease. She couldn't get proper medical care in prison."

Gray digested the information while he lifted his mug of draft beer and took a long swig, the steady hum of conversation and occasional laughter doing little to lift his sinking spirits. His parade *was* getting rained on. Hell, Derrick was delivering a monsoon blast. He stared at the half-full mug of Alexander Keith's Pale Ale. *Keep your spirits up. Glass half full. Glass half full.*

The shapely black-haired waitress returned and Derrick's eyes widened. Derrick smiled at Cassandra and held up an empty mug. "One more for me—and my friend."

Gray was about to decline but changed his mind. He nodded. He just couldn't say no to the goddess in black, posing alluringly—at least not quite yet, anyway. Cassandra smiled a million-dollar smile, spun around, and headed to the bar, expertly weaving her tray through the throngs of people munching on nine-cent chicken wings and socializing.

"I should go," Gray said, wondering why he had to go home anyway.

"Go. What are you talking about? It's wing-nut night. All the babes come out." Derrick waved a beefy paw around the richly furnished and elegantly renovated bar. Sure enough, there were plenty of attractive woman in the mix. "And it's only six. It's barely evening, for fuck sakes."

It might be barely evening, Gray thought, but already the black curtain of night had stolen away the day, a testament to the time of year and place: November 10th, 2012, Calgary, Alberta. Night came early once summer disappeared, and the short fall season had stripped trees of their leafy greenery. This year was no exception. If anything, Old Man Winter had come prematurely, with frigid minus twenty-two degree Celsius temperatures and a foot of snow, all within the last forty-eight hours. Gray stared out through the wall of tinted glass at the barely-visible snowflakes illuminated by the glowing streetlights lazily drifting to the ground. He hated winter, hated the cold. *When will this shit let up?*

He scanned the animated patrons and eventually settled on Derrick, a stunted version of The Incredible Hulk. And a sarcastic one at that. "I can tell you one thing," Gray said. "Well, actually, I can tell you more than one thing. But I'll tell you this. You're going to be freezing your ass off while I'm kicking back in the hot sun in a hammock with an Ecuadorian hottie watching the ocean waves lazily lap the sandy shoreline."

"What, you think you're a fuckin' poet or something?"

"I'm just saying."

"I know what you're just saying." Derrick's features softened. "Listen buddy, I hope you do have a good time. I hope you fuck your brains out with a beautiful, big-titted hottie. All I'm saying is be careful. Read the travel advisories before you go. Don't do anything stupid. Keep your head up."

"Which one?"

Derrick tilted his mug back, spewing a mouthful of beer into the mug, wiping foam dribble from his chin. Then he burst out laughing.

Gray laughed, probably more at Derrick's beer shower than his own joke. The laughter subsided.

Derrick coughed and cleared his throat as a few heads turned in their direction. Derrick stared them down menacingly, and their heads quickly turned to whatever it was that had previously engaged them.

"Both heads," he said finally. "Keep both heads up."

"I don't know if that's possible," Gray said. "You know how it goes. If I'm thinking with the little head, it could mean that the big head is not exactly up and working. And, if I'm thinking with the big head, that could mean the little head, or littler head, might be down. You know what I ..."

"Shut the fuck up already, will you," Derrick said, grinning. "You know what I mean."

"I'll be careful, man. I'm not exactly a rookie traveler, you know. I've been doing a little research already. Joined Latin American Cupid to try and line up a travel companion, and started reading Lonely Planet."

"Where you plan on going?"

"Well, I fly into Quito."

"Say hello to Sandra's Italian friend in prison. I hear he's still incarcerated on the cocaine rap."

"Yeah right, I'll smuggle some coke in to him."

"He'd be eternally grateful."

"And I'd be eternally incarcerated."

"Fuckin' right."

"No, seriously, I've been reading about this sleepy little village on the Costa Del Sol called Canoa. It's small and apparently has awesome beaches, a cool nightlife scene, and cheap digs right on the beach."

"How cheap is cheap?"

"Around fifteen, twenty bucks a night, something like that. And you can eat out for a couple dollars—maybe five if you upgrade your standard."

"Yeah, but not in any restaurant with class."

"Who needs that pretentious bullshit anyway? I'm on a budget."

"How much do you plan on spending for six weeks?"

"My flight was free on air miles points. Just the hundred and fifty taxes. And I've budgeted two thousand for trip expenditures."

"That's cheap for six weeks. You'd spend more than that here."

"Tell me about it."

Cassandra returned with a sexy smile and two more pints. Derrick ogled her ample cleavage and athletically-carved butt as she left.

They fell silent for a moment, listening to cheerful conversations, sipping beer and people-watching. Gray noticed an attractive middle-aged blond woman eyeballing him, made brief eye contact and then looked away. He knew it was rude to stare for too long. Didn't the flirt protocol call for only brief intermittent eye contact? He thought so, but he didn't really know; he wasn't very good at any of it.

It wasn't that he was bad looking. At forty-five, he looked much younger than his years. He stood a tad over six feet and weighed a trim one hundred and eighty pounds. His crew-cut brown hair, soft features and penetrating green eyes could still turn the odd head. With his narrow black-rimmed glasses, he had the appearance of a combination jock-nerd, although in reality he was far from either.

He could attract women all right, but it was his sarcasm that would often be misinterpreted, his humor often misunderstood. Not that he meant anything nasty, but it often came off that way.

A few months back, sitting in a bar, pleasantly numb from alcohol, he had been making good inroads with an attractive rather gothic-looking thirty-something dark-haired woman. Things had been light, pleasant and enjoyable until they began a discussion about marriage. The woman, Josie, said she was indifferent to the institution of marriage, echoing a sentiment about the strong bond of love being much more important than any piece of paper.

"According to DH Lawrence, marriage is the death of experience," Gray had said, meaning the line sarcastically rather than a statement of fact.

Josie didn't see it that way. Her face grew dark, the pleasant smile quickly replaced by a grimace. Tossing her gin and tonic on the rocks in his face (he would have preferred it neat), she stood up, declared, "What the fuck do you know about marriage?" and stormed out of the bar, leaving Gray wiping his face and shirt with a napkin to the amusement of patrons.

He didn't know, probably would never know, but he supposed most women harbored a secret desire to be married even though many served up rhetoric saying quite the opposite. Either way, it was a conundrum he couldn't solve right now.

The other conundrum he couldn't solve at the moment was working up the confidence to approach the attractive blonde periodically making flirtatious eye contact. He told himself the reason was that he was leaving for Ecuador in less than a month, and didn't want to start anything before he left. But, if he had to be completely honest, that was a lie. Truth be told, he hadn't had intimate contact with a woman in so long his confidence was at an all-time low. It didn't help matters, due to city budget cut-backs, that he had just been laid off from his job as a public relations officer with city hall. He was out of work, rapidly running out of money and, along with his confidence, his self-esteem was on a downward spiral, if not in complete and rapid free-fall mode.

But at least he had Latin American Cupid. He had completed a profile, posted a photo, indicated an interest in women living in Ecuador, and had about six leads. Now it was just a matter of following them up, although he had doubts about finding relationship material there.

"Tell me about this Cupid dating thing," Derrick said. "Have you talked to anyone?"

"A few e-mails and just last night one short Instant Messaging conversation with a woman from Reston, Virginia."

"Where did that go?"

"I got suspicious when she didn't ask very many questions during the IM. It was all about trying to get me to give up my Yahoo IM account so she could contact me there and exchange photos. I've never used Yahoo IM. I gave her a Yahoo e-mail address. She said she'd meet me there and I haven't bothered checking the account. I think she's a hooker or an internet pornographer looking for money."

"That's the thing with internet dating. You never know what you're getting yourself into, and there are so many women who use the net just to steer people to their paid sex or porn services."

"Not to mention the sexual predators who use them to target unsuspecting women, some of them underage."

"Well, by the same token, you better watch who you hook up with in Ecuador. And don't have any chick meeting you at the airport or give out your arrival time or anything like that. You could be walking right into extortion or a kidnapping trap."

Gray shook his head. He had already thought of that. He might be low on a lot of things right now, but not brains.

At least, that's what he hoped.

# Chapter Two

*I hope I'm not there. I'm not there. I'm here at home.* But as Gray opened his eyes a second time and stared at the blinding sunshine beaming through the slightly-ajar door, he realized with an all-encompassing wave of despair he wasn't in his comfortable suburban Woodlands bungalow. No. He had seen that bright sunlit view many times before, along with the yellow wall, the brown door, the white floor tile and the lone palm tree outside, gently swaying in the soft breeze.

He was in Rurrenabaque, a small Amazon jungle town in northern Bolivia. He was trapped in his hotel suite bed, staring daily at the peek-a-boo view from the open door, listening to the unsteady drone of the small electric fan that provided faint relief from the suffocating afternoon jungle heat. Oh, he could certainly get up, walk outside to the shared bathroom to answer Mother Nature's call, but that was about all he could do.

He had travelled eighteen hours by rickety bus from LaPaz and arrived at the small town on the shores of River Beni. The first decision he had made, a disastrous one, was to dine at a shack-like riverfront restaurant. Walking down the dirt road with his travelling companion, Lola, whom he had met in LaPaz, it might have occurred to him that the small gutters lining the sides of the narrow dirt road carried raw sewage directly into the river. He smelled it, saw it, but didn't register its deadly potential.

Travel-weary from the long and grueling bus ride, and starving, he didn't give it a second thought. He and Lola sat down, had a few drinks, conversed in Spanish and dined on grilled catfish. He would probably never know what kind of bacteria the fish had been contaminated with, or if some other potentially lethal bacteria from the kitchen like E. coli had invaded his body, but he knew, a few weeks later, he was too weak to move very far.

A river of diarrhea runs through it; or more accurately, through Gray. Every few minutes saw him racing outside to the brick outhouse where he would squat and shit brown and yellow-colored liquid before returning to his main-floor room with a view of the gently swaying palm tree.

And if it wasn't for the nurturing of Lola (she was a doctor. How lucky was that?), Gray figured he might well be dead by now. During those first weeks of intense fever and vomiting, it was she who had ventured to the local medical clinic, returning with medicines, specialized rehydration fluids containing necessary electrolytes, salts and minerals, and began nursing Gray back to health.

He twisted in the bed, accidentally poking one of his protruding ribs in the process. During his illness, he had shed thirty pounds and was but a gaunt shadow of his former self. He looked more like a man stricken with AIDS than a man recovering from food poisoning, if that was indeed what he had. The wheels of the portable intravenous apparatus squeaked along the tile floor. He stopped and stared as it tugged at the needle taped to his forearm. He had almost pulled it out. Again. Although he was on a diet of oatmeal and bananas, he often forgot about the IV of rehydration fluids. In the middle of the night he had occasionally ripped it clean out of his arm, and Lola would wake and carefully replace it.

An angel from heaven. But where was she now, and why had he returned? Had he merely hallucinated his recovery? He thought he had suffered for six weeks before finally becoming healthy enough to leave his jungle prison, albeit thirty pounds lighter and a hell of a lot weaker. But maybe it was merely the product of a fever-induced hallucination and he had been here all along.

Or had he died and this was his hell?

Panic knotted his stomach, which had already begun to rumble, signaling another trip to the outhouse. He called out: "Lola ... Lola ... where are you?"

He heard no sound, but for the distant and unmistakable cawing of an Amazon parrot. And the incessant, rumbling drone of the portable fan, like the muted thumping of distant helicopter rotors.

The knot in his stomach cinched tighter and Gray winced. He could feel it coming. The river of diarrhea was running through him again. He grabbed the IV pole and staggered out of bed as his vision suddenly blurred and the small yellow room grew hazy, dark and distorted.

He stumbled into the wall, steadied himself with a hand, and took a few deep breaths while his vision slowly cleared.

When the indistinct reality grew less hazy, he advanced to the door, and yanked it open. It creaked loudly. He bumped into the wall and shielded his eyes from the blinding sunlight for a second before stepping out onto the stone pathway that wound through the small garden toward the brick outhouse.

Lola appeared on the dirt road in front of the small hotel. Her brown eyes were sad, her shoulder-length black hair disheveled. A lone teardrop on her cheek caught a glint of the intense afternoon sunshine and sparkled. She stared at Gray in disbelief.

Gray hobbled down the uneven path toward the outhouse. He could feel his bowels loosening and knew he would be unable to control it. He reached the outhouse, pulled open the wooden door and stopped, mystified by Lola's expression. "What's wrong?"

Lola brushed away the tear and watched him, jaw-dropped and wide-eyed. "What are you doing out of bed?" she asked in Spanish.

"I have to ... you know, go."

"You don't do that anymore."

"What do you mean?" he asked, no longer able to control the impending diarrhea torrent. He closed the door behind him and quickly squatted on the cracked plastic toilet seat. It pinched his ass and he flinched as his bowels loosened and thrust forth a projectile blast of liquid with a loud splash.

He drew in a few deep breaths as the diarrhea and accompanying wind from his anus abruptly subsided. Sitting in blackness with the putrid stench of his bowel movement—a few tiny rays of sunshine painting misty white lines through cracks in the wooden door—he asked: "Lola, why don't I do that anymore?"

The Amazon parrot cawed, eerily punctuating her words.

"You're dead."

# Chapter Three

"I'm not dead ... I'm not dead," Gray shouted as he swam up from the nightmare's terror and realized he was at home in bed in the dead of winter. His heart pounding in his chest, he leaped out of bed, glancing at the bedside clock. It was only 6:36 am, about an hour before his biological clock would usually wake him.

He quickly changed out of his sweat-soaked t-shirt and underwear. He glanced through the bamboo curtain of his bedroom window and noticed it was still very dark outside, but for the diffused yellow rays of a streetlight casting a faint glow through the small cracks in the window covering. A white blanket of snow covered the deathly quiet and frigid cul-de-sac.

He threw on a housecoat, flicked the bedroom light on and went into the kitchen, draining a glass of cold water and relieving himself before returning to bed. A wave of memories from the Bolivian trip five years ago washed through his mind and he reminded himself how lucky he had been to survive it. He lay on the bed and stared at the ceiling as he contemplated the ambitious trek, listening to his thumping heartbeat gradually return to normal.

Lola. She was the angel who had saved his life. If it hadn't been for her, he never would have made it out alive. He didn't have travel medical insurance, didn't have a set itinerary, and flew off the beaten path by the seat of his torn, tattered and multi-pocketed travel pants.

He recalled the trip.

He had started the adventure in Buenos Aires, Argentina, before hitchhiking a ride across the border into Chile in the back of a battered pick-up truck. Once there, he had spent a few nights in a hospedaje in Puerto Montt before traveling by various buses south to Vina Del Mar, finally arriving in Santiago, where he stayed for a few days before returning to Buenos Aires by first-class bus.

From there, he eventually boarded a series of buses, which amounted to over twenty-four hours of non-stop travel through rickety roads, switchback mountain passes, on route to LaPaz, Bolivia. Halfway through the grueling bus trip, he disembarked in a small poverty-stricken village at dusk and wandering aimlessly through dodgy and decrepit streets in search of a bus stop. Finding one, he entered the crowded ramshackle building. He was accosted by many locals pawing him with stumps where once hands had been (he had heard police amputated thieves' limbs but had never verified it). It was a macabre scene right out of a horror movie. Terrified, he had finally made his way to a ticket booth and in adequate Spanish managed to purchase a bus ticket to a destination a couple of hours just outside LaPaz.

He boarded the rickety bus along with locals transporting chickens, hens, dogs and other supplies. It stank of acrid body odor and foul animal smells. The bus bounced through the night to a small village bus station, where he bought a bus ticket to LaPaz and waited, sick to his stomach, watching indigenous Indians street-side stir a vat of broth, the odd bone occasionally washing to the surface.

By the time he climbed aboard the bus which would take him to LaPaz, he was physically and mentally spent, and wondered why he had decided on such a grueling journey without factoring in travel time and the enormous poverty and culture shock that assaulted his senses at almost every turn.

On the last leg of the journey, sitting near the back of the bus, he focused on a small television screen at the front that was playing a melodramatic love story in Spanish. The volume was set to a level irritatingly low enough to barely hear, but not quite loud enough to decipher the words; exacerbated by the engine and road noise, foreign smells, animated conversations. But, concentrating on that little screen, Gray believed, was the only thing he could do that would distract him from his mental and physical pain. He was hungry but too sick to eat and had a pounding headache, the result of riding on rickety buses that bounced over rocky, switchback mountain roads. And he was sleep-deprived.

He remembered the feeling of elation when that bus finally went from bumpy gravel to pavement. He knew in an hour or so he would arrive in LaPaz, the capital city built on steep hills 11,975 feet above sea level. The epic journey was just starting to become too overwhelming—Gray had drifted into a mild hallucinogenic state—when the bus stopped momentarily and more passengers boarded.

A colorfully-dressed indigenous Altiplano Indian woman sat down beside him, calm, peaceful and perfectly composed. Gray thought making conversation with her would take his mind off his pounding headache and knotting stomach pain.

"Are you heading to LaPaz?" he asked, forcing a smile. He was chalk-white.

She smiled. "The Altiplano, just above LaPaz."

He had heard about the Altiplano and knew many indigenous Indians lived there. He had also heard it had many dodgy, poverty-stricken and dangerous areas. It was certainly not the place for a strung-out gringo to be aimlessly wandering around. He may as well paint a bulls-eye on his back and be done with it.

"Where did you start your journey?" Gray asked.

"In Buenos Aires."

"Non-stop?"

"Only stopped for a few hours to visit some friends."

*Pitiful*, he thought. He, who fancied himself a rugged and seasoned traveler, was completely spent, sitting beside a woman probably twice his age who had just completed the same journey in about the same amount of time. But she was a picture of composure. Unlike Gray, she looked perfectly refreshed, well-rested and alert.

Needless to say, the woman inspired Gray to a semi-state of alertness and calm, even entertained him with her lively conversation. And she went one step further. As the bus approached the Altiplano, Gray jumped up, believing the stop was LaPaz, and headed toward the exit door. Two young men quickly followed close behind him. The woman grabbed Gray by the arm. "You don't get off here. This is the Altiplano. LaPaz is the next stop."

The two men glared at the Indian woman as Gray stepped aside. The woman smiled at Gray as he sat down. "Next stop is yours. It's dangerous in the Altiplano for you." And she left.

Gray took a few deep breaths, realizing she had probably saved his life. The men were probably intending to rob him and do who knew what else.

When he finally arrived at the LaPaz bus station, altitude sickness had him in its debilitating grip. His eyes were bloodshot, his head pounding more violently and painfully than ever. He had a Lonely Planet map of a hotel he wanted to stay at about ten blocks from the bus station but wasn't sure in his state if he could find it.

He had heard the stories and watched the documentaries of how well-organized gangs of small kids would expertly attack tourists and locals alike and, using knives, would slice a victim's clothing to ribbons, leave him or her buck-naked in the middle of the street missing personal effects and money. The thieves were so adept with the blades they rarely injured their targets. The documentaries were specific to Peru, but he also knew the modus operandi extended to bands of thieves across the border into Bolivia.

That's why he wasn't entirely surprised when he stepped off the bus, took a few steps, glanced behind and noticed a gang of small boys rapidly closing the distance. He did the only thing he could do—run like hell.

A small lightweight backpack slung over his shoulder, he sprinted five blocks before finally stopping to catch his breath, realizing he couldn't see the kids anymore, although they had given chase; for how long he didn't know.

He finally found the hotel, checked into a modest room on the fifth floor and stayed there recovering from altitude sickness and travel fatigue for four days before even being physically able to venture out into the streets for anything other than to get aspirin, food and water.

After he had recovered and adjusted to the altitude and culture shock, he met Lola. After becoming intimately involved and spending a week getting to know a LaPaz that was friendly, rich in culture and history, they departed for Rurrenabque, stopping halfway down the treacherous tombstone-marked cliff-side road to spend a week in Coroico to enjoy life in a sub-tropical small village before finally venturing into the Amazon jungle to Rurrenabaque.

But Rurrenabaque had almost cost Gray his life. If it wasn't for Lola's tender loving care, he could have died. But in the horrific nightmare, she said he was dead. What did she mean? He was very much alive, if a little rattled. Was it a premonition dream, like he had experienced previously? He didn't know. But the dream felt damn real. And the dreams he had had previously—that had come true—felt as eerily real as the one he had just woken up from.

He shuddered as he rose from bed and pushed the worrisome thoughts from his mind. After making a pot of coffee, he carried a fresh cup into his office and decided to check e-mails. Maybe Latin American Cupid had produced some quality results. He opened the inbox to twelve women who were interested in him. He automatically ruled out four from Columbia—no point in chasing them if he wasn't planning a trip there anytime soon—and also ruled out six from the Dominican Republic. He knew only too well the types of Dominican women, who, like trolls, would be using any internet means possible to lure foreigners to their country with the promise of love. But, in most cases, unsuspecting men would eventually realize that once the money ran out, the love wouldn't be too far behind. And many Dominican women had a way of making money run out. He had first-hand experience with those kinds of predators.

But he had heard Ecuadorian women were different. That was Gray's experiment, using himself as the human guinea pig. He told himself—promised himself—he would keep an open mind to finding a soulmate in Ecuador.

He finally stopped and read Mary's profile, a thirty-six-year-old woman living in Esmeraldas, Ecuador. She had sent a form-letter e-mail saying nothing more than she was interested in him. Her profile described her as romantic, sweet and a dreamer. She had a PhD in something (her profile didn't say what) and worked in the travel and hospitality industry, which could mean anything. She occasionally drank, didn't smoke and had no religion. Her member overview read: *I am sincere and I do not like lies. I like a man that will respect me and want my only daughter. I'm seeking a faithful, loving and precise man that I be all in his life.*

Her profile picture showed a slim woman, long brown hair, with dark skin, smiling warmly while standing beside an artificial Christmas tree. The tree stood in the corner of a living room with yellow and red floral-patterned wallpaper on one wall. The adjoining white wall had a television on a small table, a pair of rabbit-ear antennas poking up from its fuzzy screen.

Gray realized Mary had also sent a message showing interest. He navigated to the inbox to read it. It was written in Spanish and said: *Hi honey. My name is Mary and I live in Ecuador in the province of Esmeraldas. I would love to meet you. With kisses, Mary.*

She had also left a private e-mail address.

*Honey? We don't even know each other and already I'm honey? With kisses? She's sending me kisses? What will she call me once she gets to know me? Asshole? Fuck face, maybe? And what will she send me once she gets to know me? A right cross? Straight left maybe? A knock-out sucker punch? Something I just don't see coming. Is that what she's setting me up for? The sucker punch? Or maybe it's just how they court? Those digs don't look that shit-hot. Maybe she's looking for a sugar daddy?*

He sighed. It was the nature of internet dating sites. You got the good, bad and ugly. And it was his mission to find a good woman. If he didn't want to take the time to weed out the predators, porn solicitors and gold diggers, he shouldn't be using Cupid.

But he couldn't help laughing at the notion of a gold digger. Since getting laid off from his city hall PR job just over two months ago, Gray's savings were dwindling fast. Many of his friends and former co-workers had said he was nuts for going on a six-week hiatus to Ecuador when he didn't even know where his next mortgage payment was coming from. As it was, he would be funding the Ecuadorian adventure on credit cards. Not very fiscally responsible, he knew, but he needed a break from the inherent stresses of North American society and the pursuit of the almighty dollar. Was his time more valuable sitting in an office or hanging out in the jungle? Did it matter, really?

He decided to pass on Mary and was just about to close his e-mail account when another message popped into the inbox. It was interest from a 29-year-old woman named Adriana Enrique from Guayaquil with an accompanying message. He scanned the photo before reading the profile summary. She had a slim body, olive-toned skin, soulful brown eyes, a playful smile and long, thick flowing black hair. *Not bad.*

He clicked to the profile: *I want a good relationship. I want someone I can trust who is respectful, sincere, tranquil with a sense of humor and loving. Someone who will take care of me, will accept me for who I am, but will also tell me of the areas that I might need improvement in. I want a companion who is a friend and lover, someone who can converse with me about anything on his mind. I want a serious relationship without lies, with fidelity, with someone who makes me feel really comfortable. I seek a relationship with a balanced equilibrium.*

*Hmm ... she's put some thought into that,* Gray thought, noticing she occasionally drank, didn't smoke, had no pets or kids, had a college education, and was also a Christian who enjoyed sports and recreation. He cut to the chase and opened the message: *Hi, how are you? I'm Adriana* ☺.

The message in its simplicity caught his attention. He noticed it had come in yesterday and wondered if she had already moved on to greener pastures. Although an internet dating newbie, he had learned that an instantaneous response is always best if one hopes to make contact. He quickly typed a message in Spanish: *Hi Adriana, how are you? Sorry I didn't respond to your message earlier. I'm going to visit your country in early December. Maybe we could have a coffee together or something? I would like to get to know you and your country. People tell me it's a beautiful country. Write to me please and we can talk. Thanks for your interest and sending me a message. Take care. Gray.*

Gray went to the kitchen for another coffee refill, cooked and ate breakfast and returned to his computer, anxious to see if Adriana had responded. He smiled when he saw another message from her. It had been over two years since his last relationship and the stirrings of desire and that often inexplicable emotion called love were already filling him with a euphoric high. He was giddy with emotion. *Don't be ridiculous. You're like a schoolboy. You don't even know her.*

But he anxiously read Adriana's response: *Hello. It would be a pleasure to have you in my country. It's very beautiful and the people are very friendly. The beaches are beautiful, the mountain ranges spectacular and The Oriente and Amazon jungle are incredible. The beaches in Esmeraldas are beautiful and our little gem, the Galapagos Islands are a paradise, teeming with many fascinating species of animals. If you want, here's my Skype contact info. Contact me if you use it. Kisses. Take care. Let's speak soon.*

Gray quickly re-read the message, cognizant of his heart thumping in his chest. He hadn't felt that kind of emotion in a long time. Without hesitation, he clicked open his Skype account and typed in Adriana's contact info. She instantly added him to her contacts and began an online chat. After the cursory greetings, she typed a question: *Is it really cold there now?*

What else was she going to ask? They didn't even know each other. After some small talk, or small type, it was she who initiated the Skype call. But Gray was relieving himself in the bathroom when the call came in, thinking he had time between messages to try and come up with something witty. When he returned to his computer, he noticed the missed call. With fluttering heart, he picked up his earpiece and called Adriana. The first conversation:

"How are you?" Gray asked.

Looking intently into the camera, she sat on a white plastic lawn chair in a small, modest bedroom, the shouts of children audible in the background. She was, Gray decided in an instant, a very attractive woman.

"I'm doing well. And you?"

"Great ... great." It wasn't quite true, but Gray knew nobody likes a whiner—especially on first impression. "I just thought I'd tell you this laptop is old and it doesn't have a camera. So I can see you, but you can't see me. Sorry, but it's the only computer I have Skype in."

By choice, Gray hadn't downloaded Skype into any of his other two computers, although both were equipped with cameras. He didn't consider himself unattractive, but he also knew he was pretty far from photogenic. More often than not, he photographed with silly or nervous expressions. He thought a camera would not do him justice, particularly a video camera. Besides, for Adriana to see him would also mean a little video screen would appear on his computer and he would see himself talking while also seeing a larger screen of Adriana talking. He found the idea disconcerting and annoying; constantly looking at your own image while talking to someone. He hated that almost as much as being in restaurants or bars with wall-to-wall mirrors. Thought it was the tackiest design scheme available to humankind.

"That's okay," Adriana said cheerfully, an infectious smile countenancing her warm features. "I'll just call you my invisible friend."

There was a pause and they both laughed. It instantly put Gray at ease and seemed to do the same for Adriana.

*Think of something smart to ask her.* "You live in Guayaquil?" *That's what her profile says, idiot.*

"Yes, I do."

"How do you like it?"

"Most of my family is here, so it's okay. I'm from Esmeraldas, though, and I much prefer it there."

"Do you live by yourself?"

"Mostly—but my brother and mother visit and stay with me sometimes."

"How many siblings do you have?"

"I have four brothers and six sisters."

"Wow ... big family."

"What can I say? My dad likes to ... you know ... different wives and girlfriends. All my family is working except for one of my brothers. He's lazy, you know. I think if you have a lot of kids you get one in every family."

"I think so."

They laughed.

Adriana went down the list of occupations of her family members but she rattled it off so fast Gray only caught three occupations. One brother was a schoolteacher, two were cops, and on and on it went. But Gray got stuck on the cop revelation. On one hand, that could be a good thing. On the other, he certainly wouldn't want to piss Adriana off on her turf with two cop brothers. He could well end up on the dark side of the dirt.

He asked about different areas of her country and she dutifully explained, even offering to be his tour guide, on his dime of course. A small red flag sprang up but Gray chucked it out of his head. On her income as a 911 dispatcher, she probably couldn't afford to do much traveling. But Ecuador was inexpensive, even if he had to foot the bill for two.

He was warming to the thought.

"Wow," Adriana said. "I don't even know you and I already trust you. But that's what the people of Esmeraldas are like—loyal and trustworthy."

"I'm a good guy. Honest and loyal to a fault."

"Who are you traveling with?"

"By myself."

"You're not going with any friends?"

"They can't make it."

"Do you live alone or with your wife?"

"Wife? I'm not married, don't have a girlfriend. Do you think I'd be talking to you now and hooked up on Cupid if I was married?" *She doesn't know me from Adam. How the hell does she know if I'm the kind of guy to commit infidelity or not? She had to ask. Give her a break. Obviously it's an issue with her. It was in her profile.*

"I'm sorry. I didn't mean anything by it."

It entered Gray's mind to ask if she had kids or a boyfriend but it disappeared as soon as the conversation moved on. They talked about possible destinations Gray might like to visit. Adriana offered to help him find a safe and affordable hotel in Guayaquil should he decide to visit her city.

"For sure I'd like to meet you," Gray said, becoming enamored with her easy smile and genuine laugh.

She promised to locate some affordable options and e-mail them to Gray. Gray glanced at his desk clock and suddenly realized he had been talking to Adriana for forty-nine minutes. Wow. The time had flown by. The conversation was smooth, easy and occasionally funny.

He didn't want to be rude. "Listen, we've been talking for a long time, and I'd love to talk to you more, but what time do you start work today?"

"At noon."

Gray quickly did the math. It was about a quarter past eleven Ecuador time. "I should let you go. And I want to get some work done too."

"Okay, but you can call me later if you like. I'd love to talk to you more."

"Me to. It was a pleasure meeting you. I hope we can meet when I arrive."

She smiled. "I'd like that very much. I get a month holiday starting in December. I'm supposed to go to New York to visit a girlfriend at the end of December but that depends on whether I get my visa approved or not."

*An attractive traveling companion for a month. What better way to see Ecuador and learn about its people and culture?* Gray liked the idea so much he was having a hard time controlling the powerful feeling of euphoria washing over him. A natural high. Wow. He had almost forgotten those emotions.

Adriana had begun rolling her long and beautiful hair into a ponytail during the last minutes of the conversation.

She blew him some kisses and said: "I send you kisses. I hope to hear from you soon. I hardly know you and already I like you."

Gray smiled ear-to-ear as he ended the call. *Wow! Thou asketh and thou receiveth. This is going to be an adventure to remember.*

# Chapter Four

"Just remember, most women who are on Latin American Cupid are there for material reasons, regardless of what they say," Derrick said later that afternoon in a bustling Starbucks coffee shop in a popular strip mall, Chinook Centre.

It dampened Gray's otherwise uplifted spirits, but simultaneously ushered forth a reality check. Did he really think he could meet a woman from a comparatively impoverished country like Ecuador who would be looking for anything more than to better her financial position? Didn't Adriana mention having to work for twenty years to afford to be able to visit Thailand, a country she eagerly wanted to explore? Didn't she also say she would be happy to be his tour guide—on his dollar? Maybe he had been blindsided by her demure beauty, easy and infectious smile and playful sense of humor. But, just because most women on Latin American Cupid might be looking for a way out of their struggling existence, did that make them all the same? Probably not—but with Adriana, there were some indicators that perhaps Gray had conveniently ignored.

The dating game could be an emotional roller-coaster at the best of times. And he didn't know if right now he had the emotional strength to climb aboard that rapidly undulating amusement-park ride. It might career off the tracks and slam him face-first into the pavement with serious and long-lasting injuries and scars; shattering his already fragile and low confidence level.

*Ah, to hell with it.* "Maybe so, but that doesn't mean they're all like that. That would be a sweeping generalization. And anyway, the action is the juice. I won't know what's at the end of the path unless I take it."

"The action is the juice?" Derrick said, eyeballing a shapely brunette who was adding condiments to a designer coffee. "What the fuck does that mean?"

"It means it's the thrill of the ride, not necessarily the result that matters. Live for today. I heard the line in a movie once but can't for the life of me remember the movie or who said it."

"Seems like rather twisted logic in this case."

"Maybe it is, maybe it isn't," Gray said, suddenly remembering at least the context of the quote. It was a bank robber commenting about why he was willing to accept the next dangerous job assignment even though the FBI was hot on his tail. *The action is the juice, that's why, never mind the risks.* "But it's my logic. I'm going to run with it. Besides, if I have a shot at a successful relationship, why not take it?"

"Just be careful," Derrick said. It was easy for him to say. A recently-married oil and gas engineer, the proud owner of a new house with a white picket fence, half a dozen income-producing revenue properties, a debt-free life. The only thing Derrick needed to complete the stereotype would be for his wife Sandy to pop out a bambino or two. His philandering days were over. He was in love. But he couldn't stop his wandering eyes—visual infidelity.

"I will. You've told me that already."

"Well, I'm telling you again. I don't want to see you wind up dead."

*You're dead,* Gray heard Lola say, and the haunting image of her teary-eyed face flashed through his mind. He winced, struggling to push the chilling image away. *Shit. My life isn't getting any easier.*

He was right about that. Prior to meeting Derrick, he had received two phone calls from bill collectors. A Rogers rep had called, saying his cell phone bill was a month overdue. His insurance broker had called, telling him he had missed a payment on his home insurance. The well had run dry. He was surfing the credit card wave, knowing full well that tumultuous swell would eventually send him crashing into a wall. It wasn't a question of if he would hit the wall, it was when. Borrowing from Peter to pay Paul was a proposition that had a clearly-defined and finite limit when you were unemployed. He only hoped he would be able to arrive safely home from Ecuador and find another job before he crashed violently into that beckoning wall of debt.

"I'll be okay," Gray said weakly, trying to think of a less disturbing topic.

But Derrick, unwittingly or not, wouldn't let him. "Don't you think you should be putting out some feelers for jobs before you leave?"

Gray had to admit, since his untimely dismissal, he hadn't looked for work. He had focused on planning his Ecuadorian adventure, believing it would pull him out of his funk so he would be in a better mind frame to find a new job on his return. But do nothing? It was hard to play the victim when you did nothing to try and change the hand you had been dealt. "I suppose you're right."

Gray suspected this conversation was leading somewhere. Derrick wasn't the kind of person to throw things like that out there unless he had a reason.

"I might be able to help you at least for the short term." Derrick's demeanor darkened.

Gray was open to suggestions. "What do you have in mind?"

Worry crinkled Derrick's brow. "You know my duplex in Forest Lawn?"

Gray nodded, glancing at the flirtatious blonde by the window. She smiled and he diverted his gaze to Derrick. He wasn't very good at the flirt game anymore. It brought back too many bad memories.

"Well, I had that property in the hands of a property management company and they royally fucked it up."

Derrick's life wasn't as idyllic as Gray thought. Sometimes having money and investments creates more problems than being broke. "What happened?"

"I had to hire a lawyer to evict the tenant, some witch managing a marijuana grow-op. They were in arrears, damaging the property, and denying access for an inspection. It turns out the property was rented by The Chosen Ones—a rather nasty bike gang; some burly, tattooed meathead and a scrawny friend of his. Anyway, to make a long story short, I have an order of possession and the bailiff has changed the locks. The bikers had a week to remove their shit and it's still there. I want to go in and burn it to the ground, have a bonfire in the backyard. Only problem is, I'll need backup in case they return during the party. I think the witch has left already."

Its namesake contradicting its seedy edge, Forest Lawn was one of the worst areas in the city for crime. Although the barrio was currently in the process of a taxpayer-funded revitalization, it still attracted all manner of riff-raff. It would be a long time coming, if ever, for it to be unanimously considered a good neighborhood. Locals still referred to it as Forest Harlem, Forest Ghetto, and sometimes just the Ghetto.

"You want me to help you burn the shit? What if they return? I just read the other day there was a drive-by shooting in Forest ... ah ... Lawn. I don't want to be another statistic."

Derrick tried a different tact. "I'm sure you could use the money. I'll pay you thirty dollars an hour. It'll take at least eight hours. I also have more paid backup. My biker friend Jimmy said he'd come. Think of it as an eviction party. I'll buy the beer. And I could really use your help. I need your help."

"I don't suppose you've had a lot of other volunteers?"

"No. I drunk-dialed a bunch of friends and invited them to the bonfire eviction party."

"No takers?"

"No. A few of them said I was nuts."

"That's a surprise."

"Maybe I am nuts. I'm just so fucking pissed off at them right now I don't really care. And at the end of today the week grace period expires and their shit is legally mine anyway. So, I'm within the law."

"Calgary allows small backyard fires in a contained fire pit ... but you're proposing a massive bonfire in the middle of the day. Don't you think some of the neighbors will complain?"

"Are you kidding? In Forest Ghetto? I've already had half a dozen phone calls from neighbors, who're so anxious to get rid of the riff-raff they've volunteered to help. The cops are too busy dealing with real crime to bother with our eviction party. They've got better things to do."

Gray hated requests that called in friendship loyalty. If loyalty could be called a weakness, it was one of his. He needed the money. And if he didn't acquiesce, he would probably be worried for Derrick's safety. And if something did go terribly wrong, he didn't know if he could live with himself if he did nothing but could have prevented it. Besides, oftentimes loyalty overrode fear.

"What time do you want me there?"

Derrick smiled at the goddess waitress approaching. "This one's on me. I'll pick you up tomorrow morning at ten."

# Chapter Five

*Ten thousand dollars*, Gray thought, scanning an e-mail from Adriana. *She's sending me links to five-star hotels and I've got ten thousand dollars to last two months.* He crunched the numbers. Really, he didn't have ten thousand dollars. It was what he had available on credit cards, which he thought should be called debt cards. It wasn't a true credit; it was a euphemism invented by banks to make debt-ridden consumers feel better about their purchases. Lull them into a false sense of comfort before broadsiding them with a 25 per cent interest rate.

By his math, he would return from Ecuador in late January with just enough money to make a mortgage payment and survive for about two weeks on Kraft dinner and rice.

*The action is the juice. Yeah, but not when it comes to your livelihood, you moron.*

He pushed the thought from his mind and returned to the e-mail. He and Adriana had had two conversations so far and exchanged multiple e-mails. Her line of questioning was becoming more personal. During the last conversation, she had told him eventually she wanted to get married. She envisioned a perfect wedding on the beach exclusive to close friends and family. At one point during the conversation, she had risen and closed the window, both for the noise and invading mosquitoes. Invading mosquitoes. No screens on the windows. He had seen that before.

She questioned him on the size of his house, why he didn't have a girlfriend, and if he ever planned on marrying. She also pointed out she wasn't the type of person that went in for casual sex. She wanted a long term, stable and committed relationship.

He tried to be as honest as possible, saying he didn't know if he wanted marriage, but "never say never," and the reason he didn't currently have a girlfriend was because his last ex had cheated on him with a so-called close friend. It still produced painful memories when he thought about it.

Goosebumps crawled up his arms as he read the latest. It was still freezing outside but toasty warm in his office:

*Hello invisible friend. I enjoyed talking to you yesterday. I think you are a good, sincere man and I want to get to know you better. I'm glad you like my accent. I speak differently because I'm from the coast. From what you tell me of the climate over there, it sounds like you live in a freezer. If I lived there, I'd only be able to shower once a month due to the cold (LOL). Here's some internet links to hotels and parts of Ecuador. If you want to talk please Skype me later tonight or tomorrow morning before I go to work. I send you kisses. Adriana.*

He thought of calling her but glanced at the desk clock and noticed it was almost ten at night, midnight Ecuador time. It was too late to call. She would probably be in bed, so he opted for a quick e-mail message, intending to try her tomorrow. He turned the office light off, drained a glass of water from the kitchen tap and went to bed.

The last thing he remembered before drifting off to sleep was the sad image of Lola's face, this time grotesquely disfigured.

*You're dead.*

# Chapter Six

"It's not like you're going to end up dead or anything like that," Jimmy Bold said as he and Gray surveyed the damage in the living room of the Forest Lawn house the next morning. Clothes and junk were strewn around the room, some hacks and fist-holes in walls and doors, the obvious signs the house had been used as a grow-op; but so far no significant damage that would involve great cost to remedy. But they had only made a dent in the debris, throwing the non-burnables into a large dump bin outside and tossing the burnables into the backyard fire, which was now raging with flames six feet high, a few neighbors sitting on lawn chairs nearby drinking beer and enjoying the unseasonably warm and sunny day.

Derrick was outside supervising the neighbors and stoking the blaze with leftover garden implements. At least the wooden handles would burn and the metal could later be tossed into the dump bin.

A car drove a little too slowly down the street and passed in front of the bay window. Jimmy, a beefy, grizzled and tattooed man, grabbed Gray by the arm, yanking him away from the window quickly. "Get down. You want to pay attention when you walk in front of the window."

"I thought you said I'm not going to end up dead."

He grunted. "I should've qualified it. Not if you keep your fucking head up, that is; and not if I can help it. But, for all we know, they could be planning a drive-by shooting."

The car slowed to a crawl, sped up precipitously and disappeared. They stood and stared out the window.

"In this neighborhood, you have to be careful," Jimmy said as they resumed packing stuff into green garbage bags. His beady eyes had narrowed to slits. "This really fucking pisses me off, that these losers would fuck Derrick over like this. I'll tell you one thing—if they show up, I'm going to beat the shit out of them."

Gray didn't know what to say so he said nothing. He tied off his green garbage bag filled mostly with clothes, left the house, wondered for a split-second whether the fire or dumpster would be a better home, and then opted for the fire. Besides, the beer cooler was beside the fire and he needed another beer.

"That burnables?" Derrick asked, tossing a pock-marked coffee table into the blaze and centering it with a shovel.

"Mostly clothes."

"Throw them in. They'll burn."

He tossed the bag into the blaze, grabbed a beer from the cooler, sat down on a plastic lawn chair, and took a long pull on it. A skinny bald man and a skinnier woman with straggly sandy blonde hair sat beside him, drinking beer. They had been introduced to Gray earlier as Rona and Tyler, and they owned the house next door. Rona was an incessant talker and it didn't take her long to get rolling again.

"I'll tell you, Derrick ... I'm sure glad that Rocky, that bitch daughter of his, and Strap are the fuck out of here. Those bastards would make all kinds of noise." She surveyed the debris-cluttered backyard. "And look at this mess. Fucking hoarders. I'll tell you if they come back, they're going to get a piece of my mind. You know they were always bringing hookers over here ... coke sluts, some of them pretty young. They'd keep me up at nights. I called the cops twice on them, even banged on the door a few times. I don't care if they're bikers. They don't scare me a bit. Do you want me to clean the house when all the stuff is gone? Me and Tyler will clean the debris up for free, but cleaning the inside of the house ... that's a big job. We'd do it for fifteen bucks an hour. I'm a good cleaner and ..."

"Done," Derrick said.

Rona stood—the nattering continuing. To Gray's ears it had become white noise and he tuned it out. There was something about her beyond the incessant babbling he found disconcerting. And the reference to Strap had brought back another painful memory. He was in fifth grade, entering the cloakroom just after recess with his friend Tony.

Mark, considered by his peers the class geek, was at the other end of the cloakroom, hanging up his coat. "Why don't we get Mark," Tony said, rolling up a ball of Plasticine from a nearby bucket.

Without thinking, Gray grabbed a handful of the pliable substance and rolled it into a ball.

"Now," Tony said, and they both whipped the balls at Mark. Tony's shot hit Mark in his nerd glasses, smashing the lens and knocking them clear off his head. Gray's shot hit Mark square in the eye as his glasses fell to the floor.

Mark burst into tears, ran and told the teacher.

In the principal's office awhile later, Tony received six lashes with the strap—three on each hand. He cried like a baby.

Gray, his left arm in a cast, the result of a broken wrist from a bicycle accident, received six lashes on the palm of his right hand. He too cried like a baby.

Gray had learned the hard way—quite literally the school of hard knocks. He would never pick on Mark again. And even though the strap was now banned as a form of punishment in schools, Gray reasoned he deserved it. Even at that tender young age, he knew right from wrong.

*But I would bet this Strap guy has a twisted sense of what's right and what's wrong. Asshole.*

Gray grabbed some waterlogged wood from a corner of the massive, treed yard and pitched it into the blaze, Derrick smiling and casting an approving glance. "I really appreciate your hel ..."

Gray heard it before he saw it; the rumbling of an engine dropping to an idle and the metallic click of vehicle doors opening and slamming shut. A black pick-up truck had stopped in front of the side driveway.

Derrick's smile was replaced by something else—fear. "Shit, we've got company."

The Chosen One's leader, Ron Misfelt, aka Rocky, stepped out of the truck alongside Stuart Treblecoch, aka The Strap.

Seeing the blaze, Rocky marched purposefully up the driveway into the backyard, followed by Strap. Although there was a healthy bonfire blazing, their furrowed features did not bear the trademarks of happy campers. Rocky, a grizzled ape of a man, was livid, large veins bulging and pulsating in his temple and neck.

"What the fuck do you think you're doing," Rocky said, coming within a few inches of Derrick's face. Strap flashed a toothy grin, the crotch of his jeans bulging unnaturally. Either this dirt bag was happy to see Gray, or he was packing heat. Gray doubted the former.

"That's my best coffee table," Rocky said, poking Derrick's chest with an index finger. Derrick stood his ground while Strap slid a hand toward his crotch. Gray doubted he wanted to play pocket pool. It was hardly the time or place for that kind of extracurricular activity.

Gray picked up a shovel as Strap neared, the distorted image of Lola washing through his mind, along with her words: *You're dead*.

"Listen," Derrick said, not backing down. "We're the clean-up crew. We were instructed by the management company that the owner has legal possession of this stuff. We were told to burn what we can, throw the rest in the dumpster."

Heads jerked as Jimmy stormed out of the house and raced across the lawn. Rona and Tyler, eager for ringside seats, followed close behind. Derrick stepped back as the rival biker tackled Rocky to the snow-covered grass. They rolled a few feet before Rocky mounted Jimmy and smashed him in the face twice with meat hook fists. Jimmy elbowed Rocky in the nose and blood spurted out.

Rocky covered his face with his hand.

Jimmy bucked and Rocky bounced and rolled along the ground, a few inches from the blazing inferno. He sat on Rocky's chest and pounded him in the face.

"Kill the fucker ... kill the fucker ... beat him to a pulp," Rona said, grinning with satisfaction.

Strap extracted a handgun and pointed it at Jimmy's head. "Get the fuck off him." Jimmy continued pounding Rocky in the face.

Gray raised the shovel and stepped toward Strap.

Strap pointed the gun at Gray's head. "Put that fucking shovel down or I'll blow your brains out." Gray didn't see the need to argue. He tossed away the garden implement but stood his ground.

Jimmy stopped pounding Rocky's face. One hand held Rocky's jacket collar while the other fist was cocked in the air, poised for assault.

"I said get the fuck off him," Strap shouted in an assertive tone. He leveled the gun at Jimmy's head. "I'll put a bullet hole in your head."

Jimmy glared at the skinny man pointing the gun. Rocky, face smeared with blood, grunted and squirmed beneath his captor.

Rona stepped toward Strap. "Put that fucking gun away or I'll call the police. You guys get out of ..."

Strap whirled and cracked her in the side of the head with a backhand. She dropped to the ground and lay there dazed, in that fuzzy place between consciousness and unconsciousness.

Jimmy released Rocky and stood up.

Gray stepped toward Strap.

Bad intentions in his narrowing black eyes, Strap leveled the gun at Gray's head. "Hold up or die."

Gray froze. The voice in his head echoed: *You're dead, you're dead.* Staring at Strap, Gray certainly believed the scrawny six-foot-four man with gangly arms and legs had the potential for murder. There was pure evil in those eyes, in that pock-marked complexion, crooked jaw, long pointed nose and mop of unkempt straggly black hair. Gray knew in an instant if Strap pulled the trigger it wouldn't be the first time the monster threatening him had taken great satisfaction in bringing about the destruction of another human being.

"Listen ... let's hold up a second," Derrick said, trying to diffuse the situation. For thirty dollars an hour, Jimmy and Gray had come very close to losing their lives, not to mention the other volunteers. "What the fuck do you guys want?"

"I want my fucking stuff," Rocky said, wiping his bloody nose on his blue jean jacket sleeve.

Derrick thought about it quickly. If he let them take the stuff, it would not only save him money in dump fees and hourly wages, it might also save a few lives. "Okay, how about this? I'll give you guys until seven this evening to clear out all your shit. If you can't do it, we carry on getting rid of it."

Rocky nodded to Strap, who, winking at Gray, lowered the handgun and re-inserted it into the crotch of his jeans.

Helped by Tyler, Rona staggered to her feet. She had a small cut on her head that trickled blood. Her eyes rolled. Tyler helped her into a chair beside the fire.

"Don't ... let them take anything," Rona said, still a little punch-drunk. "Fuck them ... you ..."

"Shut your fucking pie-hole, Rona," Tyler shouted, grabbing her arm stiffly. She frowned dazedly.

"Keep your bitch quiet," Strap said, pointing to his crotch "Unless she wants some of this."

Although his hands were trembling, Gray couldn't help grinning at the sexual innuendo. He doubted Strap was smart enough to get it.

Fists clenched, Jimmy stepped toward Rocky. "You guys going to remove your shit or what?"

Rocky wiped his bloody nose and nodded. He pulled out a cell phone, made a call, had a short conversation and hung up. "I'll have four guys and two more pick-up trucks here in fifteen minutes. We'll have my stuff out of here in a matter of hours."

Rocky walked over to the half-full metal dumpster. "Is this all garbage in here?"

"Some clothes, dishes, your shit," Derrick said. "You figure it out."

Rocky grunted and started removing garbage bags and throwing them in the pick-up truck. Strap bent, picked up the shovel and raised it slowly over his head within striking distance of Gray. The toothy grin reappeared.

Gray stepped out of range.

Strap winked and walked backwards toward the dumpster, his eyes not leaving his enemies. He waved to the assortment of garden implements leaning against the house. "Don't be throwing any more of those into the fire. We're taking them."

The tension ratcheted up as two more pick-up trucks pulled up a short time later and six bikers started removing belongings.

Derrick made a deal with Rona, saying he would tip her generously if she kept her mouth shut and didn't call the cops. He didn't want his rental property stigmatized as a former grow-op. The value would instantly plummet. Besides, Jimmy was still on probation. A police visit would likely mean he would return to the joint. Derrick didn't want that either.

Tyler helped Rona next door to their house while Gray, Jimmy and Derrick sat fireside drinking beer and watching. Strap cleaned the yard of most of the garden implements and stood guard beside the dumpster while his cohorts came and went. Occasionally he would cast a nasty stare at Gray.

*Why the fuck is he focusing on me?*

About three hours later, most of the stuff had been cleared out and the last of the biker's vehicles were pulling away. Gray had drained about seven beers, the nerve-wracking ordeal causing him to pour in the liquid confidence. Strap was giving him the creeps. Hell, the whole situation was.

Gray picked up a few fallen branches in the yard and noticed a rake buried in the dead brush. He didn't know why he did it. Maybe he hated the word strap and the psychological scars that went with it. The numbing effects of the alcohol were distorting his judgment, fueling him with a bravado that might have been absent otherwise. He picked up the dead branches, along with the rake, and threw them into the fire.

Strap was just exiting the house's side door, Derrick right behind him. Derrick had decided to monitor the last few loads in case the angry bikers decided to start destroying the property on their way out.

Strap glanced sideways, seeing the rake fly into the fire. He drew his gun and ran into the backyard.

Jimmy unsheathed a large military-issue combat knife.

Strap aimed the gun at Gray. "I told you not to burn any fucking rakes, you little shit. Do you have any idea who you're dealing with?"

"Fuck you," Gray said, balling his fists and stepping forward.

"That's enough," Jimmy shouted. "You've got your stuff—now get the fuck out of here."

Strap thought about pointing the gun at Jimmy, but quickly changed his mind. The ape scared him, even though Jimmy had brought a knife to a gunfight.

A tense silence followed.

Rocky stood at the dumpster about thirty feet away, watching. "Forget the rake. Let's go, Strap. We've got most of our stuff."

Strap lowered the firearm, scowling at Gray.

"You want your rake, go get it," Gray said, pointing at the blaze. There wasn't much left of the rake.

Strap backed away. "You're a cocky little fuck, aren't you? But don't worry, there will be a time and place, and you'll get what's coming to you."

*You're dead.* "Big man with a gun," Gray said. "Put your tail between your legs and fuck off."

Strap's eyes narrowed. His faced flushed red. He opened his mouth to speak.

"Let's go, Strap," Rocky shouted. "Now."

Fists clenched, Strap stared at Gray for a long moment, then slowly turned and walked away. They climbed in the black pick-up truck and sped away.

A few minutes later, Gray realized the thumping sound he heard wasn't some desperate soul trapped in a coffin.

It was the pounding of his heart.

# Chapter Seven

The heart. The internal organ about the size of a fist that pumps oxygen-enriched blood to every living cell in the body and sustains human life. Yet, on a metaphorical level, it's the heart that's at the center of human love. It's the heart that is touched deeply when that complicated emotion has us in its powerful and mind-altering grip.

*Is that what I want? Love? An emotion that could result in a broken heart and long-term psychological scarring? Do I want to get swept down that tumultuous torrent only to wash out on the other side emotionally crippled? Alfred Lord Tennyson said: 'Tis better to have loved and lost than never to have loved at all.' But I have loved and lost, and the notion of true love seems a lot like fiction to me. Or it scares the hell out of me and I'm just a chicken shit.*

He sighed, staring at the computer. He didn't have the answer. But he realized, in spite of conscious efforts to tell himself otherwise, he was becoming more attracted to Adriana with each conversation. He had just finished an hour and twenty-five minute conversation with her, and he twirled it around in his mind, trying to analyze it for a tell—any indication she had the potential for betrayal.

They talked about all the places Gray wanted to see while in Ecuador, and she mentioned a few more possibilities. Gray agreed, but on a few occasions he said "we'll see," not realizing the literal import of his words. Adriana insisted that "we'll see" was a diplomatic and evasive way of saying no. He had repeated it a couple of times before she became mildly annoyed, telling him: "Don't say *'we'll see'* to me."

To please her, he quickly changed the ambiguous wording to what he had meant to say: "We'll go see those attractions." Her features had brightened at the revised choice of words and that had been the end of it. She also asked him pointed questions about how long he had planned on spending in each tourist destination, to which he had answered as honestly as possible. "That depends on how much I like the place."

She had offered to accompany him to Galapagos Islands, a wondrous and popular region with awe-inspiring beauty and a multitude of interesting and exotic plant and animal species. Of course, she said if he planned on visiting the islands and wanted company, it would have to be at his expense—the broke leading the broker.

Maybe these should have been red flags, or maybe she was just being completely honest about her lack of financial resources. What was wrong with that? But she seemed perfectly willing to accompany him on his travels, probably share the same bed (she had hinted as much). But wasn't it all just a little too quick? After all, they hardly knew each other.

Gray didn't have time to analyze it right now. He had a doctor's appointment in a half hour to arrange a sleeping-pill prescription for the upcoming trip. He knew only too well that after many rough miles traveling in a developing country, sometimes sleep became the singular most important goal. He had no idea where he might end up, but he did know he could potentially be dealing with noise pollution that could drive him stark-raving mad. He had been there before, and never came unprepared. Ear plugs, sleeping pills, and if necessary, lots of alcohol to knock him out.

Leaving the doctor's office with a prescription in hand an hour later, he glanced over his shoulder as he climbed in his navy-blue Audi Quattro. He saw a black pick-up truck, the driver partially obscured by a baseball cap pulled down over his face. The man seemed to be grinning.

His heart skipped a beat. *Strap? Is that Strap?*

Strap hung a hand out the open window, shaping it to resemble a gun. He pulled a pretend trigger as his toothy smile widened. "Bang, you're dead."

"Stay the fuck away from me."

"I know where you live," Strap said, closing the window and speeding out of the parking lot in the afternoon sun.

Gray sat for a few minutes, closing his eyes and waiting for his heartbeat to resume its normal rhythm. *You're dead.*

*Shit.* His upcoming trip to Ecuador was quickly becoming complicated. The Canadian government travel advisory website warned him to stay away from the Columbian border (too many organized crime groups) and steer clear of a region near the Peruvian border (too many landmines). It also listed some active volcanoes in specific areas. The website said nothing about how to navigate a relationship with a woman with a possible secret agenda, nor did it offer any advice on how to ditch an armed predatory nutcase prior to boarding the plane.

On the way to the drugstore, Gray thought about calling the cops, but quickly ruled it out. An explanation of where the threat first occurred would lead back to Jimmy, not to mention an investigation of a former grow-op house. Jimmy hated cops and certainly didn't need any heat brought down on him now, especially since he was still on probation.

As he pulled into the Shopper's Drug Mart parking lot, scanning the stalls nervously for a sign of Strap, an idea popped into his head. Talk to Jimmy about the problem. Jimmy would know what to do.

Hell, he had someone trying to kill him right on his home turf, never mind Ecuador. The only option might be to hop on a plane and let Jimmy handle the situation while the heat died down, or Strap died down—whatever came first.

# Chapter Eight

"When did you see Strap?" Jimmy asked, sitting on the couch of his untidy one-bedroom apartment in southwest Calgary a few hours later. The coffee table was strewn with beer can empties, ashtrays overflowing with cigarette butts, and a cardboard pizza box containing crusts, crusted tomato sauce and cheese. Jimmy exhaled a cloud of smoke and it slowly drifted to the ceiling.

"Just as I was about to get in my car after leaving the doctor's office today."

"And what did he say to you, exactly?" Jimmy scratched a beer belly, burped and flicked some ash into an overfilled ashtray.

Gray hated to repeat the words. They were beginning to haunt him. But in the grizzled features regarding him, he saw something other than a tough, cynical biker. He saw his life.

"'Bang, your dead,'" and "'I know where you live.'"

Jimmy scratched his thick, graying beard and took a drag on the cigarette. He exhaled into the cloudy, blue-gray haze drifting around the ceiling light fixture. "Hmmmm. What do you want me to do about it?"

Jimmy and Gray were hardly friends. They were loosely connected through Derrick, who was a friend of the ex-con. Gray had called Derrick prior to his arrival at Jimmy's, and Derrick had promised to put in a good word for Gray, hoping it might help. Jimmy certainly didn't owe Gray any favors. His only hope would be Jimmy's friendship with Derrick—that it would be enough to tip the scales.

"I don't know ... maybe tell him to leave me alone."

"You want me to threaten him. You know I'm still on probation for that assault and drug rap. I don't need any more shit with the cops." But his eyes narrowed and he clenched a fist, slowly raising it above the coffee table.

Gray thought he might pound on the table any second and send the butts and pizza crusts rocketing into the air. But then Jimmy slowly unclenched it and scratched his stubble.

"Those aren't the kind of guys who would call the cops," Gray said.

There was a moment's pause. Part of the reason Jimmy served three years in prison had to do with The Chosen Ones. There was a turf war going on at the time for neighborhood distribution rights, and Jimmy had stumbled onto another connection that led him to a drop point in some old warehouses in one of the city's industrial districts. It had been a sting operation that Jimmy had a gut feeling about. The Chosen Ones set him up; someone else had been involved, but he didn't know who. He had learned in the joint that Rocky and Strap had organized the sting to take him out and seize control of drug operations. And they had done just that soon after he was sent to prison. So whether he wanted to admit it or not, he had a personal interest in extracting his pound of flesh from these motherfuckers.

The question was, did he want to risk another trip to the joint? He wanted a fresh start, wanted to reform his life and make something good out of it ultimately. As it was, he had disassociated himself from his former gang, The Skulls. As former second-in-command, it hadn't been an easy task. Many organized crime gangs don't let you leave. You pay for it, sometimes with your life. If it wasn't for the fact that Jimmy was one of the meanest sons of bitches in the valley, feared by many members, he likely wouldn't have been able to walk away like he had. They would have wanted his bulky ass in a shallow grave.

"They wouldn't call the cops," Jimmy said. "They don't do that."

Gray worried about dragging Jimmy into this. It wasn't really Jimmy's problem. It had the potential to land him back in jail, or worse, dead.

A bedroom door opened and a partially clad brunette—long black hair jutting out at odd angles—poked her head into the living room. She wore only black lace panties and a matching black lace push-up bra, displaying ample cleavage. Her small brown eyes framed an attractive smile. "Am I interrupting something?"

"Not really," Jimmy lied. The last thing he wanted his girlfriend to know was that he was seriously contemplating revenge on some rival bikers. He told her he had left the gang and she had made it very clear it was a condition of their union. He knew if he got involved with The Skulls—and she found out—she would leave. And one day he wanted to start a family with her. "This is Derrick's friend Gray. Gray, Julie."

"Nice to meet you," she said. "I've heard Derrick mention you."

"All bad?"

"He says you're a real asshole." Julie paused for effect as Gray felt his cheeks redden.

"Well, he calls me that to my face, so it's nothing I haven't heard before."

She laughed. "At least he's not backstabbing you."

"No."

"I'm just messing with you. Derrick says you're one of his best friends." Turning to Jimmy, she said, "Are we still going out for dinner, honey?"

"You bet, buttercup."

She smiled. "Nice meeting you." She disappeared down the hallway. The bathroom door clicked closed and Gray heard water running in the shower.

Jimmy spoke in hushed tones. "Whatever you do, don't ever tell Julie about our conversations. If I join the gang, or commit any crime whatsoever and she finds out, I'm toast."

Gray got up to leave. He hadn't even factored in Julie's opinion. "Listen, Jimmy ... I'm sorry I bothered you with this. It's really none of your business and you've got a lot to ..."

Jimmy held a finger to his mouth, stood up and extracted a business card from his back pocket. "Let me think about it a bit. And if you have any trouble, call me."

Walking down the snow-shoveled sidewalk to his car, Gray couldn't help glancing around and over his shoulder a few times. *Endanger my life for thirty bucks an hour. What the fuck was I thinking?*

# Chapter Nine

*Fuck, it could be dangerous. Maybe wait until tomorrow.*

*Yeah, but I need to pack, need to get organized.* It was only nine at night, but the overcast sky, pitch darkness and falling snow made it seem a lot later. Arriving home, Gray had busied himself packing for the Ecuadorian adventure. A minimalist traveler, it always took some time. It was easy to overload yourself with many items spread across two or three suitcases. It was something else entirely to pack everything you needed into a small carry-on knapsack. Every item had to be well thought through. There simply wasn't room in the pack for waste.

Everything was spread out on a queen-sized bed in a spare bedroom: two pairs of shorts, one pair of socks, three short-sleeved button-down shirts, two t-shirts, two pairs of underwear, two books, Lonely Planet's updated guide to Ecuador and Bruce Sterling's novel, *Distraction*. He also had a black baseball cap with a Canadian flag embroidered on the front, a steno pad, a couple of pens, some business cards, a digital camera, an inexpensive laptop computer, an extra pair of cheap reading glasses, travel alarm clock, and cheap wristwatch.

His toiletry case was a mini pharmacy. Along with the usual and permitted personal hygiene items, he had packed two sets of ear plugs, an anti-stomach bacterial medication, anti-diarrhea pills, extra-strength Tylenol, sleeping pills, multi-vitamins and fruit-flavored chewable vitamin C tablets.

He carried passport, plane ticket, travel insurance, money, bank and credit card plastic in a cloth money belt concealed around his waist, beneath his underwear. Important passwords and phone numbers were stored in a password-protected web-based drop box.

Lonely Planet recommended a pocket flashlight along with sunblock and mosquito repellent, but he didn't have space in the small knapsack. As it was, he had packed it three times, each time carefully weighing it and discarding certain items. He also wanted to leave a little room in the pack to accommodate an article of clothing or something important like a bottle of rum, should he decide to add more items during his travels.

Finally satisfied with the results, he placed the bag on his bathroom scale. It weighed in at twenty pounds, two pounds under the permitted weight for a carry-on. He carefully selected the clothes he would wear on the plane. Nothing fancy: a pair of black leather soft-soled Denver Hayes shoes, a light black polyester-cotton pull-over jacket, two t-shirts, Levi's blue jeans and a long-sleeved black button-down shirt with a collar. He knew Quito's climate could get a little cool at night, so he definitely needed more than just beach wear. Besides, he was departing in what would probably be sub-zero temperatures.

He carefully unpacked the items and went through them individually, realizing the Tylenol supply was low, the ear plugs well-worn and partially deteriorated, and he was missing a few things: namely, a travel toothbrush, two packs of gum, toothpaste, and a travel pack of tissues, just in case his dust-allergies flared up.

He wrote the items on a piece of paper, walked into the kitchen, refilled his coffee, and looked out the bay window into the backyard at the falling snow. Outside, under a large spruce tree, glinting red eyes reflected off the dining room chandelier.

He shuddered and then relaxed. It was his part-time resident, Robbie the Rabbit.

Robbie would visit throughout the year. In the summertime, he alternated between a well-worn patch of dirt underneath a small hedge, an equally worn patch of dirt underneath a year-round plastic lawn chair, or his perch under the spruce tree. Robbie was the only pet Gray had and he often put down carrots, which Robbie would eagerly gobble up. He stared at Robbie's glowing red eyes. *Strap's home. What, Strap's home? He knows where I live.*

He extracted the scrap of paper and wrote *carrots*. He turned the dining room light off, moved into the living room, carefully slid the black fabric drape to one side, and peered out at the lifeless cul-de-sac. Seven other bungalow-style homes dotted the street, most with yellow lights illuminating bedrooms, kitchens and living rooms. The lone streetlight illumed large snowflakes floating down and painting suburban landscape white. *Fucking frozen wasteland.* A pick-up truck wheeled around the corner and parked in front of Gray's house. He took a few deep breaths and strained to see its color in the suffused streetlight glow. Dark gray, not black. It was the neighbor, Trevor, who often used Gray's street-front parking stall, knowing Gray generally parked in the rear heated garage, particularly in winter.

"Am I a prisoner in my own home?" Gray said, a faint echo of his voice reverberating through the expansive abode. *You're only nuts if you answer your questions.* He remembered a quote from Edgar Allan Poe, one of his favorite poets: "*I became insane, with long intervals of horrible sanity.*"

"No, you're not a prisoner in your own home." *There you go, answering your own questions. What did you just say about people who do that? Ah, fuck it.*

He threw on some gloves, a toque and thick jacket, grabbed his keys, and headed for the garage, frowning slightly when he noticed Robbie had disappeared. Perhaps he would return later in the evening to enjoy his carrots, maybe even invite a few friends over for dinner or a jackrabbit fiesta.

Gray backed out of the garage, flicked windshield wipers on high, and cruised down the alley. A few turns later, he pulled onto 24<sup>th</sup> Street, heading south to Calgary Coop, a large supermarket he generally patronized. Visibility was poor in the falling snow.

He glanced in his rearview mirror just as another vehicle turned off a side street, following him. *Deep breaths. It's nothing. You're being paranoid.*

But the dark-colored pick-up was gaining on him. He pulled into the right lane without signaling, turned right on a side street, accelerating within the limitations of the slippery road.

The black pick-up truck followed. And suddenly it was right beside him. He felt the power boost of a shot of adrenaline coursing through his veins. He glanced to the left.

Strap rolled down the window, aimed a handgun and fired.

Gray instinctively ducked, slamming on the brakes. The bullet pierced the driver window, shattering it with a deafening pop, and tore into the leather lining on the passenger door. Shards of glass rained on Gray's head as he gripped the wheel.

Another bullet crunched into the rear quarter panel as the Quattro fishtailed, the ass end slamming into the side of the pick-up truck, careening to one side. His car still moving, Gray opened the door and leaped out, somersaulting on the street as the two interlocked vehicles drifted away.

He picked himself up, wincing as he noticed his right glove was torn, fresh blood oozing out from a gash on his palm. He glanced back. The vehicles were still tangled together, coming to a stop as the truck driver door opened and Strap stepped out.

*Come to the party, Strap. I'll buy you some carrots. I'll stuff a carrot right up your fucking ass, you bastard.*

Gray ran toward 24$^{th}$ Street, knowing there was a strip mall a short distance away. A gunshot rang out and a bullet whizzed past, inches from his head. Strap wasn't giving up easily. Gray hit 24$^{th}$, turned left, and kept running. Two blocks later, seeing the welcome lights of the strip mall brightening, he finally dared look behind. By that time, plenty of vehicles were visible entering and exiting the mall.

There was no sign of Strap. Gray sighed. *You're dead. No I'm fucking not. There's still a lot of life left in me.*

# Chapter Ten

"It's your life," Joanne Simons said, sipping a coffee and absently people-watching in a busy Second Cup coffee shop in southwest Calgary. Her insouciant tone belied the fact they were such good friends. "You do what you want with it. You asked me for an opinion, and I gave it to you."

"I don't get it," Gray said to his long-time friend. He had asked her about relationships, about the need to connect with one person on a soul level and forge a life with them. She had answered indifferently, saying it would take more than one man to fill all her needs. "How many men are we talking about?"

"Twelve."

"Twelve?"

She brushed back a lock of mid-length wavy brown hair and crossed her legs. She wore a tan business suit with a white V-neck blouse that showed just enough cleavage to leave the rest to the imagination. Ten years Gray's senior, Joanne worked as a secretary for an oil company. The two had met ten years ago to the day and had become good friends, keeping the relationship strictly platonic—even though Gray often had sexual fantasies involving her. He loved Joanne for her honesty, quirky sense of humor and often skewed value system. They met at least once a month for coffee, lunch or dinner. Gray would often pick her brain about the opposite sex. He wanted to know how the hell women processed information. Venus and Mars. He didn't think he was any closer now to solving the conundrum than when he had first started questioning

Joanne a decade ago. But Joanne had imparted some valuable information about women.

Perhaps he would never solve the riddle.

She grinned sarcastically, pushed her glasses up the bridge of her small nose and leaned forward, affording a better view of the cleavage. Her penetrating brown eyes stared into Gray's green eyes. He tried hard not to lower his gaze. "I'm not silly enough to think that one man will be able to fulfill all my needs. So, I have one for sex, one for love, three for friendship, one for intellectual conversation, one to nurture, one to nurture me, one for inspiration, one for sports and fitness, one to laugh with, one to go to movies with, one to call me on my bullshit. How many is that?"

"Thirteen, I think."

"Okay, thirteen—something like that anyway."

"Isn't there some overlap? I mean, what role do I fill?"

"Well, it isn't sex," Joanne said, lowering her voice and grinning. "At least, not yet anyway."

Gray decided not to touch that one. He valued the friendship too much.

"You cross over into a few roles," she said. "You're a friend, confidante, an inspiration, a good laugh sometimes. Tell me more about this Adriana girl."

"She seems okay, but sometimes I don't really know. It's so hard to tell through e-mail and talking on Skype. Sometimes I feel like I have a really good read on her, a good gut feeling, and other times doubts start creeping into my mind."

"Doubts about what?"

"Well, she has two cop brothers."

"So?"

"So I wouldn't want to piss her off. One of her brothers might throw me in jail. Worse still, kill me."

"I think you're reading too much into it. What would she have to gain from that?"

"I don't know. Revenge."

"Well ... maybe if you do something really nasty to her. But you're not like that. You're a nice guy with a lot to offer a woman. I wouldn't pay a lot of attention to it."

"Maybe I'm better off with thirteen women like you."

"Listen, Gray, I'm just telling you what works for me. I'm not saying it'll work for you, especially in a country like Ecuador where you don't know the rules of the game. If you want to piss Adriana off, try something like that in Ecuador, and maybe the cop brothers will throw you in jail."

"What do you think I should do?"

"Meet her on neutral territory, in her city, and see how it goes. Approach it as you would a first date in Canada. Whatever you do, don't arrive at some beach town and invite her to your hotel. You'd be laying the groundwork for a kind of expectation, similar to a hooker-client relationship."

"I don't want that kind of thing."

"Well, don't put yourself in a position where you'll have to put her up for the night. What if you don't like her? Then you're stuck with her and it could get uncomfortable real fast."

"So you think I should proceed?"

"Proceed with caution. Like a yellow traffic light."

"What about your thirteen-men philosophy?"

"That's me. No two people are the same. It might not work for you; especially not over there. You said you met her online?"

"Cupid."

"I've heard about that site. Maybe it's nothing, and it's tough to generalize, but isn't there something inherently wrong with a dating site where the men have to pay and the women don't? Especially in Latin American countries, where many of the women are probably looking for a meal ticket out of there, anyway."

"You have a better idea?"

"I'm just saying, don't pin all your hopes on Adriana. When you get there, you'll have an opportunity to meet women in the flesh and make a much better assessment of them. And ultimately, it depends on what you want out of it. What do you want out of it?"

Gray had initially thought he wanted a relationship, but now he wasn't sure. The conversation was making him confused. "I don't know. I think I want a relationship."

"Well, start with Adriana. Proceed with caution. If it doesn't work, find someone else."

After a moment's silence, in which Joanne seemed to be relishing in the adoration of a much younger man eyeballing her as he feigned reading a novel at a nearby table, the conversation shifted to Ecuador and its safety issues with respect to foreigners. Gray had read about many of the dangers, but also knew his knowledge was only scratching the surface. He had read about foreigners being unlawfully confined in prisons where they languished for years without a trial or even a trial date; read other reports about kidnapping, pickpockets and robberies.

"I just read the other day that an Ecuadorian realtor fell for a trap and almost got robbed," Gray said.

"What happened?"

"He responded to a newspaper ad for a house for sale well below market value in Quito. When he arrived, two men armed with knives tried to rob him."

"Did they?"

"No ... he got away, ran like hell after shoving one of them. Not the wisest decision. He could have been killed. And I recently read something about robbers in Quito throwing human feces at tourists to distract them before robbing them. Apparently it's so common there's a checkbox for it on police report forms."

"Shit ... I hope that doesn't happen to you," Joanne said smiling.

Gray couldn't help smiling at the pun. "The god of fools isn't shining on me." He liked the sound of it, but didn't know if it was true. After all, Strap had almost killed him a week ago, and he hadn't reported it to police. If it wasn't for Derrick helping him retrieve his car a few hours after the attack, the police might have become involved. As it was, however, when he and Derrick had arrived at the scene, his car was parked at an odd angle and riddled with bullet holes, broken glass and a little smashed up; keys still in the ignition, driver door slightly ajar. Some benevolent Samaritan had even killed the ignition. He had been lucky. He had climbed in, looked both ways for posterity, and driven home white-knuckled.

"Is something wrong?" Joanne asked.

"No." The last thing he wanted to do was involve her in this. Even though there hadn't been any further attacks, and Jimmy had been notified, he certainly wasn't going to involve

Joanne in any of his stupidity. Hell, for all he knew, he was already putting her life in danger.

Joanne eyed the ogling stud. At least Gray was leaving for Ecuador tomorrow. Whatever happened in his absence, he wouldn't have to deal with it for at least six weeks. *Unless he follows me.*

******

An hour later, he sat at his desk, contemplating a call to Adriana. *God of fools. You're dead. Shit … I hope that doesn't happen to you. The action is the juice. Everything will be fine … you're painting yourself into a nightmare before you even get there.*

He changed his mind at the last second, settling instead for a review of his flight itinerary before some last-minute packing and finally a lazy night on the couch with a good horror movie.

He opened the e-ticket. Flying Air Canada, he would leave Calgary on Thursday, December 6th at 3:10 pm, arrive in Toronto at 9:00 pm, layover for three hours before boarding a flight to Lima at 8:00 am the following morning. After a two and a half hour stopover, he would then fly for a couple of hours and arrive in Ecuador at one in the afternoon. He figured it would be at least three in the afternoon by the time he got settled into a hotel in Quito. And then, altitude sickness and fatigue would likely claim what little energy reserves he had left after twenty-four hours of travel.

*Fuck, now I know why I hate planes and airports. I always pick the milk runs. Twenty-four hours of travel; cooped up with people in a pressurized cabin, smelling their body odor, listening to their bullshit, catching their flu-bugs. Glass half full ... glass half full.*

# Chapter Eleven

"Your bottle's half full. Would you like a refill?"

Gray nodded at the bartender. He was in Chili's Texas Grill at the Calgary airport, waiting for the first leg of his journey to start. The bartender popped another bottle of cold Kokanee on the table. Gray was on his second.

He thought about pulling out his laptop and abruptly changed his mind, noticing his plane would be boarding in another twenty minutes. Just enough time to polish off the beer. He decided to people-watch instead. It was an all-male cast bellied up at the bar, watching the big television screen, talking on the phone, texting, e-mailing, eating and drinking.

Except for the guy right beside Gray. In between sips of draft beer, he eyeballed Gray curiously through Coke-bottle lenses. Sporting a mustache and a two-day stubble, the man wore a blue baseball cap, a K (for Kokanee beer) screen-printed on the front. His ensemble consisted of a baby-blue hooded jacket, blue jeans and bright white running shoes that seemed two sizes too big. His eyes were wild.

Uncomfortable with the strange glances, Gray finally struck up a conversation. It turned out Allen, who spoke with a thick French-Canadian accent, was on a two-week leave from a month mining gig somewhere in rural Alberta. He was flying back to Toronto to be with his girlfriend.

"I'll tell you, that's way too long in the bush," Allen said, studying Gray carefully. "Four weeks." He lowered his voice suddenly and looked around as if someone was about to attack him. "Way too fucking long. Lots of things suffer, like your personal life. If that's all you want is money … that's fine. I make a hundred and seventy an hour, plus per diem. Good money. But everything else? It goes to shit."

That explained the wild eyes, Gray thought. Allen was bush-wacked—frazzled by the isolation of camp life. He was starving for human contact and conversation, if only to subject someone to an incessant and disconnected monologue.

He continued. "It's been too warm out lately. Screws up our economy."

It had been minus five degrees Celsius or below for the last week in Calgary, even colder in many parts of rural Alberta. Five or six inches of fresh snow had just fallen last night and the weather channel was broadcasting news of some ugly rural storms. Gray had no idea what the fuck Allen was going on about. He wasn't interested in asking for an explanation.

"The oil and gas is dependent on cold weather. That's why our economy has stalled …"

Allen rambled on and Gray tuned out, sipping his beer and thinking about his itinerary, nodding and smiling at what he thought were the appropriate times until Allen's voice suddenly trailed off. Allen stared at Gray silently.

"Sorry did you ask me something?" Gray asked.

"Yeah, where are you going?"

"Ecuador."

"That sounds exciting."

"It will be."

"I'm hooking up with my girlfriend in Toronto," Allen repeated. "I invested a bunch of money on stocks lately and they went in the tank. Oil and gas. It's up and down, you know.

I won't be retiring any time soon, but I don't even check it any more. What's the point?"

"Exactly," Gray said, like he gave a fuck about this stranger's stocks.

"I bought my girlfriend some perfume, but you know she hates the name. I had to take it back. I told them I don't want a refund ... I just want an exchange."

Gray nodded, checked his watch. *Thank God, ten more minutes to boarding. Get me out of here. Fucking nutcase.*

The word girlfriend made him think of Adriana. They had talked every three or four days since they met online, and her e-mails, which were coming fast and furious—at least two a day—had gradually become more intimate: *I send you kisses ... I'm becoming very emotional thinking about your arrival ...* and the bombshell this morning ... *Call me any time, day or night when you arrive. TQM!* It hadn't taken Gray long to decipher it: *Te quiero mucho ...* I love you very much.

*She loves me very much. She's never met me. Maybe it's my house she loves very much. Or maybe it's a culture I don't understand?* Gray had probably committed all the cardinal sins already anyway. He told Adriana how spacious his minimalist but tastefully decorated house in Calgary was, even went so far as to snap a dozen pictures and e-mail them to her while mentioning he would be selling it on his return. He omitted the fact he *had* to sell it.

"What, are you crazy?" Adriana said during a recent Skype call. "That house is beautiful. Why would you want to sell it? I showed those photos to my sister. She also thinks you're crazy for selling it. That's men. They're crazy."

*Want to pay my mortgage,* Gray thought, noticing Allen staring silently at him. *Fuck. I'm calling him bush-wacked. I'm starting to feel like a zombie.* A hissing sound crackled from the airport speakers, wherever they were hidden, and a monotone female voice announced Gray's flight was now boarding. *Thank God.*

Gate 10 was right next to Chili's, so he didn't have to rush. His Kokanee was half full. Passengers began lining up. They still had to call priority boarding, handicapped, the elderly, children, before he could board. He had at least another half hour. But on the other hand, did he really want to listen to more verbal diarrhea? He could tell by the way Allen's lips began flapping uncontrollably that it could well amount to projectile vomiting.

Gray stood. "Excuse me ... my plane's boarding. Nice to meet you, cheers." *Merry fucking Xmas.*

"Cheers to you. What did you say?"

*Did I say that out loud? Who's bush-wacked? Who's the fucking nutcase?* "I said ... cheers."

# Chapter Twelve

*Cheers ... did I say that? I guess I did.*

Gray had made it, and twenty-five hours of travel later he was sitting in the terrace area of Casa Helbling, a house that had been converted into a hotel or a hostel—whatever the contemporary terminology nowadays was. A large Brahma beer in hand, Gray was drinking with a German guy named Peter. They were well into their third large Brahma, and Gray had very little gas left in the tank. He was exhausted—running on adrenaline and instinct. But the decent digs, reasonably priced at thirty bucks a night, pleasant vibe—European travelers happily going about their business—was enough. It had set the tone for the trip. It was going to be a positive experience. At least, that was what he kept telling himself.

He vaguely remembered deplaning from TACA flight 132 into Quito from Lima, Peru, which touched down a few minutes late, at exactly 1:13 pm in the afternoon. But the journey had confused him. During the extended eight-hour flight from Toronto to Lima, he had met a Peruvian woman, mid-sixties, who now made her home in Montreal, Quebec, and didn't have a lot of faith in internet dating. When Gray had told her he was about to meet a woman whom he had met on the internet, her features had darkened. "If you're not scared about stuff like that, I certainly am." She proceeded to tell him a story about a Canadian man who had met an Ecuadorian woman online and, after he had flown over to meet her, was kidnapped, tortured, robbed and eventually held for a large ransom, which his parents had willingly paid.

"I'm not scared about stuff like that," Gray had responded promptly. But Solya wouldn't give it up. For the next two hours she had given him variations of the same tale, some of which occurred in other Latin American countries. Finally he had drifted off, only to be awoken abruptly about an hour later by a phrase that cycled through his mind like a broken record: *You should be scared.*

The two-hour stop-over in Lima was a drama in and of itself. Gray couldn't have scripted it any better. Waiting for the connection to Quito, he had started a conversation with a Canadian woman, Abby Taylor, who was on her way to Ecuador to try to salvage a beachfront hotel she and her husband Spencer had purchased in Atacames, a small town along the coast about thirty minutes south of the town of Esmeraldas. Their plan, of course, was to escape the harsh winters of Canada forever and live the beachfront dream, running the small hotel, restaurant and bar, relaxing on the beach drinking exotic cocktails with little umbrellas inside. They had purchased it two years ago to the day. Only problem was, after they had returned to Ecuador after a short sojourn to Canada they discovered their staff, along with the realtor who had facilitated the deal, had moved into the hotel, were operating it, and keeping the profits. Through one of their Ecuadorian friends they had received word of this fraud. On searching the realtor's criminal history, Abby discovered he had child sex and fraud convictions in the United States.

So last year, they had returned, managed to evict the squatters, and hired a lawyer to sue the previous owner and the realtor after discovering the realtor and owner had filed a lawsuit alleging Abby was running a business in Ecuador illegally. If she hadn't gotten tipped off about the court date, Abby might have ended up in an Ecuadorian prison, languishing in squalor for years before having her case heard. The owner and realtor had sold her the building without a business license, something that should have been included in the deal.

"Wow, that's quite a story," Gray said, sitting across from Abby and her mother-in-law, Marnie, a 76-year-old woman who had decided to accompany Abby, even though she had just finished the first round of radiation treatment for lung cancer. Marnie looked pale, with large black circles under her weary eyes. Every few minutes the loudspeaker would hiss and loudly blast out details of incoming flights in Spanish. When the sound explosion occurred, the conversations would be forced to pause.

Gray was fighting fatigue and the haunting *you should be scared* voice that had permeated his subconscious while dozing off on the last flight from Toronto. He held his hands to his ears and winced, waiting for the next crackling blast from the loudspeaker to stop. "You're pretty brave to be returning to deal with the litigation ... to try and take control of your business back."

"It's either that or let the squatters take over, which I'm not prepared to do," Abby said with a smile. She stood about six feet tall with a curvaceous figure, long black hair, penetrating and lively brown eyes and a perfect smile that instantly put one at ease. Gray imagined she could light up any room she entered with her good humor, easy laugh and positive attitude. Earlier, she had mentioned she used to model. He didn't doubt it.

"Do you even know if anyone's at the hotel now?" Gray asked.

"No, I locked it when we left. I don't trust anyone to look after it anymore. Do you know all the staff I hired, who I bent over backwards for, ended up stealing from me?"

"It's hard to know who to trust."

"It's my own fault. I tend to be way too trusting of people. Then they take advantage of that trust."

"So what's your plan of attack?"

"First thing I have to do is see the lawyer. I have to see how the litigation is going against the owner and realtor."

"What do you have to gain from suing them?"

"My lawyer's very good."

Marnie only half listened to the conversation. Her bloodshot eyes told a story of pain, stress and fatigue. She had not slept a wink during the series of flights.

Abby continued: "His strategy is to put pressure on them with the lawsuit so that the realtor pressures the owner to turn over the business license. When that happens, we'll probably drop the lawsuit. I just need legal permission to operate. And, in this case, it means a license from the owner. So far he's been unwilling. But, when he gets served with a lawsuit, he may well change his mind. That's the hope anyway."

"Are you going to help her?" Gray said, turning to Marnie.

"That's the plan," she said, smiling weakly. "I've never been to Ecuador, so it should be an adventure."

"You didn't get much sleep on the plane?" Gray asked, immediately realizing he had already asked that question. *You're supposed to be taking her mind off her suffering, bonehead.*

"No ... but all I need is a good sleep, and I'll be good as gold."

Passengers began lining up to board the plane. Gray offered to stay at the Atacames hotel and offered his help if things got dicey. They exchanged contact details and chatted while moving along the line. Gray had told her about the details of his planned meeting with Adriana and jokingly added: "Maybe I'll get set up and thrown in jail. Be alongside you. But don't worry—we'll hatch an escape plan. I'll make a little paper airplane with the details and toss it in your cell. We'll escape by midnight, something like that."

Marnie and Abby laughed, even though Gray thought the comment was in bad taste, particularly since they were both entering unknown and potentially dangerous territory.

"Seriously, I'll come and stay there," Gray said as they moved to the front of the line. Marnie walked with a cane and was allowed pre-boarding privileges.

******

Gray played the scene over in his mind a few minutes after Peter had departed to check his laundry. He sipped a Brahma and contemplated a Skype call to Adriana. He logged in, verified she was online, and thought about what to say while the numbing effects of the alcohol, combined with travel fatigue, began to dull his senses. *At least I haven't gotten hit by altitude sickness ... yet.* He made the call.

"You're here. I don't believe it," Adriana said, beaming with excitement.

"I'm here honey." Gray had recently given up calling her by her first name. She didn't seem to mind. She looked stunning, her long black hair flowing seductively over her shoulders. They talked of his journey, his accommodations, and she had a few perfunctory questions about his thoughts on Quito, before getting to the important stuff.

"When are you coming to Guayaquil?" she asked.

Gray stalled for a few seconds. "I'm thinking of seeing a few sights here before booking a tour into the jungle." He had researched some jungle tours where travelers also got to witness a shaman perform a ritualistic healing ceremony. The idea intrigued and excited him. If he invited Adriana, he would probably have to pay for her. That could get costly. Better to knock off a few tours first.

A small frown creased her soft features. "Why don't you invite me?"

*No point in beating around the bush*, Gray thought. "Honey, I don't have a really big budget. I thought I could get this tour out of the way, since logistically I'm so close to the jungle, then head to Guayaquil to see you before traveling along the coast."

"I could figure a way to do it economically. I've never seen a shaman before. You probably will."

"Yes, I will."

"So when will you be in Guayaquil then?"

"I'm thinking probably next Saturday. Listen, we'll have lots of time to spend together. We'll have an awesome time. It's only another week or so. Will you wait?"

"Don't worry," she finally said, a smile slowly emerging on her pouty lips. "I'll wait for you. It's no problem."

Peter walked into the lobby, which was decorated with many plants. A large tree was rooted to the middle of the floor and surrounded by orange tile flooring. A circular hole about four feet had been precision-cut in the clear plastic roof, and the tree sprouted through it and into the sky. Peter held up a finger to Gray, who nodded. Peter disappeared and returned about a minute later with more beer. Gray thanked him and pointed to the image of Adriana on the computer. "What do you think?"

Peter nodded his approval.

"Do you want to say hello?"

Peter's eyes were glazed over from the alcohol. He nodded, took the headset, exchanged a few words with Adriana, and handed it back to Gray.

"She's hot," he said as Gray said goodbye and disconnected the call.

"We're going out for dinner," Peter said. "Want to come?"

Fifteen minutes later, Gray sat with three German travelers, Karina Koch, Peter Kruger and Thomas Schulze, in Vista Hermosa, an upscale restaurant in Quito with a panoramic view of the mountains and city. Most of the view showcased the spectacular old town, four-hundred-plus-year-old monuments to the city's first days. The city lights twinkled and fireworks skyrocketed into the air, lighting up the night.

As they ate dinner and sipped wine, Gray couldn't help stealing the occasional glance at Karina. At forty-five, she had a smooth white complexion, bright blue eyes, and long blond hair. An infectious smile with straight white teeth and a body with curves in all the right places complimented her assets.

"This view is incredible," Gray said, glancing at Karina. She smiled.

"I couldn't have asked for a better first day in Ecuador," he went on. "I already love the city. Look at this. Good company, an amazing view, good food and wine. What more could I ask for?"

The conversation was light and humorous as they finished their meal. Gray was beginning to feel the numbing effects of the wine combined with travel fatigue. "Since we've solved the world's problems—in two hours—what next?"

Karina stared up from her food, her deep blue eyes mesmerizing Gray. "I think we should go out and celebrate."

Thomas and Peter looked at her. With the exception of Gray, they all had to rise early the next day for organized tours around different parts of the country.

"I'm game for that," Gray said. "What did you have in mind?"

"There's a disco close to our hotel ... we can take a cab there," Karina said.

After a short discussion, Thomas and Peter agreed. "What the hell," Peter said. "You only live once. And this is our last night in Quito."

Twenty minutes later, they were in a dungeon-like bar, its dark walls decorated with colorful abstract paintings by local artists. They drank and joked as an older couple across the table tied into a twenty-six ounce bottle of vodka, a few carafes of orange juice and water for mix. The man's female companion drank mostly water, while he slammed back one drink after another. A thick mop of gray hair and grizzled beard, he looked about sixty-five.

Thomas and Karina were on the dance floor gyrating to pasillo music.

"Look at that guy over there," Gray gestured across the table. "He's going to finish off that whole bottle of vodka." It was half-gone already.

"Yeah, but he doesn't look too drunk," Peter said. Indeed, the man looked calm and composed, chatting with his female counterpart.

"Give him another hour," Gray said.

Peter nodded.

"I really like Karina," Gray said. "You sure you don't have a thing with her?"

"Strictly traveling companions."

"What about Thomas?"

"We only met him two days ago. I don't know if she likes him. I think she's just being sociable."

"I wouldn't mind dancing with her."

"Go for it."

A few minutes later, Gray escorted Karina to the dance floor. He had no idea how to move to the local music; but with liquid confidence it didn't matter. Karina admitted to not knowing any of the steps either; she just liked to dance. Gray held her close, slowly moving his hips close to hers. Their hips met. He pulled her closer and brought his face to her neck, which smelled faintly of honey and roses—a seductive combination. He pulled back, glancing into her eyes. She smiled.

"I like you," she said. "You dance very sexy."

"I like you too. I don't know what the hell I'm doing."

"But you do. It's very sexy."

He pulled her closer, thought about moving in for a kiss and then, even though the timing felt perfect, changed his mind. *Chances are, Thomas and Peter are watching.* Even though Peter had given Gray the green light, Thomas might not feel the same way. He was a strapping man of about two hundred and fifty pounds and, although a cheerful disposition countenanced his boyish features, Gray had only met him a few hours ago. For all he knew, Thomas may be fiercely jealous and have the temper to go with it.

Gray pulled back. Karina moved closer. He stared into her eyes and her face lit up with a wanting smile.

A few hours later, after the bar closed, they sat at a table in the terraced communal area of Casa Helbling, drinking beer; a nightcap before departing to bed. Gray sat beside Karina and slid a hand across her leg. He hoped the other two couldn't see.

Soon enough, Peter announced he was turning in. Thomas followed suit.

Gray was alone with Karina. He pulled her close and kissed her full on the lips. She hungrily reciprocated and they kissed passionately. "I had no idea this would happen," she said. "But I'm really attracted to you."

"The same," Gray said, kissing her soft cheek, continuing the soft pecks along her neck and ear. The fatigue and alcohol numbness was giving way to an anxious but giddy sexual tension.

Her breath came in short gasps. "I think you should take me to your room."

Gray took her hand and quietly led her into his room. Once inside, she pulled him onto the bed quickly. He lay down beside her and began kissing her lips, then along her neck and ear, and soon he had her blouse unbuttoned and was fondling and kissing her small but perky breasts. She moaned softly, unbuttoned his shirt, pulled it off and tossed it on the adjoining bed.

Soon he was inside her, feeling the tingly ecstasy of the moment. They gyrated in perfect harmony, moaning softly, before exploding simultaneously with intensely pleasurable orgasms.

Gray pulled the blankets up and cuddled her, kissing her softly on the neck while she moaned with pleasure.

"This is called a one-night stand, I believe," she whispered.

Gray couldn't help laughing. "Is that what it was for you?"

"I don't know. We don't know each other."

"Yeah, but I wouldn't mind getting to know you better. I like you."

"Me too."

"Why don't we travel together?" Gray said, knowing it was probably impossible. He had plans to meet Adriana, and Karina had said earlier she had a number of tours booked with Peter—even though during their first two weeks in Ecuador they had begun to argue over itinerary choice.

It was a question of timing and circumstance, and neither one seemed to be lining up in their favor. Karina knew nothing of Adriana yet, not that it was a big secret, but Gray was sure it would come out sooner or later during their travels.

"I don't think I can," Karina said, confirming Gray's thoughts. "We have everything planned and booked."

Gray wasn't usually so forthright with relationships. If anything, he shied away from them, and when he did become involved, he took things very slow. So, when he opened his mouth he didn't know if it was the alcohol talking or some infatuation with Karina that he had yet to fully comprehend. "Cancel your plans. You like me. I like you. A simple equation."

Karina smiled but remained silent.

"Wouldn't you like to hang around with me? I'm a good traveler, most of the time; although sometimes I overdo it and burn out. Maybe we'll become an item, and you can move to Canada." *What, are you fucking nuts? You just met her and you're talking like that. And you were whining about Adriana?*

"I don't know if I want to move to Canada. What would I do there?"

"I'll look after you," Gray said. *You will? You can barely look after yourself.*

She smiled. "I better go. You're really tired." Gray had some business cards on a small desk beside the bed that offered his services as a freelance ad-copy and SEO writer. He had dabbled in freelance promotional writing in the past but had given it up after the city hired him for a PR position he believed would be permanent. Maybe it was time to take up freelance writing again?

"Take one of my cards," he said, glancing at the travel alarm clock. It was closing in on five in the morning.

In the midst of picking up her clothes in the semi-dark room, she grabbed a card. "I'll send you a message."

"I'd like that," Gray said, while she dressed. His eyes were rapidly closing and the tendrils of sleep were clawing like black spiders inside his head.

"Don't get up," she said. "I'll see myself out."

He heard the door click shut as his mind blackened, finally overcome by alcohol, travel-weariness and the reality that his systems were still adjusting to a foreign city about nine thousand feet above sea level. Just before he drifted off, one thought materialized. It took all his concentration to push it away and allow sleep to pervade.

*Where is Strap?*

# Chapter Thirteen

Strap scratched the patchwork scruff that went only part way to covering his gaunt chin and grinned. It was two in the morning. He had just broken into Gray's bungalow, effortlessly picking a door lock. In Gray's office, he rummaged through papers. He had been watching the property for two days, confirming it vacant. He wanted to know Gray's whereabouts. Strap didn't take too kindly to people back-talking him, unless his biker boss Rocky approved of it or dished it out, as he often did. Then Strap would take it like a meek dog cowering from years of abuse. When Rocky gave an order, Strap wouldn't hesitate to follow it up. And Rocky had given the order to hunt Gray down and kill him.

Shining a pen-lite around the desk, he found a stack of papers that had a series of hand-written notes. His beady eyes lit up when he found the itinerary scrawled on a piece of paper.

*Montanita, December 11$^{th}$–21$^{st}$.*

*Perfect. This will be like killing fish in a bucket.*

Besides, The Chosen Ones had affiliates in Ecuador. It would be an opportunity to cement some of their cocaine-trade connections. He could kill two birds with one stone, almost literally. Rocky would be thrilled. Strap might be in line for a promotion.

He picked up the papers, tucked them in his pocket, and rummaged through some others. His crooked jaw contorted into a maniacal grin when he discovered Gray's flight itinerary. He fished out his cell phone and thought about calling Rocky, but at the last minute realized how stupid it was. Rocky would chastise him for calling from Gray's house.

And Strap had been chastised enough by Rocky in the recent past, not to mention the life of torment he had suffered at the hands of his abusive father. He still remembered the last thing his father said to him before he died of a fatal gunshot wound at Strap's hands: *"Put your tail between your legs and fuck off."*

When Gray uttered the exact same words only a few days ago, all the ugly emotions of his painful childhood had flashed to the surface. His trigger finger twitched while standing in front of the disrespectful fool, and it had taken every ounce of his resolve not to kill Gray then and there. But he had vowed to see to Gray's untimely end, and what better place to do it then Ecuador, where the chances of a murder being thoroughly investigated were slim to none. He rubbed his hands together with satisfaction as he slid out the side door, locked it, and disappeared into the night.

Strap had done enough time in jail. Those days were long behind him. He would rather die than end up behind bars a third time.

# Chapter Fourteen

The time had come. A few miles outside Quito, Gray rode a Panamericana bus down the twisting highway toward Guayaquil, gazing at but not seeing the lush gorges and cascading waterfalls that marked the descent to sea level. He had other things on his mind, specifically Adriana, who would be meeting him at Sweet & Coffee inside the busy terminal.

Since the unexpected one-night stand with Karina, he had mixed feelings about Adriana, like he had already cheated on her or something—even though their made-on-the-internet union could hardly be considered a monogamous commitment. His original plan had been to take a four-day tour into a jungle lodge just outside the village of Coca to see a shaman perform a traditional healing ceremony before returning to visit Adriana. But he soon realized the logistics no longer made sense—the next tour left in five days, meaning a longer stay in Quito than he had anticipated.

So, he had taken a full day to recover, then hired a taxi to help him buy a cheap cell phone for local calls. After the cell phone purchase, the taxi toured him around the old town.

He woke up the third day feeling a lot better, the result of a good sleep and a reprieve from the booze. That part wasn't easy. After all, he was a Canadian traveler. Once you secured your room, the staples were always alcohol and water. Food, well, that could wait.

For better or worse, he wanted to meet Adriana, wanted to know if she indeed was "the one."

And another disturbing fact encouraged him to start his journey north up the Costa del Sol. He had received a phone call from Abby yesterday, telling him the worst-case scenario had developed with her bar and hotel in Atacames. On her arrival, she discovered it had been taken over a second time by squatters. The police had managed to extricate the squatters, but now the locks had been changed, the doors padlocked shut. Abby wasn't allowed access to her property until the matter could be resolved legally, a process that could drag on for years. Gray had offered to help if he could when they had met in Lima, and now he was being held to his word, although he was not unaware of the risks involved.

The squatters were locals. Abby was an outsider. She was outnumbered and at a distinct disadvantage. It would not be out of the realm of possibility for the squatters to resort to intimidation, threats of violence, or actual violence to make a point. Did he really want to go there? What was he thinking?

Worrisome thoughts tumbled through his mind as he glanced out the window at the passing villages, many showing signs of squalor. He saw one indigenous woman sitting in the middle of a field, not a soul around for at least a mile, under a small makeshift tent, with a large plastic cooler in front of her. On the cooler sat ten different brands of soft drinks, samples of the products she sold.

Although the twenty-dollar ticket with the Panamericana bus company ostensibly meant a higher class ride, the bus rattled incessantly like a corrugated metal roof being pelted by hailstones. The small television screen at the front was turned off and pasillo music echoed from built-in overhead speakers. The outside temperature was stiflingly hot and the air-conditioning was not turned on. It was sticky hot inside the bus.

Occasionally, the bus stopped to discharge passengers, and street vendors would hop on and parade down the aisles, hocking their wares: snacks, liquid refreshment, fruit, in some cases prepared fruit salads and home-baked cookies. Gray purchased a bag of peanuts for fifty cents.

Adriana checked on his progress by calling every few hours. About two thirds of the way, the bus pulled over and the driver announced they would be changing buses. Apparently the elite Panamericana comfort machine had developed engine trouble. They disembarked, filed into the worn-out bus of a competitor, and carried on.

Exactly nine and a half hours after departure, they pulled into the bus terminal in Guayaquil. A few minutes later, weaving his way through throngs of shoppers (the terminal was enormous; with hundreds of retail outlets) and travelers, Gray stood in front of Sweet & Coffee and dialed Adriana, his stomach knotted with nervous tension and anticipation.

"I'm here," he said.

"I'll be there in five minutes."

He hung up and sat in the food court, exhausted from the visual sensory overload of the long journey. He recognized her in front of the coffee shop, and waved her over.

They hugged and he kissed her on the cheek.

"Are you hungry?" he asked.

"No." She smiled and looked at him with approval. She liked what she saw. Her Blackberry beeped a couple of times.

Gray frowned slightly. "Do you have some calls or texts to deal with?"

"It's my friend Jilliana. She wants a photo of you."

Gray shook his head. "I don't think so. Not right now, anyway."

She typed a few words into the Blackberry and then it rang. It was her sister, Marianna, checking in to see if she was okay. She talked briefly and then hung up.

"Do you know where you want to stay?" she asked. Gray looked at her vacantly for a few seconds before responding. He was trying to decide what to think of her, if she could be someone he could fall in love with and spend the rest of his life with. His gut feeling was already telling him no, and he couldn't put a finger on why. After all, physically she was attractive, even though that was far from everything. *Don't rush into a decision. Give her a chance. You just met her.*

He extracted a business card with the name, phone number and address of Hotel Versailles. He had heard it was reasonably priced, clean, centrally located downtown, within walking distance to the riverfront *malecon*, and close to the lively nightlife area of *Zona Rosa*.

A few minutes later, Gray rode in a yellow taxi while Adriana had an animated discussion with the driver. Something about the local government, but Gray wasn't paying enough attention to understand. He arrived in front of the hotel, located on a side street bustling with activity. It was just after six in the evening.

"Four dollars," the taxi driver said, parking. Adriana had negotiated the fare prior to boarding, always a good idea when taking a cab in Ecuador. Gray extracted four one-dollar coins, then, as an afterthought, produced a dollar tip and handed it to the driver. Adriana frowned at him as they exited.

He stood on the street beside her. "You don't tip taxis here," she said.

Gray knew the protocol. It had slipped his mind. He had read blog posts saying specifically not to tip taxi drivers in Ecuador. It sets a precedent; they begin to expect it not only from tourists, but also from locals. Apparently, the same axiom applied to local restaurants (the tip was already built into the price) with only a few exceptions.

"Sorry," he said. "I'll remember for next time."

He stared at her blankly for a moment, realizing he had no idea whether to book a single or double room. He didn't know her well enough to invite her to stay with him right away. But at the same time, would she be insulted if he just assumed and booked a single? Maybe it was polite to ask—at least that was what his muddled mind reasoned. "Am I going to book a room for two?"

She looked at him in surprise. "No, no. I'm going home later."

"Of course."

They entered the lobby. Gray arranged a room for two nights at $25 a night. As he fished into his pocket, he realized a hundred dollars was missing. It must have fallen out when he paid the taxi driver. He distinctly remembered having it earlier. He frowned, fished into his money belt for fifty dollars and paid the clerk.

Adriana offered to give him a short tour of the *malecon* after he checked in.

"I'm going to put my stuff up there. Do you want to come?" *You idiot. She doesn't even know you. Do you think she's going to accompany you to your room?*

"I'll wait here for you."

"Okay."

After returning, Gray searched the lobby floor, the sidewalk, and the road where he had exited the cab. The hundred dollars had disappeared.

"What's wrong?" Adriana asked.

"I lost a hundred dollars. I think it dropped inside the cab after I paid him."

She frowned and began searching the street, but no luck. "Sorry about that," she said a few minutes later as they strode toward the *malecon*.

Still preoccupied with the hundred-dollar hit, Gray responded with a comment that he would come to regret for a long time afterward. "If you hadn't been talking so much in the cab, I probably wouldn't have lost it. You distracted me."

Adriana immediately fell silent, frowning. Tears welled up in her eyes.

*How fucking stupid. No wonder you still don't have a girlfriend after all these years.*

After a few minutes of walking in silence, he stopped. "Hold up."

She stopped, turning to him with a distraught expression.

"I'm so sorry. That was a stupid thing to say. It was my fault and had nothing to do with you whatsoever. Please forgive me." On an impulse, he hugged her.

She didn't hug him back.

Adriana brushed away a tear and regarded him cautiously. "You made me feel so bad. I was tempted to take you to a bank machine, get your hundred dollars and tell you to have a good life."

"I don't blame you. I was an asshole. Can we put it behind us?"

Slowly her features softened and a cheerful smile returned. They walked a few more blocks in silence before she finally said: "What do you want to do at the *malecon*?"

"What is there to do? Is there some place to have a drink?"

"It's Monday, so most businesses are closed; we'll see what we can find."

They strolled along the *malecon* for a few blocks, enjoying the expansive Guayas river view and the twinkling city lights.

They crossed a street and ascended a large stone staircase. Gray wanted more than ever to sit down and drink a beer. They slowly reached the top of the stairs, enjoying the water and city view for a few minutes before finally spotting a small restaurant with one outdoor table and two vacant chairs. They sat down, ordered two Club beers, sipped and talked.

One part of Adriana hadn't forgotten about the hundred-dollar debacle. "I felt so bad back there."

"I know and I'm sorry."

They began discussing Guayaquil sightseeing opportunities. By that time, Gray was on his fifth beer, Adriana her second. Her mood seemed brighter, although Gray still felt like a complete shit about his earlier comment.

"If you want, we can go on a boat ride along the river tomorrow," Adriana said.

"That sounds good," Gray said, noticing it was almost 9:30 pm. He didn't want to walk around the downtown core too late. He still had his money belt, credit cards, passport and about six hundred in cash. He had forgotten to leave it in the hotel suite.

They discussed taking a taxi back to the hotel, and finally decided to walk the twenty minutes along the well-lit *malecon*. There were no unfortunate surprises, and Gray was beginning to enjoy the Guayaquil vibe, a pleasant and calm sensation he found hard to describe.

At the hotel, he hugged Adriana and kissed her on the cheek. He agreed to call her as soon as he got up the following morning. She promised to show him more of the city's attractions.

After she left, he went out and found a nearby supermarket, where he purchased four large Pilsner beers and a large bottle of water, and returned to the hotel.

Outside, a gringo stood smoking a cigarette. He introduced himself as Brad Ramsey, and soon they were upstairs on Gray's second-floor balcony, watching the street life and drinking. Already sporting a glow, Gray was developing a craving for more beer, ignoring the instructions of his tired body to get the hell to bed.

# Chapter Fifteen

More time in bed was exactly what he needed at 6:00 am the following morning, waking abruptly to the sound of barking dogs and the steady din of bustling traffic, honking horns and pedestrians shouting.

Gray tried to recollect the evening with Brad. Two bars, ten or more beers, two taxis, and home at 2:00 am. His head pounded like a jackhammer on concrete. He vaguely remembered tossing and turning for most of the night, before finally drifting off into a fitful sleep at about 4:30 am, with the aid of earplugs and sleeping pills. As he staggered into the washroom to relieve himself, he felt like getting on a plane and returning to the familiar surroundings of his comfortable bungalow and sorting his life out.

*What the fuck am I doing here, anyway?*

He slipped on a pair of shorts and a t-shirt and surveyed the city life from the balcony. There was a lot of free entertainment. As buses roared past below, he gawked into the windows at passengers, in some cases right down the tops of women who had decided to sport a little cleavage on their way to work.

Feeling like a pervert, he closed the balcony door and returned to bed. But the noise was too loud and it was futile to try to sleep. So, finally at 9:30 am he showered and dialed Adriana, noticing as he left the bathroom mirror that his eyes were bloodshot and pupils dilated. Space cadet was written all over his fatigued face. *Fuck sightseeing. I'll suggest something else when she arrives.*

Adriana agreed to meet him in an hour outside his hotel. She lived in Villa España, a gated middle-to-lower class community forty minutes north of the city.

"I have a different plan in mind today," Gray said to her in the lobby. "Sorry. I met an American guy last night, and we went out partying after you left. I didn't get a lot of sleep. Too much street noise." Gray had thought about changing hotels, but at the last minute changed his mind. He was sure once he acclimatized to the noise, he would be fine. He just needed a break from it for a few hours, some time to regroup mentally.

Adriana looked at him quizzically. She was fresh and alert, her black hair neatly braided and flowing down her shoulders and back. "What do you want to do?"

"I was thinking maybe we could visit your house, check out your neighborhood a bit; maybe have lunch there or something."

"Oh my god ... not my place. I haven't even cleaned it."

"I don't care about that. You say it's a quiet neighborhood?"

"Yes."

"Then let's go. Please."

She agreed and they hailed a cab. "You stand back there," she said. "Let me do the negotiating."

Gray nodded and stepped back, just within earshot. Two official and two unofficial taxis were parked in front of the hotel. One cabbie wanted six dollars and Adriana insisted on five. The man wouldn't budge so she approached another one, had a short conversation and waved Gray over. He sat in the front, Adriana in the back. *My first bonehead move for today. At least I could have joined her in the back.*

Gray turned to her. "I'm not saying a thing," she said. It was followed by a few tense moments of silence.

Finally, he asked: "What did you get up to last night?"

"I ended up drinking with my girlfriend, Jilliana."

"Really? How many beers?"

"About six."

"What did you guys talk about?"

"Of course, she wanted to know everything about you."

"What did you tell her?"

"Woman stuff. You wouldn't be interested."

The conversation abruptly ended and the taxi stopped at a red light on a congested street. Gray surveyed the other cars, and suddenly did a double-take. A man resembling Strap, a baseball cap pulled down over his face, sat in a taxi, having an animated conversation with another passenger. The man glanced at Gray and Gray quickly looked away.

The light turned green to honking horns, and the taxi merged into traffic, cutting off the car that appeared to be occupied by Strap.

*Strap? He wouldn't come looking for me here. How would he know? Wake up and smell the coffee. It's your imagination.*

"Are you okay?" Adriana asked, noticing Gray's face was as white as a bleached bed sheet.

"Yeah—just lack of sleep. I'll be fine." Gray fought to prevent his heart from exploding out of his mouth.

A few minutes later, the taxi entered the patrolled gates of the barrio, and the barrier was lifted as a friendly guard recognized Adriana. Gray was pleasantly surprised by the community. Rows and rows of concrete houses, mostly attached, lined the quiet streets, many with corrugated tin roofs.

"Right here is good," Adriana said. The taxi stopped.

They entered the house. It was a sparsely furnished three-bedroom bungalow-style home with one bath and an open concept kitchen and dining room, which doubled as a living room. Rough walls were painted white.

Slightly embarrassed, Adriana quickly started organizing some of the disarray. But the home wasn't that dirty. Some dust lined the wooden television stand in the flex room, the sink was full of dirty dishes, and there were some clothes scattered on the floor of Adriana's bedroom. But not really messy enough to be defined as a dirty house; lived in, maybe.

Fatigue was starting to envelop Gray, in part due to the adrenaline dump at seeing what he thought was Strap. *It couldn't be. You're dead.* He pushed the panic-inducing thoughts from his mind and tried to bring off a tone that sounded alert and awake, the opposite of how he felt. "It's a nice house; a very quiet neighborhood."

"It's very peaceful here."

Gray sat down at the table and asked for a glass of water. At least it was quiet. She returned with it, asking him what he wanted to do.

What he wanted to do was crawl onto the queen-sized mattress on the floor of her bedroom and sleep for ten hours. "Why don't we go for a stroll around your neighborhood?"

"Sounds good," she said smiling. "We can eat lunch afterwards."

# Chapter Sixteen

"Montanita will eat you up and spit you out if you let it," an American said.

Gray thought his name was Scott, but he couldn't be sure anymore. The small bar that also served as an administration building for Casa Del Sol, a Canadian-owned hostel, was packed with gringos, bellying up to trade travel tales over beer and rum cocktails. They were in various stages of a pickling by alcohol process.

Adriana and Gray had arrived at the small beach town early that afternoon after a two and a half hour bus ride from Guayaquil. It was now nine at night, and she was upstairs having a nap, having listened to two hours of gringos speaking English before realizing learning another language was producing a headache.

As the laughter-filled conversation hummed along, Gray thought about what the American had said. Having toured the center of the small town earlier in the day, he could certainly see the potential for Montanita to chew you up and spit you out. Restaurants, bars and street-vendors, selling stiff cocktails for two and a half bucks each, lined the crowded streets. They were joined by gringo hippies, many surviving by hocking their wares on the streets. Music blared from many venues, each playing a different song by a different band. Just when you thought you identified the sound, a blast from another band would assault your ears and you couldn't name that tune.

People walking in slow motion made their way along the street, many with glazed looks of hangovers or intoxication. The smell of marijuana was rife, cocaine use rampant.

But the nice beach and equally attractive surf seduced people from all walks of life. Montanita was still a preferred favorite among many backpackers.

He would find out soon enough. He planned on waking Adriana in an hour or so to make the fifteen-minute walk along the beach from the much quieter Montanita Baja to the center of the mayhem.

His thoughts drifted back to a conversation he had a few hours earlier over coffee at the Guayaquil bus terminal. Adriana had passed the phone to him, saying her mother wanted a few words with him. Gray had reluctantly taken the phone. The words still reverberated in his head: " "'You better take good care of my daughter, or else.'"

"Or else what?" a drunk Brit asked.

"Did I say that out loud?"

"Say what?" the man asked, gazing into his drink. "You said something. I didn't hear what it was."

"You just said 'or else,'" Gray said, wondering if he was losing his mind.

"I was talking to Scott," the man said. "He was talking about a threat from one of his girlfriends."

Gray thought better of asking what their conversation was about. He had enough of his own shit to deal with right now. Originally, he had felt safe with Adriana, particularly after a conversation they had had in Guayaquil. He had moved in for a kiss, and she turned her face away, converting it into a harmless peck on the cheek. "What's wrong?" he had asked. "Don't you like me?"

"It's got nothing to do with that," she had said. "I just know that eventually you'll be leaving, and probably not coming back. I don't want an adventure. I don't want to suffer after you leave. It's better for us to stay friends only."

That announcement had taken the heat off. Gray really didn't want to mislead Adriana. If he wasn't in love with her, he certainly wasn't going to tell her otherwise. That would be cruel and unwise, especially in light of recent developments. That meant he could have a traveling companion, albeit on his dime, but someone who could educate him on Ecuadorian culture, almost like a paid tour guide. It would be a perfect opportunity to learn about life in Ecuador from an insider's perspective, and also practice his Spanish.

But the threat from her mother had put a new and unfriendly twist on things. Anything Gray said or did could constitute maltreatment in Adriana's eyes. To what lengths would she go to exact her revenge? He had no idea. And two cop brothers?

"Get away from me with that cigarette," a thirty-something Canadian woman said to a man sitting beside her, pushing his smoking hand away.

"Why are you such a bitch?" the man asked.

"I've had too much sun and I'm irritable."

*Then why don't you take a nap*? Gray thought. He had observed her conversation earlier and noticed a definite attitude problem. She thought she was all that. In his view she was an arrogant and self-centered wannabe princess.

But her traveling companion took it in stride, at least for a few minutes. "Why don't you shut up," he finally blurted out.

"You're a fucking drunken idiot," she said. "And an American to boot; which makes you completely intolerable."

The man said nothing. A few minutes later, he found another spot at the bar and made conversation with another traveler. The woman began flirting with the bartender.

*Princess*, Gray thought. *Canadian princess.*

A few hours later, as he and Adriana stood in front of a street vendor, well into his third rum punch cocktail, Gray wondered how long Adriana's assault would continue. Adriana was keeping pace with him. Only problem was, she wasn't handling the alcohol very well. The music blared; partiers strolled along the busy noise-filled streets, many with drinks.

A local husband and wife team sat behind the makeshift bar listening to Adriana's tirade. The man frowned and eyed Gray occasionally, waiting for some kind of defense reaction.

"The Canadian culture is cold in more ways than one," Adriana said. "Canadians have no close bonds with their families like us."

"Our culture is different," Gray said. "Just because we choose not to live with one another doesn't mean we don't love each other. Besides, in a first-world country, it's a lot easier for us to be more independent."

"Well, I hear gringos are as stiff as a board in bed. No passion. Have sex, roll over and go to sleep."

At least for the time being, Gray let that one alone.

Adriana, although she had never left Ecuador, claimed it was absolutely the best country in the world to live, bar none, as well as being the most beautiful.

Gray let that one slide as well, but a few minutes later he had had enough, the alcohol, as it so often does, impairing his better judgment. "From what I hear, Ecuadorian women are terrible in bed."

The bartender rolled his eyes while his wife frowned.

"How the hell would you know?" Adriana said. "You've probably never slept with an Ecuadorian woman."

That much was true, but Gray was reluctant to admit it. Luckily, the bartender interjected with a serious comment about what a great couple Adriana and Gray made. For the time being, she forgot her subject of ridicule and put an arm around Gray, smiling drunkenly. She kissed him full and hard on the lips, biting his chin sharply while withdrawing. He rubbed the red mark and forced a smile.

A few minutes later, he apologized for the comment. They kissed and made up.

One hour later, straddling Adriana doggie-style, panting and pumping her hard like a turbo-charged piston, one thought lingered in his mind. He was entering the jaws of a great white shark. It wasn't a question of if, but when the jaws would come snapping down, chew him up and spit him out in a million broken pieces.

# Chapter Seventeen

A few days later, staring at the formidable ocean waves splashing ashore from the second-floor common balcony of the delightful Roa Hanga Hostel in Montanita, Gray struggled to put the pieces together. He wanted to get the hell away from Adriana. But why? The sex was good, falling short of being excellent because of an animalistic instinct she possessed in bed. She was a nymphomaniac, who wanted it rough, hard, fast and often. Gray, on the other hand, wasn't into macho aggressive stuff, and preferred a much gentler fashion of making love. Adriana talked about sex often, including different positions she wanted to try. Every day she would ask Gray at what time he was planning on making love to her. It made the whole process forced, sucked the passion and excitement right out of it.

That and she not only smothered him with attention, but was very demanding of his attention. Normally he would read a couple novels a week while traveling, but now, having been with Adriana almost two weeks, he had barely gotten to page ten of *Distraction* by Bruce Sterling, a novel he had planned on finishing by now. She always had to have her hands all over him, and explained it away by saying they were together now, a couple, and that was how couples in Ecuador behaved.

Gray wondered if there was a fundamental difference between the culture in Ecuador and Canada, a gap in the way they processed information that perhaps could never be bridged, at least in his case. All the passion and all the love in a matter of two weeks. Adriana had told Gray she loved him at least a dozen times. Things were moving much too fast for his liking.

Or maybe he was just on edge, still haunted by the apparent sighting of Strap in Guayaquil. Something told him there was a very real danger lurking ahead. And, if his gut was right, Adriana, by association, could also be in danger. That was a good reason to send her packing.

But of course some of Adriana's passion was appreciated. During one conversation, she educated Gray on how couples act in Ecuador. "Not everything has to lead to sex," she had said. "Like if we're sitting together and you decide you want to suck my breasts for a few hours and do nothing else, it's all good. By the same token, if I'm stroking you like this, it doesn't always mean I want sex with you. It just means we're in love."

"Let me get this straight. So if I want to suck or fondle your breasts it doesn't always have to lead to sex?"

"No. And if you want me to suck you off, all you have to do is whip it out, grab me by the hair—push my mouth to you."

"That leads to sex. That is sex."

She said nothing.

"So if I want a blowjob, I just grab you and pull your head here?"

"Or just pull down your pants and tell me to suck it."

The conversation led to one of the finest blowjobs Gray had ever received.

But it was the constant need for attention, the constant touching, staring at him in an I-want-your-attention-now kind of way that was starting to trouble Gray. He was being smothered. While it might be true that in Latin American countries, the locals carried on their relationships with intense and constant back-and-forth attention, he didn't think the same applied in Canada. Public displays of affection, the norm in Ecuador, were not so forthcoming in Canada. For the most part, people frowned at couples openly necking in restaurants and bars. Hence the saying: "Get a room!"

He flicked open his laptop and searched the e-mails, at the same time mulling over how to dispatch Adriana diplomatically. His eyes widened as he noticed an e-mail from Karina. He hadn't heard from her since their passion-filled night at Casa Helbling. He had become convinced it was nothing more than a one-night stand, and put it out of his mind.

> *Hi Gray. I had a great time with you in Quito. Peter and I had a fight and for now we separated. I have a few days free before I head to the Galapagos Islands. If you want to spend some time with me, let me know.*
>
> *Kisses, Karina*

"What are you doing, baby?" Adriana wrapped her arms around Gray's shoulders, hugged him tightly, and kissed him softly on the neck and face.

He fought to control an instinct to slam the laptop shut, instead setting it on a small plastic table beside the lounge chair. "Checking up on some business."

"Is everything okay?"

"Yes." *Think of something, and quickly, you bonehead.*

She sat down beside him, teasingly stroking his leg.

*There's only one way to do this.* "Listen Adriana ... I think it might be good to have a few days apart." Her brow wrinkled and she frowned. "I don't know how else to say this, but I need some private time."

She quickly released the massaging hand, got up and walked briskly down the hall to their suite without saying a word.

Gray waited about a half hour before getting up from his sunset view. He would have to approach this one gently. Once inside the room, he settled in beside her in bed, snuggled close, and kissed her tenderly on the neck and cheek. He felt terrible. "Adriana, this has nothing to do with you."

"That's a lie and you know it. You don't love me anymore."

Had he ever loved her? In such a short time? He had to admit he liked her. But love? That was a strong emotion. They had just met and were already vacationing together, sharing intimate moments in hotel suites. Everything had happened way too fast. But how do you tell a woman that she's probably not your type when you're in her country, she has two cop brothers, and you really don't know her that well? This wasn't going to be easy.

"It has nothing to do with you. It's just that I need some time to myself," Gray lied. "Maybe we can get together after I travel for a few days." He pulled her closer, kissing her cheek twice before finding her lips. She smiled, pulling him closer. *Give her what she wants. It'll be easier that way.*

# Chapter Eighteen

"It's that way," Lance Elms said, poking his head out of the water, only to be smashed by another enormous wave. Two heads submerged. An athletic man and a strong swimmer, Lance had thought he could handle the ferocious undertow that every year claimed the lives of numerous swimmers off the coast of Montanita. But now he and his pretty wife Lacy were far away from the shore, and being carried further and further out to sea. Lance had tried not to panic, knowing that in most cases if an undertow drags you out, eventually it will bring you back. You just had to be patient.

But he was getting tired, and Lacy had already swallowed a few mouthfuls of seawater.

Lance stuck his head out, searching for her. He saw an arm extend out of the water. She poked her head out, spit water, and coughed. He swam over and wrapped his arms around her, supporting her head. Her eyes were wide, and Lance knew she was close to panicking. "Stay calm," he said. "The tide should bring us back."

She coughed, cleared her throat, and spit out a mucous ball and a mouthful of salt water. The sticky mixture clung to her chin and spidery wet lines fanned out like a frothing canine. She was becoming disoriented. "Where's the shore?" she asked.

Lance pointed. It was dusk and the sky was a fiery orange. Small twinkling lights were barely visible on the shoreline. They had been drifting out to sea for the last two hours and the situation was worsening. Soon the ocean swells would make the shoreline difficult to see and their tender grip on life would worsen.

Lance only had time to point at the lights before another huge wave washed over them, pulling them deep underwater. Thirty seconds later, Lance popped his head out, frantically searching the black water for a sign, any sign of his wife. He felt the panic rising in his throat, mixed with the unwelcome taste of the salty sea. Now he was the one beginning to panic.

"Lacy ... Lacy ... Lacy, where are you?" He dunked his head underwater, squinting to try to find his drowning wife. But it was too dark. He felt something brush against his leg and jerked spasmodically. A large shark swam past, its eyes glowing portentously.

Lacy popped her head up, coughing and spewing salt water and mucous. Surging with adrenaline, Lance swam toward her, lifted her head and cradled her. He vowed not to release her this time, regardless of the ferocity and strength of the ocean. He would cling to her and drown with her if that was to be his fate. Bobbing in the rough swells, she stared at him, resignation now etched into those soulful blue eyes. She had no more strength for struggle and wanted it to be over.

"No," Lance said. "We're not going to die here. I promise you." He searched the ocean waters for a sign of life. A fishing boat. There must be fishing boats out here.

He heard it before he saw it. The rumbling of an engine.

\*\*\*\*\*\*

Sitting on the small fishing boat, accompanied by two Ecuadorians, Strap pointed toward the panicked cries. "Over there. I heard something."

Cesar nodded, turned the boat and accelerated toward the sound. Strap extracted a large flashlight and scanned the waters.

"Help ... we're drowning. Over here."

Strap smiled. This was going to be entertaining. Cesar pulled the boat to within twenty feet of the bobbing, coughing heads, and killed the motor. "You thought you were strong swimmers, did you?" Strap asked.

"Help us," Lance said, pulling his wife toward to boat. She was swallowing way too much ocean water. It was only a matter of time.

"You want to be saved?" Strap asked, as the Ecuadorians grinned.

"Of co ..." Lance started, before another large wave washed over them. They bobbed to the surface a while later, but Lacy had lost consciousness, a peaceful resignation on her soft features. Lance spit out mouthfuls of water and stared at his wife, eyes widening in fear. He started mouth-to-mouth resuscitation, stopped and acknowledged his tormentors. "Get us out of here ... please."

"How much is your life worth?" Strap asked matter-of-factly.

"What?"

"How much will you pay us for saving you? You heard me."

"I'll give you ten thousand dollars."

"You can do better than that. Is that all your life, the life of your pretty wife, is worth?"

"Twenty thousand," Lance shouted before another wave crashed over them. His head bobbed to the surface a few seconds later. He coughed and spit before replying. "I'll give you a hundred thousand."

"If you can give us a hundred thousand, you can give us five hundred thousand."

A CEO of a large accounting firm, Lance certainly had the money. He had hoped to escape with a fraction of his fortune, but he grimly realized his wife had stopped breathing, and he was far from being in a position to negotiate a better deal. If he didn't get Lacy aboard the boat soon, and begin immediate mouth-to-mouth resuscitation, she would be dead. She might already be beyond saving. "Okay, okay, five hundred thousand."

"No bullshit?" Strap said to the bobbing heads. "Because if you're bullshitting us, your death will be much worse than a simple drowning."

"No bullshit ... I promise."

Strap waved to Cesar, who started the motor and revved the boat toward the desperate couple. He waved to Israel, the young Ecuadorian in for a twenty-five per cent cut of the profits. This would be the third rescue the crew had performed this evening, and Strap thought they had the process down to what he would later refer to as "a fine art."

The rescue complete, the boat sped toward shore as Lance frantically tried to save Lacy. "Whether she lives or dies, you still owe the half million," Strap said, rubbing his hands together. A good haul. A few hours on the water rescuing overconfident and stupid swimmers, and the trio had hauled in a cool million dollars, fifty per cent of which went to Strap and his gang of degenerate dirt bags.

Lisa coughed, spit out a small fountain of water, and came back to life.

# Chapter Nineteen

"You only have one life, so you better make the best of it," Gray told Scott the American and Russell the Brit while sipping rum and Coke at the Casa Del Sol bar. It was eleven in the evening, and the bartender had already called last call. Gray wanted more booze. He was in a celebratory mood after diplomatically discharging Adriana while simultaneously making plans to hook up with Karina the next day in the small beach town of Canoa.

"You got that right," Russell said, grinning and scratching a head full of black fuzz.

"Why don't we go find a beach party?" Scott asked through glazed eyes. He wore a permanent grin. Gray had only met the pair a few hours earlier, but they had become fast friends, as is often the case when you're traveling. You had to trust someone, sometime. And it was often smarter to extend your trust to other travelers to watch each other's backs, or alternatively, get each other into trouble.

This conversation was steering toward the latter, not that Gray cared much at the moment. The stories of rape and robbery were parked far into the recesses of a mind pickled by alcohol. Gray ignored the voice of reason that said go to the hostel, climb into bed, and get a good night's sleep, even though he wanted to be fresh for his rendezvous with Karina; even though he was excited at the prospect of seeing the woman he had once believed to be but a mere flash in the pan of life's experiences.

Scott returned with a large bottle of local rum and three plastic cups just as the bartender pulled down the metal-slatted doors. "You guys be careful," he said, the heavy doors thudding shut on the countertop.

The three staggered along the beach and soon discovered a small blaze. About ten people sat beside it, in various stages of intoxication, a small thatched-roof shack off in the distance serving as an impromptu bar. A ghetto blaster thumped out *Metallica ... nothing else matters.*

It didn't take Gray long to engage two young Ecuadorian men in conversation. They were interested in Canadian culture, and discussing classic rock 'n roll singers. Scott, meanwhile, had parked himself down on a log beside an attractive Ecuadorian woman, while Russell purchased two rum cocktails at the bar and staggered around, double-fisted, uttering incomprehensible gibberish. Every so often he would punctuate his monologue by singing ... "nothing else matters."

"There's people leaving," Russell said, sometime later, bumping Gray's shoulder and spilling part of his drink—straight rum.

"What do you want to do?" Gray asked.

"The night's young," Russell said. "Like you said, you only get one life ... you have to make the best of it."

"We'll drive you home," one of the Ecuadorian men said. The partiers were departing, and the small incandescent bulb lighting the bar had been turned off.

Russell raised an eyebrow at the Ecuadorian men.

"I'd rather head into town," Gray said, knowing that other beach parties would be in the center of Montanita, a short five-minute drive from their current location.

One of the Ecuadorians shook his head. "It's dangerous at night for you guys to be walking around downtown—especially drunk."

"And I can't even speak Spanish," Russell said.

On occasion, Adriana and Gray had walked the short distance from their hostel into town, returning by walking along the beach. Not a single incident had occurred that might leave him frightened. But his judgment was severely impaired. At least for the moment, erased were the many stories he had heard of tragedies on the beach. People being robbed at night, raped, in some cases drugged with truth serum drugs or other memory-blanking concoctions. In one case, he had been told a man was lured into a car by two women, and his drink spiked with a truth serum concoction. After the man disclosed the location and pin numbers for all his credit cards, they had kindly deposited him over the side of a cliff. He woke up scratched, bruised and battered by the fall, fortunate to have survived the ordeal. There were even reports of victims being drugged into a state of memory loss and delirium by the swipe of a drug-laced handshake. And it was only the tip of the iceberg, Gray knew.

At least at one time he knew it. Now, nothing else mattered but the search for another party in the dangerous and dark streets of Montanita. Never mind the fact he was about to get in a car with two strangers, dragging along another unsuspecting tourist.

A few minutes later, he and Russell sat in the back of a small car, headed toward Montanita central. The driver stopped at a dark intersection, where a dimly lit street led downtown. "Are you sure you guys want to do this? I can take you to your hotel."

"We'll be fine," Gray said. "I can talk the talk and walk the walk."

"Be careful," the young man said as he and Russell climbed out and closed the doors.

"First stop, alcohol," Gray said as they unsteadily weaved down the street.

Gray approached three black men huddled under a streetlight sharing a joint. "Is there a store open nearby?"

An afro-headed man grinned, exposing crooked teeth. His eyes were glazed over, barely visible in the faint light. "Want a toke?"

Gray shook his head while Russell staggered down the street, thumping music echoing in the distance. There was a party somewhere.

"Two blocks straight and your first right."

Gray thanked the man and hurried to catch up with Russell, who by this time had approached a local man. They argued heatedly. Gray had no idea what started it, but the man uttered profanities in Spanish while Russell reciprocated in English. They appeared to understand each other. Intonation and facial expressions speak volumes.

Gray grabbed Russell's arm and pulled him along. "Sorry," he said, turning to the Ecuadorian. "He's drunk."

"He's also a fucking asshole," the man said, shaking a fist.

Luckily, the angry man did not follow as they turned the corner and saw the lights of the small store, a few locals loitering outside appraising them cautiously. It was very late, and most of the street parties and bars had closed for the evening, the few remaining stragglers likely of the dangerous strain. Gray wasn't liking this anymore.

An old woman appeared out of nowhere and approached Gray as he stopped in front of the store. She said something he didn't understand. He told her in Spanish to leave him alone, please.

"I'm American," she said. She looked to be mid-seventies, with frilly gray hair streaked red with a bad dye-job. Her face was wrinkled and large black circles framed her hollow and sad eyes. She was almost pitiful—a lost expat whose vision of paradise had turned into a morally bankrupt struggle for survival. "You're retired down here, right? I can help you. You should get with me. I'll show you a good time."

"I'm not retired. I'm working. I'm only here for a few months."

She approached Gray and gripped his arm. Two black men outside the store glared as she continued pestering him.

"Come with me," she said. "We can be together. I'll show you a good time."

"Please leave me alone."

Gray entered the store. She and the two men followed. He ordered a small bottle of rum, two plastic cups, a ten-pack of Marlboro Lights and some matches. He needed a smoke right now, even though he had given up the habit over ten years ago.

The men stood behind them. Gray could feel their cold stares.

"Can you give me some money?" the woman said as Gray paid for the items. He glanced at the woman, and at the two men, who, without saying anything, were saying you better give her some money or else.

"Leave me alone," Gray said. The woman inched closer and grabbed his elbow firmly. The men stepped closer. Gray might have been buzzed, but not so wasted as to realize he was in a tight spot. He had heard a story in Quito talking to an expat resident. On his first year there, a beggar had asked for a dollar and the Swiss foreigner had told him to get lost. A few weeks later, the same man cornered the unsuspecting expat with a broken beer bottle, saying: "I asked you for a dollar the first time and you refused. Now I want it all." The result: the expat had been robbed of $60 and beaten to within inches of his life.

The elderly shopkeeper took Gray's money and provided change nonchalantly.

Gray turned to leave, and then on an impulse said to the shopkeeper: "Hey, I'm a customer and I'm getting harassed in your store. Please help me. Get rid of these people."

The man looked at Gray, stone-faced, and said nothing.

"Give me some money," the woman demanded.

The black men nodded.

"Give me a dollar," she said.

Gray pulled out a dollar coin, handed it to her and left, sure they would pursue him.

He turned onto a dark side street and quickened his pace for half a block. He stopped and glanced back. He sighed deeply. They hadn't followed. He lit a smoke, inhaling a few deep drags and searching the streets for Russell, who was nowhere in sight. Gray quickened his pace as his heart rate sped up. He glanced behind him, turned a corner, and saw an incandescent light bulb illuminating a nondescript store. He could barely make out the shadowy image of Russell arguing with someone.

As he neared, the two, exchanging vulgarities, disappeared around a corner. Gray rolled up the plastic bag containing his staples for the evening and ran in pursuit. He rounded a corner and stopped. One lone streetlight in the distance lit an otherwise dark street. Russell had disappeared.

# Chapter Twenty

"I'll make him disappear," Strap said to no one in particular as he watched a shadowy figure stagger along a dimly lit street toward the beach. "And everyone'll think it's just another robbery and murder of a gringo stupid enough to walk around drunk in the middle of the night. It won't even be investigated." Strap didn't talk to himself often, but tonight he certainly felt a little self-conversation was in order. After all, he had just made a cool million exploiting overconfident swimmers, and solidified his connections with the Ecuadorian arm of Rocky's drug-smuggling operation. There was only one small task left to do before he could board a plane and get the fuck out of this god-forsaken place. To others it might not be god-forsaken—the Galapagos Islands, part of Ecuador, were surely one of the most awe-inspiring natural wonders of the world—but to Strap, it certainly was. His Spanish was survival at best, and he found the cultural differences spanned a gap much too wide to ever bridge. Truth be told, he was hardly a man of culture, but he was particularly offended by many of the stares he received from the locals. Sure, he was a gringo, and locals just stare at gringos. But Strap hated people who stared at him. His father used to stare at him, glare at him really, and it was almost always a precursor to the strap—vicious and repeated punishment with a black leather belt. He still remembered vividly the dark eyes regarding him with malice before the strap would be unbuckled, unleashed from the waist of the black polyester pants his father often wore, typically with a loathsome leathery snapping sound, and the lashing would commence. Strap had once hated the black belt, hated the snapping sound it made, hated even more the slapping sound as it made excruciatingly painful contact with his face, arms, buttocks and legs.

But not anymore.

Now he loved the belt, the strap. Stuart Treblecoch loved it so much he had become The Strap, a nickname that had started at childhood and had followed him into adult life. A nickname he once despised, but now wore the shortened version—Strap—like a badge of honor. He had become the embodiment of the cruel instrument of punishment that had struck fear, terror and permanent psychological scarring into the hearts and minds of millions. And he had become an expert with the strap. He unbuckled it, flicked it adeptly, snapping the instrument of torture quickly at the face of the naked prostitute sitting on his bed, staring. It lashed the side of her face with a snap and she screamed, instinctively bringing both hands to a V-shaped cut that reddened and trickled blood. Strap was better with the belt than his late father Ross ever had been. He could usually draw blood on the first strike. It was an art form. If only he could unleash it onto the faces of every Ecuadorian who cast that annoying you're-not-as-tough-as-you-think-you-are stare. That would be sweet justice. Then they would understand. *You don't stare at me. Not now. Not ever.*

He had thought of fucking the young hooker one more time just for good measure, but that thought had quickly evaporated after glancing from his hotel suite balcony and noticing the staggering man that *had* to be Gray. That son of a bitch was going to pay. He was going to get The Strap.

He was about to give her another quick flick of the leather weapon but the singular thought of revenge overrode any desire for more unsolicited violence, although he knew there would be no repercussions should he change his mind. Raul Allende, the ruthless local partner of the cocaine and marijuana smuggling operation, had assured Strap when he provided the twenty-four-year-old women: "Do what the fuck you want with her."

Strap knew that meant he could even kill her without retribution. How sweet life was when you had the right connections. But there was no time for that now. He pointed to the door, snapping the strap into the air expertly. "Get the fuck out of here, bitch. NOW!"

She didn't waste any time dressing and bolting for the door, tears streaming down her tender young cheeks.

Strap grinned. There would be hell to pay tonight.

# Chapter Twenty-One

Staggering up to a raucous beach party, rock 'n roll music echoing through the night from a small portable stereo, young people gathered around a large bonfire, Gray realized through an alcohol-induced fog this evening wasn't going to plan. Did he even have a plan? He pulled out the bottle of rum, poured a couple of ounces into a small cup, and sucked back the contents. He thought his plan was to enjoy himself with a couple of newfound friends, but they had mysteriously disappeared. Then the incident in the store, a disturbing extortion of a dollar from an unsuspecting tourist, had cinched tight the cords of frayed nerves. Why didn't he just walk along the beach to the hostel? Sure, the beach could be dangerous at night, but what were his chances of finding a cab at this hour? He didn't know, but he knew he didn't want to chance another trip down the potentially disastrous streets of this small beach town. One stupid sojourn was enough.

"How's it going?" a young surfer-like foreigner said.

"Good." Gray extracted another plastic cup from a pocket of his travel pants. "Want some?"

"Sure."

He poured a few ounces, handed it to the surfer-dude, and raised his cup. "Cheers."

A police pick-up truck drove along the beach and stopped behind them, lights flashing.

"I like how you pull out the alcohol just as the cops show up."

Gray slipped the bottle into a pocket and sipped as two cops exited the vehicle and engaged in a heated discussion with some partiers behind him. Gray and the surfer-dude, who identified himself as Ryan, made small talk and sipped straight rum. The desolate expat woman who had approached earlier returned and grabbed his arm firmly. Gray pulled away. "Leave me alone please."

"Is that your girlfriend?" Ryan asked.

"I don't even know her."

"I have a name. I'm Elizabeth."

"Okay, Elizabeth, could you stop bothering me please?"

"I told you, we can make a good couple down here. You're retired. I'm looking for somebody like you to spend my time with."

Ryan looked furtively from the cops—who dragged two resistant locals into the vehicle—back to Gray, who was trying to get rid of the woman at least thirty years his senior.

"I should go," Ryan said. "Thanks for the drink."

Ryan disappeared into the darkness. Gray saw a young couple sitting on plastic chairs, and a man standing beside them. He approached. If he could only identify with a group, it might discourage the foreign pest. But she followed him, hovering about three feet behind while the police drove away with their captives.

Gray started some small talk with the man standing next to the couple. Pedro was from Chile, the young couple sitting down in the plastic chairs, Anna and David, also Chilean. Over the loud music, words were not that decipherable.

Elizabeth approached, grabbing Gray's arm. "I said come with me. We're an item—could be an item. I'm from the States you know."

For whatever reason, Gray addressed Anna. "She's been harassing me since I arrived. Could you help me, please?" Maybe woman-to-woman talk would be better than man-to-woman talk. Gray had no idea. But he had to do something. She wouldn't leave him alone.

Anna scowled at the woman and balled her fists. She said something in Spanish that was drowned out by the music. Elizabeth grimaced before disappearing.

"Thanks," Gray said. "I appreciate that."

She nodded and smiled. But a few minutes later, and Gray had no idea why, Anna launched into a vitriolic verbal attack: "You're fucked-up ... do you know that? I mean really fucked-up." They had been conversing in Spanish. "You can't speak Spanish at all. I have to translate everything you say to my friends. I don't mean you're wasted, either. Just a fuck-up. A loser. You're an old man, washed up, fit for nothing at all. You hear me? You're washed up, a fuck-up."

Outnumbered three to one, and pretty drunk, Gray realized now was as good a time as any to bid his farewell. He was stunned by the onslaught, thought he may have accidentally insulted the pair. Her boyfriend David said nothing during the soliloquy, but Pedro's eyebrows slowly arched. Without saying a word, Gray turned and left.

Pedro caught up to him. "Sorry about that."

"It's not your fault. But what did I say? We were having a friendly conversation and she just attacked me. Did you hear me say anything?"

"No, you didn't say anything. She's a good friend of mine but unfortunately sometimes she can be a real bitch. It's just one of her traits."

Pedro walked alongside Gray on the dark beach toward Gray's hostel.

"I wouldn't walk here at night," Pedro said.

"I've done it before. It's not far."

"Yes, but you're very drunk—an easy mark. You should let me get you a taxi in town. I'll come with you."

Gray squinted to read Pedro's features in the moonlight. His face looked honest enough. Shortly cropped black hair and intense eyes. But what about that verbal assault? Was this a set-up designed to persuade him to wander off by himself so Pedro could lure him into some deadly trap? He had made many mistakes to this point, and he had an opportunity to change that. Now they were in total darkness, a good distance away from the beach party.

He heard the clapping sound of footsteps running on the beach, getting louder, and saw a dark, silhouetted figure charging toward him, arm raised, a machete silhouetted against the ominously glowing full moon.

And he froze.

Pedro stepped back to avoid the trajectory. The attacking man swiftly altered his course, charging toward the Chilean.

Pedro turned to run, but Strap was already upon him. With a swift motion, he brought the machete down expertly and sliced open Pedro's jugular vein. Pedro brought his hand to his throat, uttered a low guttural cough, and a fountain of blood sprayed from his mouth and fatal neck wound. "Ahhhhgh ... ahhhhhhhhhgh." He dropped to the sand and twitched spasmodically, blood squirting out like a water fountain.

Gray's brain, along with his motor functions, finally registered the murder. He raised the rum bottle as Strap lunged. "You're dead," Strap said, swinging the machete powerfully at Gray's throat. Gray ducked and simultaneously swung the bottle in a wide arc. He heard it crack against Strap's head, and the tall, scrawny man said "fucking bastard" before staggering a few steps and falling to one knee, the bottle dropping and rolling along the sand.

Adrenaline took over and Gray felt his head immediately begin clearing. *Get the hell out of here. Now.*

"Put your tail between your legs like a dog and fuck off. Afraid of a little fight. Big man when you're with friends," Strap said, wiping a small cut on his forehead and struggling to regain his equilibrium.

Gray didn't waste any time. He raced toward the hostel, wondering as he ran what protection it could possibly afford, given the circumstances. But he didn't know where else to go except into the blackness. He glanced back and noticed Strap was in pursuit. Luckily Gray had a few paces head-start. He had better make the best of it. He ran toward the small lights that marked the buildings dotting the beachfront, restaurants, hotels, bars, trying to remember the light configuration of Hanga Roa. *Three small bulbs on twelve-foot poles spaced maybe ten feet apart. And, right ... an artificial Christmas tree ... red twinkling lights. And it wasn't the last hostel on the beach ... but maybe six, seven buildings from the last ... something like that.*

He reached a vacant, thatched-roof bar with a lone light glimmering inside. *No one around. Shit.* Not noticing a small wooden step, he ran full-tilt into it, stumbled, and somersaulted before crash-landing and sliding along the sand on his back. His shins stung with the force of the blow, and he realized with a grimace that both legs were scraped and bleeding.

"You're dead." But it wasn't some twisted nightmare in his mind anymore. It was Strap, and he was rapidly closing the gap.

Gray scrambled to his feet and ran into the darkness, down a small path toward the dirt road fronting the buildings. The road was a much better bet. Streetlights ... and with any luck, people. It was probably his only chance.

The darkness slowed his progress. He couldn't move too fast without being able to see the ground beneath his feet. Who knew what obstacles might send him sprawling to the dirt again, making him an easy target for the madman.

"Arrrrrreeeee ... arrheeee ... arrheeeeeeee."

He stepped on a small dog's tail, startling the canine from its slumber. It darted ahead of him, yelping and providing a helpful sound indicator of the path to salvation.

He heard a crashing sound and glanced back quickly. Strap's shadowy figure, machete raised, vanished into the darkness. "Fucking cunt!"

*Good ... the fucker wiped out.* For a second, Gray thought about turning around and attacking, turning the tables on the son of a bitch. But he was unarmed, and Strap probably still had the machete. *Not a good idea.*

The yelping dog burst into the street-lit road, Gray right behind in full stride. *Hope that fall keeps the fucker down.* A small girl ambling along started and screamed at the intrusion. Gray thought of stopping to ask her something, but what the hell was he going to ask? Instead he sprinted past, saying: "Get the hell out of here now. There's a man with a knife chasing me." The girl looked at him like he was an alien before dashing into a nearby building.

Gray spotted the bamboo fence marking the entrance to his hostel. He hoped Strap didn't know where he was staying. It had a small chain looped over two bamboo poles. He lifted it, pushing open the gate a crack, slid through, looped the chain back in position, and ran up the stairs to his room. He sat on the bed, watching his arms quiver and the blood drip from both shins. To say he was a little jumpy would have been an understatement.

# Chapter Twenty-Two

"You seem a little jumpy," Karina said, lying beside Gray in the double bed mid-afternoon the following day in the hostel they shared in the little coastal town of Canoa. The shuttered windows were wide open, and their prostrate position afforded a beautiful ocean view. She stroked his arm gently as they cuddled and stared out at the crashing waves beneath a brilliant blue sky.

They had just made sensational love. Karina was a soft and gentle lover, sensitive to Gray's desires, seductively arousing him before bringing him to an intensely enjoyable and shuddering orgasm. And the pleasure was mutual. She had become so aroused, small high-pitched screams had burst forth, which she had muffled with a hand for fear other hostel patrons playing billiards and socializing at the bar below might hear. In spite of her efforts, the pair couldn't be sure they hadn't been heard. The screen-less, open windows were only a few feet above all the hippie types and socializing surfers.

The crashing waves could drown out a lot of noise, but perhaps not the high-pitched squeals of carnal pleasure. But Gray didn't care. He had other things on his mind at the moment. After his close call with Strap, he had swiftly packed and dialed Acilino, a taxi driver. He had called twice before the sleepy driver had picked up. He asked him about the standard taxi rate to Canoa from Montanita, to which Acilino had said one hundred and fifty dollars. "Come and get me now and I'll give you two hundred," Gray had responded. Acilino had agreed. Fifteen minutes later, Acilino arrived. Three and a half hours later, Gray had arrived in Canoa, the town with "a heart of gold," according to many travelers. However, informed tourists refused to walk alone on the beach at night due to reported incidents of rape and robbery. Heart of gold? Yet Gray could think of nowhere else to go. Besides, he had made plans with Karina and hoped, in spite of the danger he was in, to make his way to Atacames and help his friend Abby with the squatters who had overrun her hotel on the beach.

But the more he thought about it, the more he realized how nuts the whole thing sounded. *The shaman has the answer. Shaman?* During his narrow escape from Strap, he had chucked his flip-flops in the sand just before darting away. Perhaps the flip-flops could be traced to Gray, and it would be easy to discover from Pedro's friends that Gray was the last person who saw Pedro alive. And Pedro's friend Anna hated Gray for reasons Gray knew not. She would surely tell the police Gray was a lunatic murderer. What would stop her? For all he knew, cops were hunting him right now. Yet he wanted some blissful nights with Karina—was he in some surreal state of denial? Afterward, he would journey off to try to help Abby with the squatters who had probably already threatened violence. Abby was outnumbered and holed up in a beach town, culture and country that were not her own. Really, what were her chances of regaining possession of her business?

But, on the other hand, if Gray was currently wanted by the law, even if he did show up to the airport to return home early, surely he would be detained and imprisoned, with no idea of when or if his case would ever be heard. If that were the case, didn't his life come down to this very moment? Didn't it always come down to this very moment? *We don't have the past or the future, only the present, and we have to make the best of it.*

"Maybe I'm still adjusting to the culture or something," he lied, turning and kissing Karina gently on the cheek. She moaned softly.

"I can't be beside you like this without getting turned on," she said, inching closer and massaging his chest.

He smiled and stared out at the magnificent vista. Should he be starting a relationship based on lies? Wasn't he endangering her life? He was sure Strap wouldn't go away. Probably Strap's murderous intentions would be sanctioned by police. He could see the headline: *FOREIGNER TRACKS AND KILLS MURDERER.*

With Adriana, it had been different. He had only thought he had seen Strap, thought his confused mind had created Strap's image. But now he *knew* it was Strap; he had almost died at the lunatic's hands. Didn't Karina have a right to know? He thought about how he would explain everything, whether he should omit Adriana from the story. Did Karina really need to know about Adriana? He had slept with Karina once prior to meeting Adriana; but for all he knew at the time, it was a one-night stand. Karina had said as much. And he certainly wasn't in a committed relationship with Adriana at the time. Had he done anything wrong?

Karina circled Gray's nipple slowly with her forefinger. He was getting aroused in spite of a head full of worries. *I should tell her.*

There was a knock on the door and Gray jerked convulsively, frayed nerves unraveling. "Can I clean the room?" the chambermaid asked. It was a perfect opportunity to walk to the beach and get everything off his chest before making-love-to-Karina-round-two could continue.

He kissed Karina, staring into her deep blue eyes. "Let's go for a walk." He gave her a grin that said to be continued.

Walking along the sparsely-populated beach hand-in-hand in the hot sun, he told her the story, concluding with his plan to visit Abby in Atacames despite the mess he was in. But he omitted the part about Adriana. He only had three more nights with Karina before she would depart on an eight-day boat tour of the Galapagos Islands. He didn't want to ruin it.

As they walked, Gray did a double-take of every passerby. He felt at any time police sirens would blare, a police vehicle would whip across the sand, arrest him at gunpoint, toss him into the vehicle, and disappear. And maybe take Karina along for the ride—just because they could.

As he finished, she stopped walking, released his hand and stared into his eyes, her brow creased with worry, a small frown on her pouty lips. "Wow ... that's quite a story. I thought I had it rough when I mentioned two good friends of mine passed away just before I left."

"If you want to leave now, I'll understand." Gray knew she and Peter had parted company over some itinerary disagreements, but, since it had been booked and paid for long before the friction, the Galapagos trip would move forward.

"What are you going to do?"

"What can I do? I'm sure going to the police would accomplish nothing, probably get me thrown in jail. And if I am wanted in connection with murder," he lowered his voice as a man jogged past them, "they'll get me at the airport anyway. I may as well enjoy the time I have in case everything does go to shit. Leave when I'm supposed to leave at the end of January."

Karina sat in the sand, pensively staring at the ocean and weighing her options.

Gray remained standing, respecting her space. "The last thing I wanted to do was endanger your life. But I really wanted to see you. I like you."

She extended a hand. He took it, sat down and put an arm around her. For a few long moments they stared out into the infinite sea vista, as if it were there they would find answers. Occasionally, Gray glanced furtively around the beach, half-expecting to see Strap, machete raised, charging toward them. But they were at the north end of the beach, close to the jagged and protruding cliffs and caves that were home to many bats, and few people could be seen, none of them close by.

Karina's features softened and she stared sadly into Gray's eyes again, a gaze he found transfixing and mesmerizing. In those eyes, all his problems seemed to disappear. "I like you too. And I don't want to leave." She kissed him softly. It transformed into a long, passionate kiss.

"Are you sure? I don't think I could live with myself if something happened to you that I could have prevented."

"I'm staying with you until my trip with Peter." After a moment's pause: "And maybe you should come with us."

"I'll think about it." Gray had given his word to Abby. If he wasn't good for his word, what was he good for? For better or worse, he would travel along the Costa del Sol to Atacames. He planned to spend Christmas with Abby if he could stay alive and not incarcerated for the next week.

"You figure out something to do, though," Karina said.

"As strange as it sounds, there's only one thing that's come to mind."

"What's that?"

"Well, I was thinking of seeing a shaman—you know, a traditional medicine man, and get his guidance."

"Do you think it would work?"

"Who knows, but I've always wanted to see a shaman perform a ritualistic healing ceremony anyway. Why not get him to do one on me?"

"I've heard some people who take ayahuasca have enormous spiritual enlightenment regarding their purpose on Earth. Exorcise demons, things like that. Are you going to do that?"

"I don't think so, even though I've heard the Amazonian shamans have used it for hundreds of years as a window into the soul. Ayahuasca might just make me paranoid. I'm already getting that way. I've heard of a woman getting really messed up. I don't know if the concoction was prepared improperly or what. But she's fucked to this day."

"What's wrong with her?"

"Not all there, mentally."

"Better not take the chance," Karina said with a nurturing smile.

"I just feel I need to speak to a shaman," Gray said. "If he can do all that healing stuff, maybe he can help me with my problem."

Karina scratched her small nose and contemplated it. "It sounds like a long shot."

"Got any other suggestions?"

She shook her head. A mischievous grin appeared on her face. "Do you think our room's ready?"

# Chapter Twenty-Three

Gray was ready to leave after three lazy days in Canoa. It was a sleepy village, to be sure, but there was a negative and unnerving undercurrent. He had heard one foreigner at his beachfront hippie-commune-like hotel say: "You don't want to walk around town late at night pissed, nor do you want to walk the beach late at night by yourself. If you must walk at night, at least do it in numbers." Waking from a fitful sleep in the middle of the night, Gray saw the hippie staggering around aimlessly in front of the hotel, shirtless and shit-faced. The old "Do what I say, not what I do" adage, and it sounded all too familiar.

Maybe it was the increasing tension of the recently-transpired drama that had tainted him. He didn't know. But he seemed to be getting a lot of strange looks lately. Every weird stare was ratcheting up his stress level. He looked in the mirror one day, trying to determine if it was a vibe he was giving off, and had to admit his face looked angry, his eyes drawn to slits, mouth fixed in a combination grimace of pain, anger and anguish. But he couldn't help it. It was Gray's cautious face. *Must be me. People react to how you look. If you look angry, you get anger; if you don't smile, how do you expect people you meet to smile?* Gray brought fingers to mouth, trying to curl his lips into a happy expression. It came off more like he was in the middle of a troublesome bowel movement.

At least Karina had proven to be an awesome companion, and an affectionate and passionate lover. In that department, things couldn't be better.

He stuck a Lider cigarette in his mouth, lit it, took a sip of Pilsner beer and stared out at the crimson sunset and the nearly-deserted beach. He made up his mind to enjoy himself with what little time he had left here. He turned to Karina, who lounged in a neighboring hammock at a small thatched-roof bar and restaurant. They were the only two patrons, and planned on having dinner there in a few hours. Karina's eyes were closed. She was either contemplating or sleeping, but either way Gray didn't want to disturb her peaceful reverie. A resilient woman, Karina was handling the scary revelations with an air of calmness. It was Gray who had started chain-smoking and was on a steady diet of sleeping pills.

He couldn't seem to get the shadowy image of Pedro gurgling on the sand, one hand clenched to his throat, taking his last gasps of breath as blood drained into his lungs. And the demented face of Strap also haunted his waking and sleeping hours. He pushed the thoughts away and brought his gaze back to sleeping beauty. Her soft features were the only thing that gave him any amount of peace these days. In spite of the dark and haunting thoughts, Gray had gone out of his way to please Karina, and it was working. She couldn't get enough of him, in and out of bed. She was in sync with his need for space and allowed him his privacy and alone-time. And, unlike Adriana, she enjoyed the moment with Gray, without expectations or promises of what would or could be. She had a liberal attitude: enjoy the good times while they last, without reading too much into it. After all, they lived worlds apart, and long-distance relationships were difficult to manage at the best of times. Who knew what the future would bring? But it was exactly that lack of expectation that had so endeared Karina to Gray.

Gray thought he could spend a lot of time with this woman—maybe even a lifetime.

She opened her eyes and from her comfortable slumber. "What are you thinking?"

"You really want to know?"

"Of course."

"I haven't been that successful at relationships, but I really like you. Sometimes I wonder if it might be possible for us to, you know, be an item." It hadn't come out the way he'd hoped. It all sounded rather stupid. He barely knew her. "Sorry, that's presumptuous of me. You probably haven't even thought about that." *Insert foot in mouth. Slowly slide it in deeper until you feel the gag reflex.*

"I have. I've been single for two years since my fiancé and I broke up." Gray didn't want to hear the details, so he didn't ask. She went on, "Since then, I've wanted to remain single for a while. Maybe I'm still healing, and not ready for a relationship. I don't know. But I'm forty-five. Not getting any younger. Sometimes I do think about another life partner."

Now it was Gray who was talking with expectations. Ruining an otherwise near-perfect romantic tryst in an almost idyllic setting. "Would you come and see me in Canada?"

Karina smiled. "Maybe."

Gray tried to pull the foot out before the gag reflex ejected it like an intercontinental ballistic missile. "Sorry. I'm getting too serious."

There was an uncomfortable silence.

Then she said, "Yes, I would visit you in Canada, if you invited me."

The foot slid out, not uncomfortably. "I'd like that."

"Let's see what the future brings."

Gray liked the answer. To do otherwise would make him a hypocrite, so what choice did he have?

Gray went to the bar (service was non-existent at best), ordered another large Pilsner, a *Cuba libre* for Karina, returned and handed her the drink. "Cheers—to our time together. I'm glad I met you."

They clinked and drank. He bent down and kissed her sensuous lips. God, she turned him on. He couldn't wait to get her back to the raucous hippie commune. *Who gives a shit what the hippies want to do with their exclusive group?* Gray planned on having his own party. He nestled into the hammock, watching the last of the crimson sunset disappear on the horizon.

Her next question surprised him. "Would you visit me in Germany?"

"If I was invited ... yes. I'd come in the summer, though. I hate the cold."

She smiled and his problems seemed a world away. "Me too."

He changed the subject. "You've covered a lot of ground in your travels—the coast, the Andes, the jungle, lots of indigenous cities. What do you think of Ecuador? I mean, besides the beautiful country. The culture—the people? Would you come back?"

"I like Ecuador, but I don't know if I'd return. There are too many other countries to visit."

Karina's Spanish was survival at best. She couldn't possibly develop the same understanding of what made the people tick as Gray could.

She continued: "I find a lot of the people very friendly, but I also find a lot of them indifferent to tourists. Maybe they've been mistreated and become tainted. Or maybe it's the exploitation of Ecuadorian resources by more developed countries? Or maybe it's just me?"

"Who knows, but I find the same thing," Gray said. "I thought maybe it was just me, but a few other travelers have said the same thing. You know, one of the reasons I came here was to see whether I could spend three, four, maybe six months of the year here. I'm not sure I could. Maybe I'm barking up the wrong tree thinking I can find peace and tranquility in a developing country. There are cultural differences that I don't think I could ever be happy with. Maybe learn to ignore, but never be comfortable with."

"Like what?"

Gray paused a moment before responding. "Listen, I don't want to come across as prejudiced, ethnocentric or xenophobic because I'm not. I'm sure Ecuadorians would have as many problems with my culture as I have with theirs. And let's face it, there are good and bad in all cultures. I'm just pointing out things I have a hard time getting used to."

"Go on."

"Take the music, for example. Always brutally loud."

"Yes. They do it with televisions too."

"I've noticed."

"Did you notice the private party in that restaurant a block away?"

Gray nodded. "They were just setting up the speakers."

"Didn't you think it strange they set up two massive speakers outside, angled only slightly toward it? When the music starts, the whole town will hear it."

As if on cue, the distant speakers came to life, belting out pasillo or merengue or something else Gray couldn't identify. The peaceful moment was drowned out, but at least they had maybe a hundred yards separating them from the noise pollution.

"It doesn't matter to me right now," she said. "We're in Ecuador. We can't expect everything to be the same as in our cultures. That's why we travel to places like this—to experience the cultural differences and learn something from it."

"Great minds think alike. I won't entertain the flip-side of that."

She laughed. Her command of the English language and comprehension was excellent, Gray thought. He grinned as he imagined the intense pleasure he would soon derive from that shapely bikini-clad body lounging in the hammock.

# Chapter Twenty-Four

"What did you do with the body?" Rocky asked over a crackling cell phone. He was referring to Pedro, the unfortunate Chilean who happened to be in the wrong place at the wrong time.

"I cut him up and buried his torso in the country," Strap said.

Strap had learned of Gray's whereabouts by threatening the life of Gray's taxi driver. The diminutive Ecuadorian didn't take the first verbal threat seriously enough, but when Strap produced the belt and flicked him upside the head, instantly drawing blood, Acilino quickly sang like a well-trained parrot.

Strap's private driver Joachim whisked past Puerto Lopez, heading north along the Costa del Sol. With narrowing eyes, Joachim glanced at Strap occasionally as he drove. Strap was about two hours away from Canoa, and knew it wouldn't be hard to find Gray once he arrived in the tiny village.

"Why'd you have to cut him up if you buried him anyway?"

"Cut off the head, feet and hands and dropped them in a concrete foundation. He's been immortalized in a Montanita hotel under construction. Anyone finds the rest of the body they'll never be able to identify it."

"Why didn't you dump the whole fucking body in the concrete?"

"Dunno, boss. Didn't think of it at the time, I guess."

"Never mind." Rocky had been briefed on the profits from project stupid-swimmer-exploitation and brought up to speed on the alliance with the Ecuadorian drug cartel. The strengthened partnership with Raul's group would increase the flow of cocaine and marijuana into Canada and the United States. It was turning into a productive trip.

"Don't worry, boss, I'll get the job done and get the hell out of here."

"You do that." Rocky wasn't into small talk. The cell phone clicked dead.

Strap felt completely invincible in Canada. But in Ecuador, he didn't know what friends might turn to enemies on a dime. He could tell from Raul's stone-faced, business-like expression the kingpin would just as soon put a bullet through his head as make a deal. The partnership was tenuous at best, and the only reason Strap was being treated like royalty, albeit most of the time with Raul's facial expressions bordering on dismissive indifference, was because Raul needed that distribution route currently controlled by The Chosen Ones. But it might be only a matter of time before Raul decided he didn't want the Canadians involved anymore. At any point, he could decide to take them out and keep all the profits.

That might well happen in the future, but Strap knew there were pieces of the puzzle that Raul had not put together. It was a complicated web of opportunistic alliances that tied the drug route together, and Raul was not familiar with all the players and their propensity for swift and ruthless retribution. But he could figure it out. He had already begun hinting at the different players. So far, Strap had evaded the questions, but he knew it was only a matter of time before the kingpin resumed the interrogation or turned to other sources.

He had to take care of business and leave. He was sure of one thing: Gray would regret the day he ever said a nasty word to him. It was just a question of when, but certainly not how. Strap planned on a slow and torturous death for Gray, a death that would involve the use of a machete, gun powder, a disposable lighter and, of course, the strap. Things were going to get downright medieval.

"How much longer?" Strap asked, glancing at Joachim as he caught glimpses of blue-gray ocean water. The heat was stifling. Although he had been promised air-conditioning, the older black pick-up truck was not thus equipped. Raul had organized the truck and driver, and Strap wondered if it was his way of subtly saying he can't always get what he wants, Raul asserting his authority in *his* country. Strap didn't know, but for the first time he was starting to feel a little nervous.

And that was an emotion he wasn't at all comfortable with.

# Chapter Twenty-Five

Gray felt slightly more comfortable after he kissed Karina goodbye and watched her, weighed down by a bulky knapsack, trudge along the dirt road at nine in the morning to catch a bus that would take her to Guayaquil, where she would spend a night in a hotel before flying to the Galapagos Islands with travel companion Peter. Her options were limited. She would be sharing a room with Peter, who had already blown up on her on more than one occasion, accusing her of being inflexible with her travel plans.

Gray had no idea whose fault it was; nor was it top priority. He had enjoyed his time immensely with Karina, and in his eyes she was a stellar companion, sensitive, caring and flexible with her plans—not to mention, a passionate lover. In the short time he had spent with her, they never had a single argument. She possessed an inner peace and tranquility that he found rejuvenating and reassuring. Her presence suffused him with a calmness he had rarely experienced before.

But, like the incoming tide, his problems came flooding back as he watched her wave and smile, wondering if he would ever see her again. What was important, he supposed, was they had lived for the moment and enjoyed their time together.

What he didn't know was how it would be with Abby, Adriana, the cops, or Strap. He saw his bus pull up and stepped off the curb just as he noticed a black pick-up truck overtake the bus and speed toward him. He saw the eyes and they didn't lie. Strap sat in the passenger seat, anxiously scanning the passengers. Gray ducked and hurriedly pushed ahead of some passengers, garnering some nasty looks and an elbow in the face for his trouble.

He jostled through the crowd and found a seat, seeing the pick-up stop alongside the bus.

******

Strap continued scanning the boarding passengers, peering in the windows. A vehicle pulled up behind the pick-up, horn honking repeatedly: *Beeeeep ... beeeeeeep ... beeeeeeeeeeep ... beeeeeeeep.*

The bus driver muttered something unintelligible and roared away. Gray glanced back as the pick-up followed, beads of sweat popping out on his forehead. Two anxious blocks later, the pick-up veered down a side street. Gray wiped his brow with a hand as an attractive young Ecuadorian woman stared at him like he was a demon sent from hell.

"You look a little stressed," a gringo traveler beside him said.

Gray jumped. It took a few seconds to compose himself. The Ecuadorian woman stared along with a few other curious locals. He glanced at her and she flashed a smile—perfectly straight, gleaming white teeth. He had to admit she had a rack to die for. At first, Gray didn't know how to respond to the traveler, who resembled a skinny GI Joe, complete with a neatly-trimmed black beard. "It's just the culture. It stresses me out sometimes."

"I know what you mean."

Gray had no clue if the man sensed the panic clawing through his stomach lining. A few minutes later, when he had regained a semblance of composure, they discussed traveling and local culture. Crane said he was American, and had been traveling in South America for fourteen months already.

Gray hoped the conversation would take his mind off his worries. Right now, he felt like having a smoke and a *Cuba libre,* or ten. "How long are you planning on continuing?"

"I don't know," Crane said with a relaxed smile and oversized white teeth. "I don't want to jinx the trip, so I don't want to fix a date."

"Fair enough," Gray said, although he had no idea what Crane meant.

He learned Crane worked as a realtor and had saved a pile of money, given up his US address and hit the road.

"Travel is always the best education," Gray said after they had discussed highlights of their trips. Gray had omitted details of the danger lurking in his path.

"For me, it's also a trip for self-improvement," Crane said.

"I always learn something about myself when I travel, particularly when I travel by myself."

"I know what you mean. It's more than that for me, though. I mean real self-improvement."

"Explain."

They rumbled along the coastal highway as the day heated up, and Crane relayed his story. "I've got social anxiety issues."

"You could have fooled me. I saw you socializing with a bunch of people in Canoa. You seemed to be getting along famously."

"You thought so?"

"Yeah."

"That makes me feel good. But it's like this. If I'm in a social group situation, having dinner, something like that, it's really stressful for me to converse with people. Over time the anxiousness leads to extreme fatigue, and I have to leave the group. Like if there's a gap in the conversation or something, and I can't think of anything to say, I get really nervous."

"I think that happens to everybody, to greater or lesser degrees."

"Yeah, but for me it's much worse. For example, if I'm with a group of travelers, partying with them or something, I generally run out of things to say and retire early to bed, to the safety of my room. Then I stay up analyzing everything I said, things I might have said wrong, things that may have offended people, what their reaction might be, whether they like me or not. Stuff like that."

"Wow ... that is serious social anxiety issues."

Crane's expression turned stern. "Don't say anything to anyone."

"I won't."

"So for me, traveling by myself is forcing me out of my shell, forcing me to interact with others, forcing me to be comfortable in my own skin."

"And how do you think you're doing?"

"I think I'm making progress ... but I've got a long way to go. What do you consider yourself ... an introvert or extrovert?"

"It's not black or white for me," Gray said. "I love socializing with people, but I also need my downtime. I like to do some creative writing occasionally, and I need my own space for that. Then I don't want people around—don't want to listen to the phone ringing. I also like living by myself and would have to be very comfortable with a woman to live with her. I'd have to get to know her a long time, maybe two or three years. Even then, I might have problems sleeping in the same bed with her. I tend to thrash around a lot, and sleeping really is such an individual thing. Are you looking for a girlfriend here?"

"I don't know. I'd have to be comfortable in my own skin first and I'm not there yet. I've met a lot of nice women in my travels who've willingly given me their contact info, and I haven't followed up on it. When I was flying to the Galapagos I met a woman from Germany, and I'll tell you, she was drop-dead gorgeous. As it turned out, we were going to be in Quito at the same time so we exchanged contact details. When I got to Quito I stressed about contacting her for two days and then finally decided I'd be much happier—or rather that it would be much easier just doing my own thing. The whole notion of interacting with her and maybe getting intimate stressed the hell out of me."

Gray thought Crane needed more than fourteen months—even fourteen years for that matter—traveling in South America to repair his issues. He needed intensive psychotherapy, maybe even multiple visits with a psychiatrist, a doctor legally allowed to prescribe medication. He realized he was frowning at Crane, and tried to force a smile.

"Don't get me wrong," Crane said, misinterpreting the frown. "I'm not trying to toot my own horn or anything, but I know I'm a damn good-looking guy. It's very easy for me to attract women. I just can't close the deal. How about you?"

"I've had two intimate experiences with women since I've been here. I met an Ecuadorian and traveled with her for a while, another German woman for a few days. I think there might be possibilities with the German, but the Ecuadorian, just not my type." Gray felt like he was bragging now. "But don't get me wrong—the Ecuadorian's a great chick. And the sex was out of this world."

"You don't seem to have any issues with meeting a woman and closing the deal."

"I don't know. In Canada I did. Maybe this trip is also giving me more self-confidence. Like I said, travel is an education—maybe also a journey of self-discovery and self-improvement."

"In my case, self-improvement," Crane said, staring Gray up and down as if making an assessment of his physical attributes, or lack thereof. His frown suggested the latter.

"You have to remember," Crane said. "Women think differently than men. For them, it's not about physical beauty, it's about what's inside. Men think that women are looking for physical beauty, but it's not true. So, in your case, you should be fine."

It was more of a round-house punch than a sucker punch. Gray had seen it coming, and winced on impact. But it was going to take a lot more than names to break his bones. He had a psychotic killer on his ass, not to mention the shit-storm in Atacames. He might not be a Brad Pitt look-a-like, but some women found him attractive. Adriana had even commented that he was beautiful and could have almost any woman he wanted. He didn't necessarily believe her flattery, certainly didn't let it go to his head anyway, but it was nice to hear it. Beauty, after all, was in the eye of the beholder, and for all intents and purposes, although Gray found it hard to believe, Adriana seemed very much in love with him.

But now, all he could think about was getting rid of Crane. As the bus rolled into the bustling station of Pedernales, where he would have to change buses, Gray asked: "Where are you off to, anyway?"

"I'm going to Sua to meet some travelers, then maybe check out Atacames. Want to travel with me?"

Gray had read Sua was a peaceful fishing village near Atacames. "I'm going to Atacames," Gray said as a brainstorm struck. As they disembarked amid the bustle of Ecuadorian travelers, and searched for a booth to purchase another ticket, he continued: "My Canadian friend's hotel has been overrun by Ecuadorian squatters, and I plan on seeing her. Her life's been threatened. If you're seen with me in Atacames, you'll be found guilty by association. I don't want to put your life in danger."

Crane stared at Gray in disbelief.

As an afterthought, Gray said: "But I'll travel with you as far as Sua. I think we have two more buses to take: one to San Jose de Chamanga, the other to Atacames, which also stops at Sua."

After a moment's pause, Crane smiled nervously. "Okay. I didn't know there were two more buses. Someone told me this goes direct."

They bought their tickets and fifteen minutes later boarded the bus, Gray glancing around nervously the entire time.

Once they sat down and the bus rolled out of Pedernales, Crane resumed dolling out pearls of wisdom and profundities. "I'm a big film buff. But I don't read at all, unless it's educational stuff. I blew off most of my friends in the States because they pretended to know how to analyze a film, but didn't know the first thing about it. You know how you have to be able to discuss themes and things like that?"

Gray nodded.

"I'm just starting to get into themes and, you know, the main components of a story."

Gray doubted Crane, who had just accused his former friends of being pseudo-intellectual, knew anything about the main components. "Which, in your opinion, are what?"

"Oh shit ... I used to know. It'll come to me," Crane said.

Gray decided to save Crane the embarrassment. Besides, other people were beginning to stare, as if they knew where the conversation was going. "You mean exposition, conflict and resolution?"

"That's it. Isn't there a fourth and fifth one? Isn't one of them a climax?"

"Suppose it could be. But I just threw it in with resolution, but I guess in some cases you have a climax in a story and then a resolution in the form of an epilogue. I'm thinking more along the lines of a novel."

"It could be a sub-category," Crane offered.

Maybe he wasn't as stupid as Gray had originally thought.

"I never took you for an intellectual," Crane said.

Now was his chance. Gray didn't know when another one might come along; however at this rate Crane might start flinging insults like projectile vomit. "That's a coincidence. I never took you for an intellectual either."

"Really?"

"Yeah, when I first heard you open your mouth at that restaurant in Canoa, I just thought you were an idiot."

"Another dumb tourist?"

"You said it. But during our conversation now, it's obvious you have some intellectual depth. Mensa material."

"What's that?"

"You know—the Mensa intelligence test."

"I've never taken one of those."

"You'd be in an exclusive group ... trust me."

"You think so?"

"Now I do ... after talking to you for a while." Gray was beginning to feel bad and decided to end the ridicule. Besides, there was no one else to share the laughter with. "I can tell you one thing: you certainly seem relaxed in social situations."

"I'm really enjoying this conversation," Crane said. "Do you want to exchange e-mail addresses?"

"Are you going to contact me? I thought you said you get a lot of contacts but rarely follow up?"

"I'll contact you."

"Okay."

Stepping off the last bus a few hours later in a noisy public square in Atacames, Gray was relieved to be rid of Crane. Maybe Crane had a big heart, was more intelligent than Gray had given him credit for, but Gray had enough on his plate to attempt to solve the issues he had listened intently to. It was a job for a professional.

He dodged noisy traffic in the intense mid-afternoon heat, found a shady spot on a park bench, plopped his small knapsack down, and surveyed the locals while puffing on a smoke. They went about their business, some ogling him oddly as they strolled past in no particular hurry. His senses were immediately assaulted by the noise pollution. Although travel guides indicated the raucous beach town's population was 10,200, it seemed much larger to Gray. He extracted a cell phone and called Abby. She could direct him to the Hotel El Marques, which he knew was near the beach, quiet and well-priced. The phone rang four times before going to a Spanish-speaking voicemail. Gray didn't leave a message. She would recognize his number. He slid the phone in his pocket, wondering if something had happened to her. Was he too late? Even if he wasn't, what could he possibly do against an army of Ecuadorian squatters trying to gain control of a business in their country? It was blatantly obvious which way the scales of justice would be tilted.

He focused on clearing his head. He was travel-weary from the seven-hour bus ride and his nerves felt like violin strings pulled tight enough to pop with a discordant twang at any second. Two small local boys approached with outstretched hands asking for money, while a third approached from behind. A distraction for a pickpocket attempt?

Gray politely said no and asked to be left alone. They loitered, continuing to beg, ignoring the request. He glanced behind. The third boy had inched closer. He spotted a small café across the street from the small square and crossed the street to it. He sat down and called Abby again—four rings and voicemail. The heat was stifling, with no breeze. It didn't help that he had dressed in blue jeans, a t-shirt and a long-sleeved black button-down shirt with a collar.

The boys approached again. Just as he began wondering what in the fuck he was doing in Atacames, Abby called.

"Gray, how are you?" she asked cheerily. Maybe the troubling situation had resolved itself in a positive fashion.

"I'm good ... a little burnt out and hot. I've got three little kids stalking me and asking for money. You?"

"You need to go the hotel and wind down. I'm tied up with legal issues right now. We can talk later."

"How do I get to the El Marques?"

"It's not far. Take a motorcycle taxi and just say the name. It's close. Don't pay more than fifty cents. I'll call you in a few hours, once you settle in."

"Okay." Gray hung up. On pay-per-minute phones in developing countries, you keep conversations short. It was the unspoken protocol. He glanced around as the boys neared, noticing several rickshaw-style motorcycle taxis, some customized with box speakers installed in the open two or four-seat rear passenger compartments—efficient and inexpensive transportation about town.

He climbed in one, telling the driver the destination. A few minutes later he arrived at the spotlessly clean and gleaming reception area of the El Marques. He viewed a well-equipped and modern room on the second floor for $75 a night. When he asked about a room with an ocean view, he was told $150 a night.

In the reception area, he said he would think about it. He sat down on the plush tan leather couch in air-conditioned comfort and considered his options. He realized it was well above his budget. Unless he wanted to continue jacking his credit card balances up and then be forced to return home early, the El Marques really wasn't an option. He stood up, smiled at the receptionist, and left, silently chastising himself for not doing a little pre-arrival research. He had a Lonely Planet guide, which at best scratched the surface of available accommodation options in Atacames, but at least it would point him in some direction. As it was, he didn't even know where he was going or where he was going to sleep.

For a moment, he thought about going back into the hotel to check Lonely Planet. The last thing he wanted to do was sit outside in public reading the travel guide. It smacked of dumb tourist. "Fuck it," he muttered to himself, and turned toward the noisy beach *malecon*. Surely there would be lots of hotels there. Besides, he felt like a beer anyway.

A local in a white pick-up truck trained binoculars on Gray. As Gray rounded the corner, the man started the truck and pulled away from the curb slowly, simultaneously dialing a number on a cell phone. "Another gringo in the hotel," he said into the phone.

"Is he with Abby?"

"Abby hasn't returned yet. I don't know."

"Keep an eye on him."

"I'm following him right now."

"Good." The phone went dead.

Gray surveyed the buildings along the *malecon*. It was lined with restaurants, bars, discos, gift shops, a hodge-podge of various sized hotels, convenience stores, street vendors and the like. At four in the afternoon, the street was lively with thumping music, partiers and the steady drone of vehicular traffic intermingled with hissing ocean waves.

He weaved through the crowds and entered a small store to purchase a pack of smokes. A middle-aged local woman, indifferent to the arrival, swept a cloud of dust in his face. Another younger woman sat stone-faced at the counter. "Can I help you?"

"Pack of Marlboro Lights, please."

She extracted it. "Four dollars."

Gray pulled out a five as he heard a voice from behind. "You can't charge him four dollars for that. That's fucking gringo prices. You're ripping him off."

Gray stared at the man. He had short blonde hair, a ruddy and red-veined complexion, glazed eyes and face stubble. Perhaps in his early fifties, he was definitely not from these parts.

The man continued, snatching the package from Gray's hand. "Look ... it says three dollars right on the side." He showed it to the teller.

"Four dollars," she said, unfazed.

"Listen," Gray said. "I appreciate that you're trying to help me, but I'll pay the extra dollar."

"You can walk three blocks and get it for three dollars," the man insisted.

Gray was starting to feel exhausted from the afternoon heat coupled with the visual-stimulus-filled bus ride. The disorder, poverty and sheer culture shock of developing countries did that to him sometimes. He didn't think its effects were anything a person should downplay. "Listen, I appreciate what you're doing and I respect it. But I don't want to walk three blocks for a dollar. I want a smoke and a beer."

The man smiled; straight white teeth in spite of his ruddy, alcoholic appearance. "You from Canada?"

"Yeah."

"Whereabouts?"

"I live in Calgary right now."

"You?"

"I'm from Toronto."

The cashier stared while the other woman continued sweeping. The small store was filling up with more dust.

They exchanged introductions. The man's name was Ray Thomas. "Why don't you join us for a beer?"

"Sure," Gray said. "Can I pay for those so we can get out of here?"

Ray handed the pack to Gray. "I hate seeing tourists getting ripped off by the locals. They do that everywhere here."

Gray paid for the smokes, added three large Pilsner beers to the barebones shopping list, and left.

A few minutes later, they sat at a wooden table facing the beach. They were in a restaurant/bar shaped like an antiquated ship. By all accounts, it was closed. A few people occupied some chairs and sipped bottled beer purchased from nearby convenience stores. Ray introduced Gray to his girlfriend Karen, a local who was mid-sixties but looked no older than forty. Her long, flowing black hair parted in the middle accentuated her dark, slightly bloodshot eyes, white teeth, easy smile, and soft features. She was slim and fit, dressed in a white summer dress dotted with bright purple flowers.

Gray enjoyed Karen's easy manner, but there was something about Ray and his husky voice that he found disconcerting. They were both drunk; that much was clear. But there was an uneasy nervousness about Ray's mannerisms and disposition. He seemed unable to relax.

Over beer and cigarettes, Ray told Gray his bittersweet story of his life in Ecuador. He had met an Ecuadorian woman in Toronto, fallen in love, married her, and they had returned to her homeland. He had lived there for twenty years, arriving first to the vibrant city of Quito, where he had opened a bar in the popular business district of *La Mariscal*, or "new town" as it was often called.

After two years, the bar was a huge success. After eight years, his childless marriage disintegrated. As part of the split, his wife got the bar. Ray got paid out half of its estimated value.

Ray continued: "It didn't take her long to run it into the ground. I think a year. But as far as I know, it's still there." Gray didn't bother to ask if the business had been sold or what had happened to it. Ray was on a roll, so Gray let him continue as Karen picked up the empties, held up three fingers to two nods, and disappeared across the street to purchase more beer and collect the fifty cents per empty, bringing the cost of a large beer (the equivalent of two regular-sized Canadian beers) to one dollar each. It was going to be a cheap night of drinking. For the time being, Gray had forgotten all about the hotel quest.

"Not that I'm any better," Ray said, as kids played merrily on the beach and another low-skilled group of teenagers played volleyball at a makeshift net that was impossibly high. Four of five shots hit the net or flew underneath it. "What do you think I did with my half?"

Gray didn't think he had to answer the question. He was going to get told.

"I blew it in the casinos. Now, you know what the government has done with the casinos in Ecuador?"

"Closed them down?"

"That's right. Casinos are now illegal in this country."

"That could be a good thing if people can't control themselves."

"In my case it's a good thing. At fifty-five, I'm just now trying to figure out what the fuck I'm going to do with my life." He waved a hand to the empty chair once occupied by Karen. "And guess who's supporting me now? Fancy that—an Ecuadorian woman supporting a Canadian man. Have you ever heard of such a thing?"

Gray shook his head while lighting another cigarette.

"You know what else the president has done?"

"No."

"Made it illegal to buy alcohol on a Sunday. It applies to bars, restaurants, liquor stores, and the like."

"That doesn't sound too bad."

"It isn't," Ray said. "Forces the men to be home with their wives and kids. A day totally put aside for family."

"I don't necessarily disagree with that."

Karen had returned with three beers. Gray suddenly remembered he was supposed to meet Abby later and checked his phone to see if she had called. There were two missed calls from Adriana, but nothing else. "Excuse me. I'm expecting a call from a friend I'm supposed to meet later."

"No problem," Ray said. As Ray and Karen talked about dinner, Gray dialed Abby's number to four rings and voicemail. He hung up and put it in his pocket. He was hoping to get a recommendation for a hotel. *Wait a minute. I'm with two locals.*

"Do you guys know of a decent and inexpensive hotel around here?"

"Why don't you stay at our house?" Karen said. "It would be an honor to have you as our houseguest."

Gray paused. *Are you fucking nuts? You don't even know these people. He could be a serial killer for all you know.*

Ray smiled, as if reading Gray's mind. "You're welcome to stay. But, honey, we don't even know this guy. He could be a serial killer for all we know."

Ray stared at Gray, a twinkle in his bloodshot eyes, waiting for a reaction. Gray forced a smile and they all laughed—two low chuckles and a high-pitched cackle, all with an undertone of nervous tension.

"Trust me ... I'm not a serial killer," Gray said.

"But we don't know that, do we?"

"Do you know I'm a witch?" Karen said.

That would explain the cackle, Gray thought. But, as the crimson sun began setting over the vast ocean and sky horizon, this idyllic and alcohol-laced day at the beach was all starting to become a little too creepy. Gray reached for his small knapsack and stood up. "I should get going. I need to find a place and I'm supposed to meet a friend later."

Ray's expression turned sad. "No, don't go. Come up to our place, at least for dinner and a drink."

"You know," Karen said. "I've never seen him so happy. Come over. He has no Canadian friends here. We moved here six months ago from Quito, and he hasn't a single foreign friend. Not a lot of foreigners around here."

Gray was starting to understand why. No wonder Lonely Planet called Atacames a town that "inspires pure excitement or dread depending on how you like your beach vacations."

"I really should find a hotel."

"Come over for a beer," Ray insisted. "I'll help you find a cheap place later."

Maybe it was the sadness in Ray's eyes. Or the pleading look in Karen's eyes. But Gray was starting to give in, even though a small voice of reason told him to get a hotel and regroup. *What happened to Abby?* "What's that about you being a witch?"

"It's true," Ray said. "She's a white witch. She reads palms and does spiritual healing. She's been doing it for twenty years. She's got clientele here and in Quito. She travels there once a week for a few days—makes good money."

"What kind of a vibe do you get from me?" Gray asked, staring directly into Karen's eyes.

"You're a good person ... an intellectual. And it would be an honor to have you in our house."

"She likes you," Ray said. "Come over. You're Canadian. I'm Canadian. We look after each other. I'll help you find a hotel later."

Gray had finished off five beers and hadn't eaten since breakfast when he had shared a fruit salad with Karina at the hippie-commune in Canoa. That seemed so far away now. A pleasant alcohol buzz settled over his body and mind. Gray nodded. "Do you live far away?"

"Not that far," Ray said. "Maybe fifteen-minute walk."

"Can we take one of those cool motorcycle taxis? I'm not up to walking."

Ray nodded. As the last oval-shaped slice of the fiery orange sun disappeared over the black and blue horizon, three inebriated people piled into a three-wheeler and buzzed toward an apartment building.

# Chapter Twenty-Six

"It's not a bad apartment, really," Ray explained perfunctorily as they sat out on the fifth-floor balcony and enjoyed a twinkling light view of a small valley and rolling hills dotted with residences. Black clouds drifted along an ominous blue-gray sky. A few dogs yelped in the distance, and the faint hum of traffic and music drifted up. Somewhere, someone was having a party.

They had eaten a dinner prepared by Karen: rice, salad and chicken. She was inside doing dishes in the modest two-bedroom apartment, which, although sparsely furnished with inexpensive and utilitarian furniture, was immaculately clean. Karen kept a tidy household and, although the apartment often had no running water (they bathed and flushed toilets with buckets), Ray's computer had recently crashed and the television had blown up, the monthly rent was only $150 and the location was reasonably quiet and safe.

Over dinner, Ray had gone into detail about how he no longer had any interest in returning to Toronto. Last year, he had returned to visit his parents, two brothers and a sister and ended up working for six months in the dead of winter as a sales representative at Home Depot. At his age, it was hardly the career he had dreamed of. There was sadness and a resigned acceptance in his tone that underpinned a tragic tale of loss, despair and broken dreams.

"You have an amazing view," Gray declared, trying to lighten the somber gaze in Ray's disillusioned eyes. "Do you mind if I take some pictures?"

"Go ahead." It was delivered without enthusiasm. Ray's mood had changed on a dime.

Gray stepped through the sliding-glass doors into the suite, grabbed his camera, popped onto the balcony, snapped five pictures from various angles, returned the camera, and sat next to Ray.

"I should get going. I need to find a hotel." He was in unfamiliar surroundings, and the black curtain of night had enveloped the strange town—the worst time to be looking for accommodations. Gray wasn't exactly in love with the vibe in Atacames—or in the apartment, for that matter.

"How much do you want to spend?"

"I don't know ... twenty, maybe thirty dollars."

"I can get you a crash pad for ten bucks a night. It's nothing fancy."

*But for the first night it would work. Besides, I'm better off walking in pairs now. I don't even know where I am. Regroup tomorrow ... get a better place.* "Sounds good."

A rickshaw-style taxi dropped them off in front of a small hotel. Gray paid the driver and they stepped out. Gray followed Ray into the lobby. Ray waved over a local man, said something in Spanish and walked out onto the street to wait while Gray viewed a room on the main floor that was in front of a small swimming pool, cascading water spewing from the mouth of a large concrete shark and splashing loudly inside the oval-shaped orifice.

Gray only glanced at the room, but quickly realized it was clean and the double bed appeared comfortable. It was late. It didn't really matter right now. He was half in the bag and he only needed a temporary crash pad. He would upgrade tomorrow in the sober light of day. "How much?"

"How long?"

"One night."

The man glanced at Ray, pacing on the sidewalk, returned his gaze to Gray and said: "Ten dollars. He's a friend."

"I'll take it." He paid, took a key, tossed the bag into the tiny suite, locked the door and joined Ray on the noisy street. "Can I buy you a beer?"

# Chapter Twenty-Seven

"They're drinking beer," Strap told Rocky over the phone, pressing a finger into one ear. He stood on the moonlit sand, staring intently at the second floor of a terraced bar with bench-style chairs that offered unobstructed views of the action on the *malecon*—people strolling, cars passing, music thumping, dancing and drinking. He could hardly hear Rocky over the noise, but he could see Ray and Gray peering over the wooden railing, ogling the nightlife crowds that were getting thicker by the hour. A few days before Christmas, the party town was filling up with mostly local vacationers craving a raucous party.

"Who's they?"

"Sorry?"

Louder: "Who are they?"

"The other guy is Ray. Some fuck-up from Canada who lives here now."

"Will he be a problem?"

"Doubt it." Asking around at the hostel where Gray had stayed in Canoa, it hadn't taken long to learn Gray was headed for Atacames. In tight and crowded lodgings, paper-thin walls have ears. It had taken Strap less time to find out the story on Ray. Being one of the few gringos who lived in the small town, almost everyone knew him, had seen him drunk many times, and had heard his sad story. He would hardly be missed if he disappeared. But Strap was convinced he could get rid of Gray without interfering with the loathsome life of Ray. That was if Ray didn't get in the way. If he did, well then he would be expeditiously dealt with. End of story.

"Well get it over with and get back here then," Rocky said. "And leave the other gringo out of it if you can. I don't want to make any unnecessary waves. We're not exactly getting the red carpet treatment from Raul anymore. You never know what he decides to get pissed off at."

The phone went dead.

******

"During the week it's dead," Ray said. "Well, dead for Atacames. But today's Friday, don't forget. Friday it's always like this, maybe a little less busy. But it's close to Christmas. It's filling up."

"Lots of people," Gray said, pulling out his cell phone and checking for missed calls. Nothing. *What happened to Abby? You're dead.* "Do you want another beer?"

"I don't have a lot of money."

"Don't worry," Gray said, flashing a peace sign to a passing waiter. "I'll get it." The bar was crowded with locals eating pizza, drinking beer, and socializing.

Two large beers appeared on the table.

"What do you think of Karen?" Ray asked, lighting a smoke.

"She seems nice."

"She's my fuck for now."

"I thought she was your girlfriend."

Ray wiped his brow, ran a hand through his hair. "You're right. I shouldn't talk about her like that. We've been going out four years now. She's not exactly what I had in mind, but she takes good care of me. But ... I don't know. She could be waiting for my mother to die. You know I'm in line for a big inheritance."

"I don't know about that."

"I'm fucked right now. No money. She's paying the bills. What can I do?"

"If you can't be with the one you love, love the one you're with."

"That's true. You know we've had some real fights in the past. But we're okay now. I mean, like throwing plates around ... shit like that."

Gray wasn't interested in the sordid details of Ray's personal relationship. He tried to shift the conversation. "But you're good now?"

"Yeah ... I should call her, though. She thinks I was helping you find a hotel and then coming right home."

"Do you have a phone?"

"No. Lost it. Lost three phones, so I've given up. I don't need a phone anyway. Phones are fucked. People calling all the time. Who's going to call me, anyway?"

Gray didn't have an answer. "Do you want to use mine?"

Ray nodded, dialed a number, and listened. "She doesn't pick up. I knew she wouldn't."

"At least you called."

"Yeah, but she's going to be pissed."

Gray checked the time—10:36 pm—before inserting the phone in his pocket. "Why don't we go get her, invite her out? Then she has no reason to be pissed."

Ray stared out at the revelers, scratching his chin. "You want to walk back to my apartment? I've been robbed a couple of times crossing the pedestrian bridge over Atacames River. Both times, trapped me on the bridge, couple guys held me down while a third robbed me."

"We'll take a taxi. For the price, it's not worth taking a chance."

Ray waved over the bar owner, introduced him as Diego, and had a short conversation with him.

Diego took the beers and left.

"He'll keep them cold for us while we're gone. You know, he's my only Ecuadorian friend. But he's Americanized. He and I used to drink a ton of beer together all the time before he got his shit together and opened this place. He's doing well. He bought it. Two leaseholds below that generate money. You know what's weird? We both owned bars in Quito, both got divorced and both exes got the businesses. Isn't that weird?"

"Strangely coincidental," Gray said as they stood to leave.

"He's got his shit, together but I didn't," Ray said as they walked down the narrow, steep staircase to the *malecon*.

They waved over a taxi. "You will," Gray said as they climbed in and the vehicle pulled away.

# Chapter Twenty-Eight

*He's going to get away. Where the fuck's my driver?* Strap thought as he finished urinating in the ocean. Many beachside bars didn't have bathrooms. For bar patrons, the sea and surrounding sand was a public urinal. Waiting and watching, Strap had given in to the temptation to drink; even flirting with a hooker at a beachfront disco. Three beers later, Mother Nature had called.

Joachim, his driver, had disappeared, promising to return after running an errand.

Strap was just zipping up his fly when he felt it. Two hands grabbed one shoulder from behind, while two hands grabbed another. A third man shoulder-checked Strap's chest, winding him. He toppled to the sand, while a fourth and fifth scurried forth from the darkness and pinned his legs.

It happened so fast. Arms and legs pinned to the ground, one man sat on his chest, smacking him in the face while another cleaned out the contents of his pockets. They took cell phone, cash, machete, a small pistol, and disappeared before Strap even had a chance to retaliate.

For good measure, one black-booted man kicked him hard in the side of the head before they scattered.

"Welcome to the Ecuador," a man said as Strap, dazed and confused, panting for breath, rose to his feet. The man stood beside Strap, urinating. He stared out to sea. "Such a beautiful night in paradise."

Still gasping, Strap reeled around and round-house punched the man on the chin. *Whack.* The man gurgled and dropped to the sand like a sack of hammers—a sucker punch knock-out. Strap clutched his head, staggering up to the mayhem that was the *malecon*. His head hurt. He was mighty pissed off.

# Chapter Twenty-Nine

Gray awoke at 6:43 am with a head that throbbed like it had been kicked full force by a booted attacker. He felt like shit. It was the splashing of water and the shrill screams of children playing that snapped him awake. At first he had no idea where he was. Then slowly, the memories flooded in. They had returned to Ray's apartment, woken up Karen, and invited her to join them for a drink. She refused, so the two had found a nearby cave-in-the-wall restaurant that served beer. He and Ray drank another four, five, six beers each, Gray couldn't remember now, before he had hitched a cab back to his hotel, staggered into the room, hit the bed, and fallen into an alcohol-induced slumber. He glanced around the room, saw his knapsack in the corner and immediately felt under the pillow. His money belt was there.

He breathed a heavy sigh of relief, stood up shakily, and went into the bathroom. No toilet paper, no toilet seat, no towel, no shower curtain. Well, what the hell did he expect for ten dollars, anyway? He splashed some cold water on his face and used a t-shirt to dry it. He could still feel the numbing effects of the alcohol and steadied himself on the wall for a few seconds before reaching for a smoke, opening the door, walking outside and lighting it.

A few children stared at him while others splashed loudly.

He studied the small outdoor pool surrounded by a concrete patio. Other higher balconies overlooked it. Acoustically, the V-shaped design was not unlike a theatre. Gray wondered if higher-floor guests could hear the children's shouts and screams reverberating louder than on the main floor. It wouldn't surprise him. Beyond the pool were tables and chairs, an open door for what he presumed was a kitchen and a reception area. A woman behind a desk stared at him. He was a gringo after all, and one that looked like death warmed over. He had noticed small black circles under his eyes in the mirror, and the once four o'clock shadow was now a scraggly four-day patchy brown growth. He never could grow a decent beard.

To the annoyed eyes of the receptionist, he butted out the cigarette in a nearby flowerpot and returned inside the room. His throat was parched and dry. He needed water. He looked around for the trusty liter bottle of water but it wasn't on the night table. Then he remembered. He had left it at Ray's house. *Fuck sakes!* He quickly pulled the travel guide from his knapsack, scanned the pages and stopped: Hotel Tahiti. It would have to do for now: water, taxi, and Tahiti, in that order.

He found a store, bought a liter bottle of cold water, and guzzled about a third outside on the street before hailing a taxi.

"Tahiti," he said before getting in. "Fifty cents?"

The driver nodded. Twenty-five minutes later he had checked into a third-floor functional, clean but sparsely furnished suite on the quiet end of the *malecon* with a balcony, peek-a-boo ocean view and a shower with piping hot water. The first thing he did was shower, shave, change into a pair of green travel shorts and black t-shirt, curl up on the double bed and fall asleep. He wanted to clear his head a little before calling Abby. He awoke at 9:46 am, walked out onto the balcony, sat on a small wooden table (there were no chairs to be had), lit a smoke, fished his cell phone from his pocket and dialed.

She answered on the first ring. "Gray, how are you?" Her voice sounded bright and cheery. He didn't know how she did it.

"I'm good. I met a Canadian guy last night. We had a bit of a party—drinking on the *malecon*."

"That's great. You had fun?"

"Yeah ... How are you?"

There was a pause. Finally, she said: "I've got problems. My lawyer advised me that I should move from the El Marques. It's not safe for me there anymore. I'm getting death threats from the squatters. They knew where I lived. I found a new hotel, but I can't say where right now. Something else: the owner's lawsuit against me—it's dangerous. For all I know, he might win. If people sue you in Ecuador, you can't leave the country. Now this new lawyer I got doesn't even speak English. And my Spanish is okay, but far from perfect."

Gray could only think of one word to say: "Fuck."

"You got that right. The other thing—and I'm sorry about this."

"What's that?"

"Did you go to the El Marques yesterday?"

"Yeah."

"Are you staying there?"

"No ... I'm at the Hotel Tahiti right now. It's basic but decent, and it seems pretty quiet—even has an outdoor pool and ocean view."

"You shouldn't stay at the El Marques. And I'm sorry I sent you there. I didn't know at the time, but it's being watched by the squatters. They're dangerous. They already might've seen you, connected you to me somehow. Not many gringos here."

The irony wasn't missed on Gray. He had a nutcase following him around, bent on his destruction, and now Abby had a gang of nutcases bent on her destruction. Why had he been so stupid as to want to even see Abby, while he was being followed by a psychopathic murderer? Something about the different cultures—one day he would pin it down—that clouded his judgment. Perfectly simple decisions at home became perfectly impossible in Ecuador—at least for Gray. He was unwittingly leading the lion right to the front door of the prey. If Strap wanted him so badly, wouldn't Abby just be collateral damage if she got in the way?

He knew before Abby spoke where the conversation would go from here. It appeared she was the only one with a functioning brain.

"I don't think we should get together," she said. "If you haven't already been spotted, if they see you with me, they'll view you as an ally. I don't want to put your life in danger. Sorry, Gray, for making you come all the way down here. And I could really use your help ..."

Gray heard sniffles on the other end of the line. He brought a finger up to a watery eye and, frowning, brushed it away.

"... but I'm not prepared to play Russian Roulette with your life. I won't see you right now."

"It's okay. I understand." There was no point going into the drama with Strap. He felt stupid enough as it was. "What about Marnie ... your mother-in-law?"

"She left a week ago, before the shit really hit the fan."

"That's good. How's she doing?"

"Actually, her health improved quite a bit once she got to the coast."

There was an uncomfortable silence before Gray said: "Get a good lawyer. The Canadian Embassy in Quito has a list of approved lawyers—more expensive, but worth every penny. And, if you can, Abby, leave the country. No amount of money is worth risking your life for. Not like this."

"I'm gonna fight for my business."

He admired her courage, however naïve and misguided it was.

"Listen," she said. "I've got to go. Enjoy your stay here. I'll try you in a few days if things get better. Right now, I don't think we should talk."

"Good luck ... and take care."

"Bye."

Gray often considered time by himself enjoyable and relaxing. He rarely used the word alone, disliking the implied negative connotation of loneliness and despair. He preferred "by myself." But at that very moment, he felt very alone and afraid. "I'm alone," he said, and shuddered at the thought. He went inside the compact room, butted his smoke in the ashtray, sat down on the bed, and pondered his next move.

He checked the date on his cell phone—Saturday, December 22$^{nd}$. In a few days it would be Christmas. What kind of a Christmas would he have? It certainly wouldn't be a white Christmas. Would it be a red Christmas? He pulled out his laptop to check his e-mails, maybe Skype-call Derrick. He could use some contact with a familiar and friendly voice. Besides, he wanted to tell Derrick about Strap. He hadn't even bothered to e-mail his good friend since his departure.

He entered the hotel internet password and got a connection. Thank God for technology. He knew Derrick would be taking time off over the holidays and hoped he could reach him. He was in luck. Derrick's green online icon was illuminated.

After Gray had given Derrick highlights of his two affairs, and been congratulated on his newfound confidence and success with the opposite sex, they dismissed the preamble and Gray got to the point. "Listen, I'm in a little trouble down here."

"What do you mean?"

He relayed the story of Abby's troubles and provided an edited version of the near-death experiences involving Strap.

"Funny you say that," Derrick said.

"Why's that?"

"Jimmy's been asking about you lately, like he knows you're in danger. He's also been asking if I've heard anything from Strap and Rocky."

"What'd you tell him?"

"The truth. I hadn't heard from any of you guys. Why didn't you tell me this before?"

"I don't know. There's a lot of adjustment down here culturally and ... hell, I don't know. I'm telling you now."

"So you think Strap is still after you?"

"I have no reason to believe he isn't."

"Why don't you get the hell out of the country?"

"I don't know. I want to go to the jungle and see the shaman."

"Do you think a shaman can help?"

"I don't know, but I feel like I have to see him, like I have no choice. It popped into my head the other day: a voice—*see the shaman*—something like that. It was really weird. Not like anything I conjured up on my own."

"Sounds like you're losing your mind."

"Maybe I am. But before I return, I'm going to the jungle to see the shaman."

"Are you going to take that mind-altering drug ...?"

"Ayahuaska."

"That's it."

Gray had initially thought not, but had since changed his mind. "Probably."

"I've heard it can be dangerous. People freak out."

"Whatever ... I'm going to take it. What harm can it do? I'm in enough shit. I'm already fucked-up."

"What do you want me to do?"

"Do you think Jimmy will help?"

"I don't know. He's been asking. Should I tell him?"

"Yeah, tell him. Maybe he can threaten Rocky to call off his dog. It would be nice to enjoy my holiday without someone trying to murder me."

"Right. Merry Christmas," Derrick said.

"Merry fucking Xmas to you and yours. May the holiday season fill you with everlasting peace, happiness and glee."

"Fuck you Scrooge."

"Anyway, can you tell him?"

"I'll tell him."

Gray gave Derrick a brief and unappreciative description of his current location, promised to keep up more regular communication, and hung up.

He stifled a sudden urge to call Karina, powered down the computer and prepared to leave—in search of breakfast and coffee, the first challenge of the day. His phone rang just as he closed the hotel suite door. He glanced at the number and pressed the Ignore button after seeing Adriana's name appear. He locked the hotel suite and left.

He had no idea what he was going to do about the Adriana conundrum—he didn't know what to say to her. It would require more thought. In reality, she had been good to him. She deserved an explanation, deserved the truth. But on the other hand, with two cop brothers, what if she didn't like what she heard? He doubted she would resort to anything nasty, but after what happened recently with Strap, he didn't want to take any chances. If anything, he was erring way too far on the side of caution, his judgment skewed by recent terrifying events. And then there was Karina, with no expectations whatsoever. And he had no idea what to do about her.

He was confused.

Maybe some eggs and coffee would help him think better.

# Chapter Thirty

"It used to be way better here," Helmut Schwarz said. He sipped a *caipirinha*—sugar cane rum, sugar, lime and ice—and stared out at the setting sun. He and Gray sat at a picnic table on the sand at the quieter east end of the beach, where the thumping disco music was barely audible over the white noise of the splashing Pacific Ocean waves and incoming tide.

The bar, directly across the street from the slightly upscale Costa Paraiso Hotel, was a makeshift two-story wooden structure constructed on the sand perhaps fifty feet from the shoreline. It didn't have a name. Multi-colored incandescent light bulbs were fastened to handcrafted oceanfront tables. They twinkled in the moonlit night, creating a romantic atmosphere. It was nothing short of mesmerizing. Chairs and tables were handcrafted from twigs and branches. Branches had also gone into the construction of the actual bar, which had a small residence on the second floor, but no evidence of running water or a bathroom. A Mulatto-skinned, lean and muscular hippie lived in the tree house of sorts with his attractive spouse and infant son. Gray knew there was a story here—one that perhaps he would never know.

Walking past the structure earlier in the day, he was convinced it was abandoned. On another pass, he saw the hippie urinating nearby on the beach and noticed the spouse breastfeeding her son through the open door upstairs.

The hippie, long black dreadlocked-hair, had smiled warmly at Gray as he walked past.

It was that warm and inviting smile that brought him back to the thatched-roof structure now. After all, the Tahiti was only a block away, and he wasn't in the mood for the nerve-wracking sounds of the west part of the *malecon*. If there was a quiet and tranquil romantic paradise in Atacames, Gray had found it.

He had met Helmut about an hour ago at the atmospheric establishment. Helmut had been sitting with his wife, Alejandra, their seven-year-old son, Domingo, having a drink, before she and boy disappeared in a taxi to put the boy to bed. Recognizing Helmut as one of the very few gringos in Atacames, Gray had approached his table, asked him where he was from (Germany), and before long they were exchanging travel tales. Gray had not spotted Ray during his earlier walk around town so had sought out another companion. He needed as many friends and alliances as he could get.

Gray believed Helmut was a good man with a good heart.

But Helmut also had a dark side. Gray noticed an angry countenance about him, a palpable dissatisfaction seething below an ostensibly calm surface.

He was well-traveled, spoke very good Spanish, had been married to Alejandra for nine years, and had lived in Ecuador for seventeen years.

Maybe he was just having a bad day? Everyone was entitled.

"How is Atacames different from before?" Gray asked, sipping his *caipirinha*, enjoying the last of the setting sun, the soothing sound of the gently lapping waves. They were the only two patrons.

"They never used to gouge tourists like they do now. Have you noticed there are hardly any tourists here?"

Gray nodded. He knew the stalky man with long gray hair and a grizzled beard had a point to make.

"Take my hotel, for example. I looked at over fifteen places before my wife got here yesterday. I finally found one, negotiated a price of $20 a night, stepped out to call Alejandra, and when I returned to book the room I was told the price had gone up. Thirty-five fucking dollars they wanted. Because it's Christmas. It's fucking bullshit, I tell you."

"I haven't been getting the best vibe here. But they do that everywhere at Christmas," Gray said.

"And the people. Have you noticed how unfriendly they are? How indifferent to tourists? And the drinks. Six, seven dollars for a fruity cocktail or a rum and Coke. Tourists won't pay those prices, not to mention most of the food in the restaurants is overpriced."

"Most of the restaurants are dead. But you can't generalize and say everyone's unfriendly. I've met some very friendly people here, to be fair. They're not all like you say."

Helmut shook his head. "They are. I hate this place. I don't know why I keep coming back. I met my wife here. Maybe that's why."

"How much are these drinks? It's very good." Gray took a slow nursing sip.

Helmut lit a smoke and grabbed his glass. "These are two-fifty. It's because it's sugar cane rum. Some people hate it, but a lot of locals drink it 'cause it's cheap."

"I like it."

"Me too," Helmut said. He seemed to relax a little, his breath coming slower and more even.

"Have you always lived in Quito?" Gray asked.

"No, I used to own a farm just north of Esmeraldas. I had cows and used to grow fruits and vegetables."

"You sold it?"

"Eventually, yes. Things didn't go that well." A darkness precipitously enveloped Helmut's weathered features.

"What happened?"

Helmut paused, wiped a hand over a wrinkled brow, took a sip and told his story. "It was before Domingo was born. I always wanted to own a farm. It was my dream. So after I married Alejandra, I bought a hundred acres with a house, some outbuildings, and began life as a farmer. Things were good for about two years, and then they got ugly."

Gray didn't dare interrupt.

"About ten armed bandits raided the farm one evening. Shot and killed one of my farmhands, wounded another in the shoulder and almost killed my wife and me." He exposed his forearms, revealing several slash marks. "Took all our money—what was in the house anyway—some valuables, and stole all my cattle. Thirty cows."

"That sucks."

Helmut nodded. "Anyway, it didn't take long to realize that farming wasn't safe for us, not to mention the fact we wanted to have a child."

"You sold it and moved to Quito?"

"Eventually—but after I got my revenge."

Gray raised his eyes as Helmut's expression turned somber. Helmut reached into the crotch of his jeans and quickly glanced around the beach. Satisfied that no one was around, he pulled it out and set it on the table—a black polymer Smith & Wesson M&P45 pistol.

There was a tense silence as Helmut stared at Gray.

"What can I say? I have a nasty temper. And I don't take kindly to people fucking with me, my family, my possessions or my employees."

"I can see that."

Helmut took a long pull on his beverage, set it down, staring at its contents for a few seconds. "I killed six of them. Then we heard the rest were out for blood. That's when we sold the farm, packed up and moved to the city."

"What happened to the other four?"

"Those scumbags raped and pillaged one too many farms. They were all killed off by some of the other local farmers. One day six bodies were discovered in the forest—shot up and slashed, some beyond recognition. I guess there were more of them than I thought."

"Any repercussions?"

"There are no repercussions for killing criminals down here. It's the wild west."

"But you still have the gun?"

"That's why I still have the gun." He tucked it back in his crotch. "I would rather err on the side of caution. It's long in the past ... but you never know. It isn't like having a farm in Germany or Canada, you know. I learned *that* the hard way."

Their drinks were finished.

Helmut waved a hand and caught the attention of the bartender. "I presume you want another one?"

"Sure."

"Two more, please."

The bartender took their glasses.

They stared at the ocean for a few moments in silence before Helmut spoke: "You know, I had to give him money first to buy ice, the lime and the booze before we could even order these things."

"He seems pretty laid back. Business doesn't seem like a top priority."

By this time, the bartender's wife had climbed down the ladder from the makeshift loft abode, smiled at them, and began helping with the drinks.

"He's laid back," Helmut said. "I can't figure out why no one else is here. I guess they all like the insane noise at the other end."

"They must. But this is an awesome spot."

The drinks arrived. They simultaneously raised and clinked glasses, a silent but meaningfully bonding toast, and drank.

"It is," Helmut said. "And I'm glad I met you. I told you some of my story. Now it's your turn. What's your story?"

# Chapter Thirty-One

"That's a bullshit story," Jimmy said, delivering a hard backhand to Rocky's ruddy cheek. Blood sprayed from a cut lip and tiny droplets splattered onto a cracked and uneven concrete floor, illuminated by a single incandescent light bulb dangling overhead. "And you know it."

"I'm telling you, he doesn't answer his phone. If he did, I'd call him off. I swear."

Jimmy had retaliated in part out of a sense of loyalty and friendship to Derrick. He didn't know Gray well enough to consider him a friend. But if he had to be completely honest, there was another reason—revenge. The Chosen Ones had set him up. As a result, he had spent time in the joint. He could never completely forget that. One part of him found it difficult to leave the gang life, the hardened, desensitized part that refused to be pushed around by anybody. He knew he was taking a chance with his relationship with Julie, with his parole officer, with the shitty job he had managing a Rocket car wash in the city, but right now the need for revenge overrode those concerns. Anyone who had ever fucked with him had paid dearly. But with The Chosen Ones, he had put his tail between his legs like a frightened puppy dog and retreated into the tenuous sanctity of his relationship, his shitty job, his shitty little flat. Over time, it just wasn't good enough. Maybe all he needed was a reason to exact his revenge—and now he had one.

He walked over to the small wooden table containing the instruments of torture and examined them: a cordless drill, ball peen hammer, a pair of vice grips, needle nose pliers and, for good measure, a jerry can of gasoline to disinfect flesh wounds. Beside the instruments were the contents of Rocky's pockets: a wad of cash, a bag of weed, a bag of coke, two cell phones, some keys, lighter, wallet, handgun and military-issue combat knife.

He picked up the combat knife. Why not use the man's own weapon as an instrument of torture on him? He unsheathed it, held it to the light, and eyeballed his victim. Rocky sat in a wooden armchair, arms and legs zip-tied and duct-taped to the utilitarian piece of furniture. The light bulb dangling overhead cast a gray-white glow over his cut and bleeding body. The remainder of the warehouse—arranged compliments of his still-intact connections with The Skulls—was enveloped in darkness. With help from his connections, Jimmy had kidnapped Rocky earlier.

His torture session was young. After tying the gang leader up, for the last thirty minutes, he had only used fists, slaps, backhands, and on one occasion, a kick to the side of Rocky's head, which had sent the small chair toppling to the puddle-filled concrete. Setting the chair upright, he had realized that tactic was a mistake. Crashing to the floor, the small wooden chair creaked and cracked, almost breaking with the weight of Rocky's formidable bulk. He had made a mental note to self. *Be thoughtful in your torture.* The Skulls had left the warehouse, and he was on his own with this monster. And he didn't want things to get out of control. He knew Rocky wouldn't hesitate to get downright medieval on his ass if an opportunity presented itself.

As it was, he might have to kill Rocky to send the right message anyway.

Brandishing the knife, he stepped out of the darkness surrounding the torture table.

"Wait ... wait," Rocky pleaded. His eyes bulged. His long hair was matted to one side of his head, sticky with blood and dirty water from the floor. "Call him yourself if you don't believe me."

Jimmy stopped and considered it. Maybe Rocky was telling the truth? Returning to the table, he set the knife down, picked up a phone and waved it at Rocky. "Is it this one?"

"The black one ... the other one."

He set it down, retrieving the black phone. He scrolled through the directory, stopping at one name before Strap. The name rang a bell. But he couldn't remember the man behind the name. "Who's Raul?"

Silence.

"I said who's Raul?" Jimmy approached Rocky, cell phone in one hand, knife in the other. He put the point of the blade onto a bound forearm, applied pressure, and carved a two-inch incision. Blood squirted out and Rocky winced, emitting a small squeal like a wounded puppy dog.

*Now who has their tail between their legs, cowering like a fearful dog?* "Maybe you need some gasoline in that?" Jimmy said, spinning around and approaching the torture table.

"He's our Ecuadorian connection," Rocky blurted out. This was going to be easier than Jimmy thought. He remembered the man suddenly. The Skulls were involved in a negotiation with Raul for distribution of Ecuadorian-produced cocaine. Things had cratered because ... because Jimmy got busted, because Rocky set him up for a fall. Now he was beginning to see the whole picture. Maybe he could kill two birds with one stone?

But first things first.

He found Strap in the contact directory and pressed call—four rings and voice-mail. "If you get this, Strap, you better call off your attack on Gray ASAP or your boss will never see the light of day. I want your word now." He hung up and approached Rocky with the ball peen hammer.

"I guess you were telling the truth."

"I told you ... I left two messages."

"There must be someone else who can reach Strap."

Rocky didn't answer. The alliance with Raul was precarious at best, and he didn't want to go there. Raul would likely do more than call off Strap's attack. He would kill him and say it was an accident. That was if he hadn't already killed him.

Jimmy scratched his grizzled chin. "What about Raul?" Jimmy knew for Rocky to backtrack on an order to assassinate Gray could be a fatal blow to Rocky's credibility. And Jimmy suspected Raul was tacitly involved in the planned execution of Gray. He was at least turning a blind eye; facilitating it to some degree. He had to be. It was Ecuador. Logistics were a challenge at the best of times. Strap would need help.

"Raul doesn't know anything about this," Rocky said.

The hammer cracked down so hard on Rocky's baby finger it crushed bone and sprayed splintered wood into the air. He emitted a short, shrill scream while Jimmy watched, satisfied with his efforts so far. He knew Rocky was going to sing like a parrot in short order.

"That's bullshit and you know it," Jimmy said, when quiet prevailed in the dungeon.

"Okay, okay, call fucking Raul and give the phone to me. I'll tell him to call off Strap."

# Chapter Thirty-Two

This wasn't the scenario Strap had anticipated. He wanted to be long gone from this raucous beach town by now, with a fond and sentimental memory of the painful expression on Gray's sarcastic face as he breathed his last breath on Planet Earth. He wanted to categorize the memory neatly in the archive of his mind, keep it close so he could retrieve it when the need for reassurance possessed him.

Then, like he had done with so many other victims before Gray, he could draw on it to give him strength and remind him that he had power and control. He was the one who made people wish they had never uttered a foul word or cast him an askance glance. He was the one who would make them pay for their sins, replacing whatever deity possessed their puerile minds and demonstrate emphatically that The Strap was indeed the meanest son of a bitch in the valley. Or, in this case, the beach.

But as it was he was sitting in a shitty apartment in a shitty barrio in Atacames staring at some punk teenager named Adelmo who was lying spread-eagled, cut and bleeding, tied to a double bed with duct tape wrapped around his wise-ass little mouth. And the little shit—clad only in a pair of cheap polyester black shorts—was crying.

Crying, because after Strap had caught up with Adelmo the evening of the robbery, he had fist-smashed his face twice—just to demonstrate who was boss—and dragged him back to the vacant apartment. Adelmo, after receiving five or six stinging blows from the trusty strap, had spilled his guts, admitted his responsibility in the robbery and revealed a hiding spot where Strap was able to retrieve his pistol and the machete. But his cash and cell phone were still missing, and he didn't know the whereabouts of the other perpetrators.

But he was going to find out. Of that he was sure.

He had just returned from retrieving his belongings. Now, brandishing the machete, he approached the bed, made some hand gestures to the frightened, tearful brown eyes forlornly regarding him. The hand gestures said: When I remove this duct tape if you scream you get the machete embedded deep in your chest.

Adelmo nodded, his eyes widening.

Strap reached over and, in a swift motion, stripped the tape from Adelmo's mouth.

"Aaaahhhhh."

"That's enough," Strap ordered, raising the blade.

Adelmo shut his mouth.

"Where are the others?"

Adelmo shook his head, fresh tears streaming down cheeks. Strap realized, not for the first time, there was a language barrier. Even if Adelmo could understand him, and confessed the whereabouts of the other perpetrators, Strap wouldn't understand. He needed a fucking translator.

He retrieved a paper and pencil off a dresser, returned to the bed, cut a bound hand free, stuffing writing materials into it.

"Write the names and addresses of the others. Names and addresses." He stood up and provided a little pantomime until Adelmo finally nodded.

Adelmo scrawled on the piece of paper. *Like taking candy from a baby*, Strap thought. In a few minutes, he had the names and addresses.

He smiled reassuringly, picked some clothes off a small chair, and tossed them on the bed. The teenager's expression brightened, sensing freedom was close at hand. Strap cut the remaining ties and motioned for Adelmo to get dressed and get the fuck out. Adelmo dressed with his back to Strap.

It was all the time Strap needed. He rushed at Adelmo and plunged the blade deep into his back. It pierced his heart, blood squirting from both sides of the fatal wound.

Strap extracted the blade as Adelmo grabbed his chest, spit blood and dropped face-first on the bed, a gasping-gurgling sound escaping his lips.

Strap flipped Adelmo over and stared at the eyes, growing lifeless. *One more for the archive.* "There is no second chance when you fuck with Strap, you little shit. No second chance, you hear?"

But Adelmo couldn't hear. He was dead.

There was a sudden pounding on the door of the abandoned apartment that Raul's appointed driver, Joachim, had arranged for Strap's macabre interrogation.

"Strap … open door … we talk," Joachim said.

Strap cleaned the machete on Adelmo's shorts, set it on the fresh cadaver's blood-soaked chest, and opened the door.

Joachim's eyes widened when he saw the carnage. He thought Strap would beat and torture the boy, but there would be no deaths involved in the plan to catch the culprits. Although he was a hardened criminal, this caught even Joachim by surprise. "What you do?"

"What do you think I did? He's dead ... and that's what his friends are going to get for fucking with me."

Only problem was, Strap had killed the wrong boy. Not that Adelmo hadn't committed the robbery—he was guilty—but Joachim was connected to Adelmo. In the darkness, he hadn't recognized the teenager earlier. But now, seeing the lifeless eyes staring at a ceiling of broken plaster and peeling paint, he recognized Adelmo.

He was good friends with Adelmo's mother. In light of current developments, Joachim couldn't let this go without retribution. He might have done nothing, if Raul hadn't informed him an hour ago to call Strap off the planned hit on Gray. Raul had said: "If he gives you any trouble, don't hesitate to take care of business. I'll look after things on my end."

In a lightning-fast motion, Joachim unsheathed his combat knife and attacked. He had a holstered gun, but right now his bravado and seething rage called for taking care of business the old fashioned way. He sprang forward.

Strap instinctively dodged and seized the machete. He swiftly rolled as Joachim's knife embedded itself deep into the mattress, inches from the lifeless corpse of Adelmo.

As Joachim extracted it, Strap lunged forward and thrust the blade downward.

Joachim rapidly dodged and Strap's machete stabbed into Adelmo's chest. Clutching it with both hands, Strap began extracting it.

But Joachim was on him, delivering a hard kick to the side of an already bruised temple.

"Aaaaaaahhhh ... you little fuck," Strap said, as he freed the embedded blade and rolled onto the floor, crashing into a bedside table with a flailing arm and sending a small lamp toppling down, the light bulb exploding into fragments as the machete slid across the floor.

Dazed, Strap outstretched his arms, grabbing Joachim by the wrists as Joachim fell on top of him.

Joachim tried to plunge the knife deep into Strap's chest, but strong arms and hands prevented it.

For a few seconds, they wrestled for control of the blade before Strap delivered a fierce elbow from the bottom that cut Joachim above the eye and distracted him just long enough for Strap to push him off, scramble to his feet and retrieve his machete.

Strap moved to the center of the room, brandishing the weapon. "Get up, you piece of shit ... you come at me for no reason. Get up, you little coward."

Joachim scrambled to his feet, circling Strap while slicing at the air with the knife. Strap held his weapon in both hands, taking full swings as soon as the small frame of Joachim stepped into range. After five near misses, Joachim put his head down and charged, head-butting Strap square in the chest.

Strap crashed into the wall, his head slamming into plaster so hard it left an imprint. A cloud of plaster-dust exploded around his head and chunks fell to the floor. Both men slammed to the floor, Joachim landing on top of Strap, still brandishing the knife. Strap's machete fell from his hand and clattered along the floor.

*This little fuck is going to get the better of me. I better do something.*

Joachim thrust the blade down, aiming for one fatal blow to the heart. The tip connected and blood sprayed out, just as

Strap punched the knife. A sideways incision narrowly missed vital organs. As Joachim slid the blade out, raising it for another downward thrust, Strap bucked him upward long enough to scramble to his feet.

He retrieved the machete and attacked, diving on his downed opponent. He wasn't going to take any chances standing this time. He swung the machete at the knife-wielding hand flailing from below and felt the machete's blade slice a deep gash in Joachim's wrist. Joachim released the knife. It flew through the air and stuck into the wall.

His eyes growing helpless, Joachim reached for his holstered pistol.

As Joachim gripped the gun, Strap raised the machete with both hands and thrust it forcefully into the bucking chest below him. As the blade sunk deep into Joachim's chest, he swung the pistol, striking Strap's head with a loud thwacking sound.

Eyeballing his chest wound, Joachim uttered a slow gurgling, gasping sound.

Strap fell sideways, slamming his head on the wooden floor with a hollow thud. He saw the room spinning for a few seconds before his entire world was enveloped in blackness.

# Chapter Thirty-Three

"Tomorrow's Christmas," Ray said, sitting bolt upright in a plastic bed-style lounge chair. "And it's going to be a Christmas filled with blackness."

"You shouldn't say that," Gray said, sipping a *Cuba libre* while lounging beside his new friend. To distill the tension in Ray's demeanor, Gray had invited him to the Hotel Tahiti for a pool party. It was mid-afternoon, hot and sunny, with barely a cloud in the sky. They had the large, fenced-in pool all to themselves. They were both on their third drink, and Ray's dissatisfaction with his life was becoming more evident with every beverage.

Gray raised his drink. "Look, the glass is half full; not half empty."

"Easy for you to say. I'm fifty-five, stuck in Ecuador with a girlfriend who's supporting me in a shitty apartment with no job prospects and no money. You're traveling ... and tomorrow you could decide to get the hell out of here, go wherever you want and start a new adventure."

"Could be worse. Your health could be failing and you could be freezing your ass off in Canada, working at Home Depot."

"I guess that's true," Ray said, his somber expression brightening marginally. He set his drink down, stood up and dove into the pool, making a large belly-flopping splash, not the dive he had intended.

Gray couldn't help laughing as Ray's flushed face emerged from the water. "That must've hurt."

Ray coughed and spit water. "I didn't want to dive too deep. So I over-corrected."

Ray swam a few lengths while Gray smoked and mulled over his situation. He still hadn't heard from Abby; she hadn't returned his last three calls. He had made fast friends with Helmut, telling him everything about the drama in Ecuador, including his recent status as unemployed in Canada. Ray didn't know it, and Gray had yet to tell him, but Gray's situation was not that far removed from that of the lost soul swimming lengths in the hotel pool.

Helmut's eyes had perked up somewhat at the mention of the shaman, saying he would like to accompany Gray to the jungle, meet the shaman, and participate in the mind-altering experiences of ayahuasca. Helmut admitted some anger-management issues of his own. He thought the shaman might help.

The news about Strap's attack on Gray had gone over with more composure than Gray had anticipated. Helmut had reached for his gun, brandished it, and said: "Don't you worry about anything. If I'm around, I've got this. And I'm prepared to use it."

But Gray no longer felt it would come to that. He had received an e-mail from Derrick last night saying that Jimmy was dealing with the problem. Gray had some ideas of how the former biker might go about this, but he didn't want to entertain them right now. He was thankful that Strap's attack on his life would be, or had been, called off. He was taking very simple pleasure in one of life's small favors—namely, that he could breathe.

He reflected on the status of his relationships with Adriana and Karina. He had received an e-mail from Karina saying she was enjoying the many natural wonders of the Galapagos, but the situation with Peter had not improved. Although they shared accommodations in the archipelago, their relationship had degenerated below the level of friendship to one of mutual avoidance. Karina had hoped to salvage the friendship, but the reception from Peter was indifferent and non-reconciliatory. He was a wall of ice. Gray longed to see Karina again.

Adriana kept calling. On a whim, Gray had picked up the phone and talked to her for a few minutes. Without going into too much detail, he had said he planned on going to the jungle to see the shaman and, if he had time, he would call her on his return to spend a few days together before he departed for Canada. Although he still harbored some reservations about her level of sincerity, he did want to see her again and had started to view their brief relationship in a much different light. After all, she hadn't freaked out when he left, hadn't freaked out at the fact he was now traveling single and available. She had only reiterated that she loved and missed him.

Adriana was a caring individual with a high degree of emotional intelligence. She had relayed a story during their travels of a 911 call she had received from a panic-stricken woman, screaming over the phone that her husband was brandishing a gun. Adriana had dispatched the police immediately and done everything she could to calm the woman. But there was a loud popping sound, a horrifying scream, and the line went dead. The police had arrived—a few minutes too late—to a macabre murder-suicide. The man had shot his wife and young daughter before pointing the gun to his head and blowing his brains out, a shocking news story that rapidly reached the attention of the international media.

Gray shivered in spite of the hot sun, took a long pull on his drink as Ray, dripping with water, exited the pool. He dried himself with a towel as Gray reclined in the chair. Was Gray endangering the life of Ray by hanging around him? He had no confirmation on Strap. And the squatters stalking Abby didn't have a lot to lose.

Ray poured another drink and resumed an upright sitting position in the lounge chair.

"Do you ever relax?" Gray asked. "Chill out, man. Kick back and enjoy the sun. You never know what the future holds."

Ray reclined, but a few seconds later he bolted upright. "I should call Karen."

Karen had caught a nasty stomach bacteria from something she had eaten last night. Her condition dictated she stay close to a toilet, so she had politely refused the pool-party invitation.

"Here's my phone."

Ray dialed. The call went to voicemail. He didn't leave a message. "I'm worried about her. She's sick and I should be at home looking after her. Not here with you."

"Thought you said she encouraged you to come and have some English conversation with a fellow Canadian for a change. You said you've got no other foreigner friends here."

"It's true ... but I should still be at home looking after her. She's going to freak out."

"I don't see why. She knows where you are and knows how to reach you. Enjoy the moment." Gray raised his glass. He was feeling a little tipsy. "Cheers. It was great to meet you." Gray was determined not to tell his new friend about the attacks on his life, or about the possibility that some deaths might occur as a result of Jimmy's recent involvement in the cat-and-mouse game with Strap. In his humble opinion, Ray didn't have the emotional intelligence or the emotional stability to handle it right now. His physical and mental world was crumbling around him and Gray wasn't prepared to risk a potentially shattering blow to a glass menagerie. He had no idea how, but he wanted to be a positive influence and a stabilizing force in Ray's troubled existence. Ray didn't need to hear any bad news. The path he had chosen had pushed him to the edge of a dangerous precipice where the black abyss bellowed threateningly from below.

For the time being, Ray forgot about Karen. "Likewise." He forced a smile.

They clinked glasses and drank.

Gray had mentioned a Canadian friend whom he had plans to visit in an earlier conversation, but he was sure it was long gone from Ray's mind. At least Ray hadn't mentioned it.

"When are you leaving Atacames?" Ray asked.

"After Christmas. Boxing Day or the day after. Probably Boxing Day."

"You're not hanging around for New Year's?"

"No."

"Where are you going?"

"Dunno ... kicking around Quito, from there the jungle."

"Where in the jungle?"

"Been reading about the Cuyabeno Wildlife Reserve, just outside the town of Lago Agrio. Some Siona Indians living in villages along the river. The shaman's there, too. In Puerto Bolivar."

"You going to see the shaman?"

"I'd like to. You ever seen a shaman?"

"No ... never been to the jungle."

"It'll be my third trip."

"So for sure you're going?" Ray's tone was pleading.

"I'm going. I just don't know when exactly. I never have an itinerary etched in stone. In case I meet some people ... *that's not going to go over well* ... or sights I decide to see. I find if you plan too far in advance a better itinerary almost always presents itself. Then you're locked into something and it has the potential to ruin a better plan."

"I like how you travel. We could plan something for New Year's?"

"Sorry, Ray. I do know I won't be here for New Year's."

"What about Christmas?"

"We can do something for Christmas if you want," Gray said. "That's tomorrow, right?"

Ray nodded and his eyes went far away, before glistening with tears.

Gray took the cue, stood and dove in the pool, the cool water calming his nerves and refreshing his body. He emerged, wiped his face, coughed, and smiled at Ray. "That's how you do it."

Ray dove in with much better form than before.

Drying himself off, Gray noticed his cell phone ringing. Ray swam laps.

He recognized the number. "Derrick, how's it going?"

"Are you planning on hanging around there for a while?"

"A few days. Why?"

"There's been a development—well, some developments."

"Tell me."

"You want the good news or the bad first?"

"The good."

"Rocky called off Strap. I hear Strap's disappeared. I don't know if that means he's dead or not. But you better not take any chances. Get your ass home."

"Is that Karen?" Ray asked from the pool.

Gray covered the earpiece. "No, it's a friend wishing me a happy Christmas."

Ray dove underwater and resumed swimming.

"Okay, tell me the bad now."

"Rocky's dead. Jimmy tortured and killed him. Jimmy's in hiding now—gone underground."

Gray processed the information through a haze. Would Rocky's Chosen Ones travel to Ecuador to exact their revenge? What happened to Strap? Would Strap come for him again? What about Derrick? Was his life now in danger? He didn't have the answers, but he also didn't want to alarm Ray, who approached the lounge chairs, wiping his face with a towel.

"Okay, thanks for that. You have a good holiday too. I'll call you later."

"Watch your ass ..."

Gray clicked the phone dead before Derrick could say more.

# Chapter Thirty-Four

"I suppose it's a question of what you can tolerate more," Gray told Helmut while they sipped *Cuba libres* at the familiar beach haunt with romantic lighting. Again, they had the entire bar to themselves. Alejandra had taken her son Domingo to their hotel about an hour ago. "If you can't tolerate all the laws in Germany, it becomes a question of how much you can tolerate the relative lawlessness of Ecuador."

"It's more than too many laws versus lawlessness," Helmut said, gazing out at the splashing waves while rock 'n roll music played in the background.

"It's just how slow the bureaucracy works and the cultural things. You know, I used to have an Ecuadorian friend, Juan. He was the best man at my wedding. We were close for three years. I gave him everything, was very good to him. I helped him build a hotel in exchange for a few days stay there. Anyway, we took him up on the stay. After a week, he presented us a bill for over two hundred dollars. I bought toilet paper for the place, there was no water, we had to bring a bunch of furniture, blankets, all kinds of shit. I worked for him for free." Helmut's face reddened. "Then he has the nerve to tell me I owe him two hundred dollars."

"That's bullshit. But that can happen in any country. What did you do?"

"I complained but he wouldn't listen. Insisted I owe him the money. So I paid him and terminated the friendship. Haven't talked to him in over three years. And fuck him. I have no Ecuadorian friends. Acquaintances, sure, but no friends. No one I would invite back to my house. And I'm not counting my wife's family. If we split up, you know whose side they'd take."

"That's sad. Don't you think you're generalizing? I'm sure they're not all like that. You're starting to sound prejudiced."

Helmut's face reddened. "Are you kidding me? Prejudiced? I'm married to an Ecuadorian woman, have an Ecuadorian son. I don't care about all that shit. I live here for fuck sakes. I know the dangers and know what it's all about. Besides, we're all prejudiced in one way or another. We just don't want to admit it. We're products of our culture, our upbringing. There are cultural differences and they're real. That's how I feel."

"What about the gringo prices?" Gray knew it was a topic that would send Helmut ranting again. But, hell, they were on the topic.

"Tell me about it. You think Atacames would be booming with tourism, maybe like Montanita. But Montanita doesn't gouge on prices. At least, not as much. See all the bars here. Most of them empty, and the only reason they're doing any business now is because it's so close to Christmas. Locals mostly, not gringos. Gringos come here once, get mistreated and never come back. Would you come back?"

Gray shook his head.

"See what I mean. Six, seven dollar cocktails, most of the stores charge gringos extra ... like four dollars for a three-dollar pack of smokes. Do you know I had to walk twenty minutes to the center of town to get these?" He held up a blue pack of Philip Morris. "Six stores later and a twenty-minute walk and in Quito I buy them for two dollars and forty cents a pack. That's the real price.

"And the restaurants ... that's another story. A friend of mine ate in a restaurant one day and they tried to charge him over the menu price, saying the prices had just gone up." Helmut was rolling now. "And my German friend, he owns a restaurant here. He went into town to buy some chairs a while ago. There was a big banner on the window offering the chairs on sale. You can guess what happened. They tried to charge him the regular price, even though the banner clearly advertised forty per cent off ... something like that."

"It's a beach town though. Beach towns rip you off."

"Not all of them ... and not as bad as here. Trust me. Compare Canoa, Puerto Lopez or Montanita to Atacames any day, and you'll see what I mean."

"So that's clearly one of the issues in Ecuador," Gray said. "Gringo prices versus local prices."

"Not as much in the big cities or the areas concentrated with expats like Salinas or Cuenca. And trust me—it's not like this in Quito, where I live. The city is too big. The shopkeepers can't keep a handle on who lives there and who's a tourist, so for the most part you don't get ripped off."

If Helmut wasn't happy living in Ecuador, why didn't he just leave? But, on the other hand, not an easy proposition when you factor an Ecuadorian wife and son into the mix. "What were you saying about the cultural differences?"

"I don't want to get into it. It just makes me angry. It's something I have to learn to live with or leave." Helmut returned to his drink and paused for a few seconds. "I'll say one more thing and then leave it alone. Do you know how many cars have almost run me over, even though they see me?"

"I've dodged a few bullets."

"I don't know how many times I've punched, kicked the fender, door or whatever, and called them out."

"Anyone ever return?"

"Would you?"

Gray regarded the angry, intimidating face watching him and quickly shook his head.

"When most people see my temper, they want nothing to do with me."

"Can I tell you one more story and then we'll move on?" Gray asked.

"Go ahead."

"I'm not saying this to be prejudiced. I'm just pointing out cultural differences."

"No problem."

"I was waiting for a bus here ... can't remember where I was going. I'm second in line, making conversation with this attractive young Swiss woman. She's loaded down with travel bags. I have my little carry-on knapsack. Meanwhile, the line is building behind us. There's a few people standing wherever, but not in the line. The bus finally arrives. The Swiss woman, Elena I think her name was, is struggling to get on because she's got a mammoth knapsack. She's wrestling with it, ends up carrying it to the side of the bus, you know, the luggage compartment. She returns and by this time there's mayhem in front of the bus. The Ecuadorians are pushing and shoving to get on. The line is now non-existent."

"What did you do?"

"I felt so bad for Elena I waited for her, pushed my way through, and tried to help her board. But by then the bus had already filled up, and there was room for only one more."

"What did you do?"

"A foreigner comes along, who apparently also got railroaded from the line-up while dealing with his knapsack. I ask him his level of urgency and he says he has a plane to catch. I give him the last spot on the bus, he thanks me profusely, the doors close and off they go. I'll tell you that guy was so appreciative for the last spot, even though I was supposedly first in the so-called line. And was he ever pissed off."

"What about Elena?"

"I couldn't believe Elena. She stood there, an island of calm and inner peace, without the least expression of annoyance on her pretty face. She was even smiling. I tell you, I could learn a lot from that girl. I gave her my e-mail, but I doubt she'll contact me. You know how it goes, different travel plans."

"So what about the next bus?"

"I planned for that. We took our rightful place in line and waited a half hour, maybe. The bus comes along after a bunch of people had gathered in the so-called line. I grab a rail at the side of the door and hang on for dear life—blocking passage—while she deals with her bag. While it's getting stuffed into the luggage compartment I'm scrambling to hold our place in line. Anyway, finally she gets to me and I get her through, releasing my hand long enough to get both our asses aboard. I don't care what happens after that."

"She must've been happy?"

"She thanked me. I'll tell you that chick was an absolute doll—an island of calm in the face of chaos."

"I wish I could be like that," Helmut said matter-of-factly, a split-second before the violence erupted.

Three men emerged swiftly out of the darkness surrounding the beach, their black shapes silhouetted by the distant moon overhead. Two appeared to be helping a third, presumably drunk. They ambled toward Gray and Helmut.

Helmut didn't waste any time. He extracted his piece, finger poised on trigger. "What do you guys want?"

There was a clicking sound, followed by another clicking sound, before Gray realized what had happened. The three on the beach served as a distraction for two men who approached from behind. The barrel of a gun was pointed at the back of his head, another pointed at Helmut's head.

"Fuck you," Helmut exploded, ducking and swinging a fist that connected with the intruder's jaw. A shot rang out that grazed the corner of Helmut's ear. He pointed his pistol at the attacker and started shooting while Gray dove to the ground and rolled as a bullet penetrated the sand a few inches from his head.

More shots rang out as the two armed attackers retreated, ducking behind the wooden bar and returning fire. The bartender and his wife scattered.

Helmut glanced behind. The three decoys had vanished. Gray was crouched in the sand.

Helmut fired two shots at the bar and a loud groan echoed in the night. "He's hit," Helmut said. "Wait here. I'm going in for the other one."

Gun drawn, Helmut cautiously moved toward the bar. He didn't duck. He didn't run. He plodded forward methodically, as if he was impervious to bullets. You could say a lot of things about Helmut and his strange ways. But you couldn't say he was afraid. In times of chaos, he thrived.

Gray stood up, watching, pulled out his cell phone and shoved it down his underwear. Helmut stood behind the bar, firing. Gray heard the groans and gasps of the dying. In the suffused light from a streetlamp, Helmut seemed to be smiling.

Was there another man running away from the bar? Maybe it was the bartender? Gray couldn't be sure. It was too dark. He heard footsteps in the sand behind him and spun around. But he was too late. He was clobbered hard over the head with a blunt instrument.

*Thwack.*

Gray faded to black.

# Chapter Thirty-Five

Black dots swirled around as Gray slowly opened his eyes—symptoms of a concussion. He remembered getting whacked hard in the head. And that was the last thing he remembered. Rays of light seeping through a curtained window did little to enhance his view. He twisted on the ceramic tile floor and realized three things immediately. His hands and feet were zip-tied, his head throbbed with a dull pain, and a sharper pain pulsated from his tailbone.

The kidnappers had dropped him roughly on the hard floor. He blinked a few times, closed his eyes and winced, then slowly opened them. He thought it might clear his vision, but the black dots, some of which had morphed into bright purple, still danced in and out of his periphery.

He surveyed his surroundings. He saw the silhouette of bars behind the dark curtain. He gazed around. In the corner was a small cot with a white blanket, beside it a small end table with a nondescript lamp. Black and purple circles danced around the surroundings, creating a surreal and hallucinogenic effect. All he needed was an eerie soundtrack. The distant hum of traffic noise outside went some way to providing it.

He closed his eyes, counted to ten, and opened them—less purple dots than before. He gazed at the whitewashed walls, noticing a black steel man-door securely locked with three steel deadbolts.

Tailbone throbbing, he swept his gaze back to the cot. It would be an improvement from the hard floor. He slowly inched his way over to it. When he was within three feet, he stopped, beads of sweat dripping into his eyes from the pain and effort of dragging himself along the floor.

There was something black on the pillow. And it wasn't a shadow. As his night vision adjusted, he realized the white sheet was crumpled, the lumps resembling a body. A body? What? He was being held captive with someone else? Who? The hair was much too dark to be Helmut, or Ray for that matter. Maybe Karen, Ray's girlfriend? Or maybe Alejandra, Helmut's wife? What had happened to Helmut anyway? He killed at least two people. Did he get away? That was entirely possible.

What about Ray? Had he been there that night? Then he remembered. By four in the afternoon—was it yesterday?—Ray, two-thirds in the bag, had opted out of the beach bar invitation and staggered home to care for his ailing girlfriend.

Who was in the cot? And were they dead?

The black mass of long hair suddenly moved and Gray jerked his head, terrified.

He opened his mouth to scream but the woman on the cot reacted too fast.

"Nooooooo ..."

In an instant, Gray recognized her. "Abby."

She stopped the mono-syllabic enunciation and stared. As her head slid into the tiny spears of emanating light, Gray could see her black hair was matted to one side, her extremities zip-tied. "Gray ... is that you?"

"It's me."

"Are you okay?"

"Yeah ... a little dozy, but okay. You?"

"A little dopey too. But okay." The realization slowly dawned on her. "All my fault. I got you into this mess. They must've spotted you at the hotel and made the connection. I'm so sorry."

"Don't worry. Forget it. It's behind us. I wanted to come, wanted to help you. No one put a gun to my head." He realized as soon as he said it—that wasn't entirely accurate. Someone *had* put a gun to his head. Someone had whacked him over the head with one. He winced, the throbbing in his head serving as a grim reminder. He looked behind him. He thought he could make out a small puddle of blood, a trail of smears snaking along the floor leading to his current location.

"When did they capture you?" he asked.

"I don't know. I ... my drink was drugged—a bar outside my hotel. I don't remember anything. I don't know how long I've been here. What about you?"

"I don't know. Could've been tonight. Could've been last night. Do you realize it might be Christmas today?"

"Merry Christmas," Abby said weakly.

They both burst into laughter. Gray had no idea what was funny about it. Maybe it was the irony of the situation? But, after the laughter, there was a long silence, an eerie quiet that spoke volumes.

Finally, Gray asked: "Do you know what they plan on doing with us?"

"Either kill us, or tell us to leave the country, or else."

"Has anyone come to talk to you?"

"I don't think so. But this drug is just starting to wear off. I can't remember anything while I was on it. I've heard it can last forty-eight hours or more."

There was a moment's pause while Gray thought. Kidnapped, tied up and incarcerated in an unknown location. He inched closer to Abby. His tailbone was screaming in pain. "Listen ... if I can get up there, do you mind if I sit beside you? My tailbone is killing me."

"Go ahead." She inched toward the wall, making space.

He pushed up with his hands, grunted a few times, and stood shakily. Purple dots shrank and grew, dancing around the room. He closed his eyes.

"What's wrong?"

"I'm seeing stars. Well, actually, purple dots."

"Your head—it's bleeding at the back."

"Compliments of the squatters." He lowered himself gingerly on the mattress and groaned as he found a comfortable spot.

"We have to get out of here," Abby said.

One of the zip-ties binding Gray's wrists was too tight. He felt a sharp pain and warm wetness on the palm of his hand as it finally sliced through flesh and blood oozed out.

Abby saw a small rivulet of blood from Gray's hand pooling on the white blanket. "What are we going to do?" she said in a tone giddy with tension.

"We're going to get out of here."

"How?"

"When they come in, we'll say we'll leave the country without telling anyone what happened."

"Do you really think they'll believe that? Besides, when I'm free I plan on continuing the fight for my business."

Gray didn't know Abby that well. But that didn't prevent him from giving her a reality check. "Are you crazy? You've had your life threatened. You've been kidnapped. You're tied up, incarcerated. And if we ever get free, you're going to continue the fight in Atacames? How many times have you had to change hotels? How many times has your life been threatened? Abby, it's time. If we ever get out of this alive, please leave the country and never look back. I don't know how much you paid for the hotel business, but all the money in the world isn't worth your life. What does your husband say?"

"Spencer told me a long time ago to leave. So did his mother, and my mother. But has it ever occurred to you that running a hotel is my lifelong dream? I'll be damned if I'm going to let some punk-ass Ecuadorians take it over. I've worked my whole life for this. I'm not giving up this easy."

"Look around. Your dream has turned into a nightmare. Even if you want to leave the country, you don't know if they'll let you. You said if a foreigner is sued by an Ecuadorian, they can't leave. Aren't they suing you?"

She nodded, eyes resolute but welling up with tears. "They sued me. I went to court already. There's another court date set. I have a new lawyer. I don't think the judge believes them."

"You don't think the judge believes them? But you have another court date. That means this isn't over. You have ongoing litigation. You can't leave the country."

"We've counter-sued. My lawyer said the best defense is a strong offense."

"It doesn't matter. Can't you see? You're stuck in litigation. They'll never let you leave. And if the kidnappers know that, what's to prevent them from killing you—killing us?" As soon as he said it, Gray realized he had gone too far.

The tears now ran freely down her cheeks. And although she had propped herself up on the wall, she made no attempt to hang her head and hide her emotions. She had been through—was still going through—a horrific trauma and all the emotions she had buried deep inside were bubbling up to the surface.

Gray inched closer. He wanted to hug her, but all he managed was to slump his muddled head on her shoulder. She leaned her head on his, her long black hair falling over his face. He felt the wetness of her tears on his cheek. He swallowed a lump in his throat. "I'm sorry. We should be talking about something else. It's Christmas." *Now that sounded stupid.*

"It's okay," she said. "Maybe you're right. I don't know why I'm so stubborn"

"Your courage is admirable." Gray couldn't think of anything else to say.

"Thanks."

"Don't mention it."

Gray closed his eyes, watching the dancing purple dots, shrink and grow, shrink and grow.

They sat silent for a long time.

He didn't know how long he sat there, but when he opened his eyes and peered up at Abby, she was sleeping. He moved his head to her chest, held his breath and exhaled as he heard the reassuring steady rhythm of her heartbeat. For a split-second, he thought she had died. *Don't go doing that. I need you.*

*A red Christmas … it's going to be a red Christmas.*

# Chapter Thirty-Six

"Merry Christmas," a man wearing a black balaclava, said.

Gray opened his eyes. The purple dots had disappeared, replaced by the bitter reality of hot and acrid-smelling breath. Someone had drawn the black curtain and bright sunlight enveloped the utilitarian room. Gray blinked, believing at first he was dreaming, and looked again. Through the balaclava, about six inches from his face, beady black eyes regarded him intently.

He lifted his head from Abby's ample bosom, realizing he had fallen asleep in a fashion as close to cuddling as was possible given the confines of zip-ties that bind. He was curled into a fetal position, legs crossed over hers. His throat was parched; head and tailbone still ached. On an impulse, he lowered his head onto the inviting breasts, for what he believed might be the last time. For all he knew, the balaclava man had come to kill them.

Abby opened her eyes. He lifted his head, embarrassed. She smiled weakly.

The man grabbed Gray by the shoulder and jerked him upright. "Merry Christmas." He waved an arm to the ajar door. Two masked men armed with AK-47 assault rifles guarded either side. In front of them was a small table, two chairs, an assortment of food—room service.

A woman dressed in a nurse uniform, holding white towels, a first-aid kit and a bucket of water stood beside the table. She waved them over.

*Why would they feed us first if they were going to kill us? Deception, that's why.*

Balaclava man unsheathed a combat knife. Gray's jaundiced face turned chalk-white.

The man bellowed laughter. The guards joined the chorus while the nurse kept up her repose.

"Don't worry. I cut you free. You eat. Then the Boss speaks to you." He waved the knife a few inches from a throat already caked with dried blood. "But don't do anything stupid. Otherwise you have a red Christmas." The guards bellowed laughter again as the man cut Gray's wrist zip-ties, sliced those binding his ankles. He then cut Abby free.

The nurse unlocked a small door in the corner of the room. It opened to a bathroom. Gray gestured to Abby and she shook her head. Gray pointed to the bathroom and the hooded man with the knife nodded. "Make it quick." Gray relieved himself and sat on the bed beside Abby.

She used the toilet and sat down beside Gray.

Balaclava man pointed to the nurse. "Let her clean you up. Then you eat. I return in an hour with the Boss. He tell you what to do."

"I want to talk to the Boss now," Abby said.

"Your time will come," the man said, twirling the knife adeptly with a thumb and forefinger. "Now shut up and let her clean you up."

The nurse cleaned, disinfected and bandaged Gray's wounds.

Then she cleaned, disinfected and bandaged some cuts on Abby's forearms. Fully clothed in a white t-shirt and black shorts, Abby received a towel-bath of sorts to the appreciative and gloating eyes of the captors. Abby was too scared to object. When the nurse was finished, the men followed her out, clanging the heavy metal door shut behind them and locking three deadbolts.

They were silent as they ate eggs, toast, refried beans, freshly-cut fruit, and fresh mango juice. There was even a thermos of coffee with milk and sugar. Gray looked around the room as they ate, realizing some of his things were scattered on the floor: cigarettes, lighter, hotel key and a few business cards he had collected during his travels. These guys had some bravado to leave him with a cigarette lighter. How did they know he wouldn't burn the house down?

He lifted the thermos, unscrewed the cap and took a whiff. "Smells good. Want some?"

Abby lifted a white mug across the table and Gray poured. She sipped black coffee while he added a few drops of milk and a quarter teaspoon of sugar.

A smile slowly crept over Gray's face.

"What?"

He stood up, cringed as a sharp pain from his tailbone shot up through his spine, grabbed his smokes and lighter and returned to the table. Lighting up, he said: "I hope you don't mind?"

"Don't mind if I do," Abby said, extending a hand. He lit her up. "Now what are you smiling about?"

"Excuse me." He went into the bathroom and extracted a cell phone from the cheeks of his ass. Then he removed the phone from a clear plastic bag, washed his hands, returned and sat down. He slowly revealed the phone. "Merry Christmas."

"Give it to me," she said. "I know who to call."

"Wait. So do I. Check the window. See if you can figure out where we are."

She went to the window, peering out in all directions. "All I can see is a black rooftop. I don't know this location."

Gray approached the window. As for directions, he didn't know shit from Shinola. He saw the black rooftop, near the edge, two armed guards, smoking and talking animatedly. "Are you sure?"

"I don't know where we are. I'm pretty sure we're still in Atacames. But it's just a feeling."

"Okay. There are two people I'm going to call. My friend's girlfriend and my friend Helmut." Gray quickly told her the story of how Helmut had killed some of their captors. "Karen's a psychic and Helmut's a psycho. She can tell him where we are ... he can do the rest."

"Are you sure it'll work?"

"Do you have any better ideas?"

Abby was going to mention her lawyer, then the police, but she bit her tongue. They hadn't gotten her out of many jambs lately. Gray gave Abby a number to remember and dialed Helmut. Surprisingly, he picked up on the first ring.

"Gray? Is that you?"

"Helmut. Thank god. Listen, I'm being held captive. Remember my friend Abby? They've got us both. We don't know where we are. I want you to call this number." He rattled off the digits as Abby recited them. "Her name's Karen, Ray's girlfriend, the Canadian I told you about. She's psychic. Maybe she can tell you where we are." There was a momentary pause before Gray said: "I don't know, but please, we need your help—badly. Don't phone me. I'll call you."

Gray hung up, killed the power on the phone and shoved it down his pants. It would find its way up his ass later. "He's coming. He sounded really pissed off. He's got anger-management issues."

Abby smiled and hugged Gray. Fifteen seconds later, the metal door burst open and two men rushed inside the small room, pointing AK-47s at two captive and surprised heads. Gray recognized the voice of the man in the background as soon as he spoke. "We're moving you." It was the balaclava man who had invited them for Christmas dinner.

Sixteen minutes later, new zip-ties binding extremities, black hoods covering heads, they bounced around in the trunk of a car as it barreled down a dusty and pot-holed country road.

*This isn't a white Christmas*, Gray thought gloomily. *It's not a red Christmas either. It's a black Christmas.*

# Chapter Thirty-Seven

"Yes, it's Christmas, honey, but I'm also expecting a call," Karen said, watching Ray talk on the phone.

He was talking to his ailing mother, feeling homesick like hell, and trying to sound all positive as he wished her happy holidays. But the damned phone had started beeping. And, being pretty far from technologically savvy, Ray had no idea how to put the call on hold, or even switch to the incoming call for that matter. So he had ignored it for a short time, until his mother had commented: "What's that beeping noise?"

Now he pulled the phone away from his ear and stared at it like it had grown horns.

"Give it to me and I'll tell them to call back," Karen said, taking a sip of wine. They had just finished a fine chicken dinner with all the trimmings, owing to the exemplary culinary skills of his common-law wife.

Sitting beside him on the couch, she extended a hand.

Ray wasn't about to argue, not least of all because she was the breadwinner in the household, and occasionally reminded him of that fact. He handed her the phone and she switched to the incoming call. "Hello?"

"Are you Karen?"

"Yes, who's speaking?"

"This is Helmut. I'm a friend of Gray's. He's in grave danger and we need your help immediately."

"Just a second."

"Don't hang up. I need your help."

She put a hand over the earpiece and looked at Ray's intoxicated eyes. "It's Gray. He's in trouble. It's an emergency."

"Let me say goodbye."

She handed it over. "Mom, I'm sorry. I've got an emergency here. No, I'm fine. But a friend needs help. I'll call you back."

He handed the phone to Karen, who disconnected one call while reconnecting another. "What do you want us to do?"

"Give me your address," Helmut said. "I'm coming over right now."

Handing the phone to Ray, Karen stood up. She needed a glass of water. Reaching the fridge, it hit her so hard she had to steady herself on the appliance—a vision so powerful it enveloped her senses completely. First, she saw Gray and Abby, arms and legs bound, sitting on the small cot together, talking. Then the scene fast-forwarded to the two, fitted with black hoods, arms tied behind their backs, being led to a waiting green car, where they were stuffed into the trunk.

She knew in an instant what the next scene was—a vision of the future, what might be but not necessarily what would be. Karen knew from experience the future could be altered. But it didn't change the deleterious effect of the macabre horror movie that played out in her mind. She saw Gray and Abby standing in a clearing, surrounded by woods, hands bound behind their backs. Abby wiped tears away. Gray stood beside her, resolute but petrified. Then, in an instant, it happened.

AK-47 drawn, the man approached. He stopped ten feet in front of them, peeled off his balaclava, revealing short black hair, dark skin, beady black eyes—an evil grin on chiseled features. "We have no choice."

Abby screamed as the first staccato-burst of bullets sprayed her chest and head. She dropped dead, and Gray cast a worried glance at her, then sprinted ten feet or so before the second blast of machine-gun fire mowed him down. He dropped to the ground and a small cloud of gray-brown dust billowed into the air surrounding his lifeless body.

As the vision slowly faded, Karen, glass of water in hand, realized she was falling forward. It had hit her like a speeding bus. The living room came into focus and she saw Ray reaching for her as she pitched the glass in the air. The water sprang out. The glass shattered as it struck the wall. Everything seemed to play out in slow motion. She extended her arms to grab Ray, and the momentum of the fall sent them both careening onto the glass coffee table. It shattered on impact and she landed on top of Ray, whose head had taken the brunt of the force.

He stared at a fountain of blood pulsating out from a triangular piece of glass protruding from his forearm. His other arm was securely wrapped around Karen. His concern was not for his bleeding arm or his injured head. The light bulb in his head popped and darkness slowly enveloped his senses. He said three words before he lost consciousness: "Are you okay?"

# Chapter Thirty-Eight

"It's not okay," Abby said. "They're going to kill us."

It was mid-afternoon the following day. The hot sun beat down on the thatched-roof wooden house where they sat beside one another, hands and legs still bound. Other than the sound of a few birds chirping, punctuated by the odd rooster squawking in the distance, the rural, barebones dirt-floor house was quiet. Dirt stains smeared their faces, arms, legs and clothing. Gray sported a small cut above his left eye, a souvenir for a sideways glance he had shot one of the captors after the blindfolds had been removed. The red carpet treatment had ended. They were being treated like pigs in a pen.

"The Boss," as he was known, had visited in the morning. There had been questions and answers. He learned the nature of Gray's relationship with Abby, the tourist nature of Gray's arrival in Atacames, and Abby's objectives with respect to her hotel. What the Boss wanted was simple—Abby to go home with her tail between her legs, forget about the hotel, and Gray to follow. "If we arrange transport to the airport in Quito, you'll both leave?" he had asked.

Gray had nodded quickly but Abby's answer wasn't so immediate. Her initial reaction probably led to the Boss's skepticism regarding the truthfulness of the captives. "Why do you have to exploit foreigners to make a living?" she had asked in understandable Spanish.

The Boss's expression had hardened as his hand slid over a gun holster. "It's you and your people who exploit our resources," he had said, approaching threateningly to within an inch of her face.

"Abby" was the only word Gray said before she had realized the slip. She quickly apologized and promised, if they were released, they would return to Canada and never breathe a word of their captivity or the loss of the biggest investment of her life to anybody.

The Boss had stared at them long and hard, worry etched in a furrowed brow, before answering. "Tomorrow we take you to the airport."

Gray watched Abby. It didn't matter what she had said. They were probably marked for death from the very first moment of their capture. It was just too complicated for the Boss to simply release them and take their word they wouldn't squeal like pigs. Too many variables—too many loose ends. Why would he take the chance? It was much easier to kill them. No loose ends. Clean and simple. Two cases that probably would never be investigated. If they were, it would be a perfunctory and cover-up investigation at best.

"I know," Gray finally said. Nothing seemed okay anymore. "I didn't know what else to say."

"Don't worry about it," Abby said it with no conviction. She had suffered too much trauma in a foreign country where the laws did anything but favor the foreigner. Her voice had the tone of a defeated woman who knew with a dreadful certainty her days were numbered.

Gray did his best to cheer her up. "Helmut will come for us."

"How? He doesn't even know where we are. And even if he did, how's he going to get past them?" She waved a hand to a partially opened door that revealed three AK-47-armed-guards just out of earshot conversing under the shade of a tree. The guards no longer wore masks.

Abby continued: "I don't know how stupid I could be to trust the realtor who helped us. I told you, he's wanted for more sex charges and fraud in the United States, not to mention the convictions. And let's face it—there are no tourists in Atacames. If they do come, they get treated like shit and ripped off. Do you think they'll ever return? They'll tell two friends and on and on. Atacames isn't a tourist destination no more than this fucking pigpen were sitting in is. What the fuck was I thinking?"

Her eyes welled up with tears. "But I know what I did wrong. I'm too trusting. I trusted the wrong people. I'll never do that again. The school of hard knocks, eh? What's the point, anyway? How much longer do you think we have?"

Gray didn't know what to say, so he said nothing; the well of platitudes had run dry.

Through the open door, Gray saw a green Datsun 510 suddenly appear, a cloud of dust announcing its arrival. It stopped in front of the shade tree for a moment, and a man barked out some faintly audible commands. A guard climbed in and the car pulled in front of their ersatz prison and stopped.

Two unmasked men entered and trained machine guns on two frightened captives. "Get up and get in the car," one said, while the other hoisted them to their feet.

Abby was beginning to come apart. "Where are you taking us?" she asked in voice tense with anxiety.

"We're getting you cleaned up to leave Ecuador."

Gray eyed Abby as a look of resignation swept over her soft features. They were frozen to their spots.

"Get moving," a man said, striking Gray in the back of the head with the AK-47 just hard enough to reinforce that he meant business. Gray grunted as they were pushed outside and ushered into the back seat of the idling Datsun.

It sped away.

*This is it,* Gray thought. *Everything in my life has come down to this one moment—the moment of truth. It's the time I ask myself if I've lived with no regrets, accomplished the things I wanted to, loved others deeply, touched their lives in a meaningful way. What're the answers? Yes, I've lived with regrets. No, I haven't accomplished all the things I wanted to. Have I lived selfishly? Probably. Fuck, no. It can't end like this. It can't. It just can't.*

"Let's just do this," Abby said, reading the panic growing on Gray's features. Her face had become serene. She inched closer, leaning her head on Gray's shoulder. "I want to be close to you before I die."

"I love you," he blurted out. "As a friend, I mean. I know you're married."

She searched his eyes, precipitously smiling in the face of danger. "I know what you mean. I never took you for a low-life. By the way, I never asked. How did things go with Adriana? Did you fall in love?"

"No," Gray said as the car pulled off the road and into a small clearing where two shallow graves had been prepared. "A great woman—just not my type."

Now it was Abby doing the reassuring. "It's okay, Gray. It was great to meet you. I love you too, you know."

"I know."

"I'm sorry about all this."

"Forget it. I had a killer following me around. I probably put you in danger. And you didn't do any of this. I came of my own volition, for no reason other than I wanted to help a fellow Canadian. It's what we do, isn't it?"

"It's what we do," she said as the car stopped. A man opened the door, grabbing her arms roughly and hauling her out.

Gray didn't care anymore. "Easy on her—at least let us die with some dignity."

The man's eyes narrowed as he seized Gray roughly and practically dragged him from the vehicle. The men ordered them to walk toward the graves, pushing them forward and following. As they walked, Abby glanced back. "I want to die looking into his eyes, please. Shoot us at the same time."

The anger had evaporated from the executioner's features. He looked almost sorrowful. He nodded.

They stopped a few inches from the graves, sweating in the hot afternoon sun. The men, a few feet behind, aimed the AK-47s.

"Wait," Abby said. She turned to Gray. "Kiss me."

Two metallic clicks sounded.

"Where?"

"On the cheek ... on the lips, if you want. It doesn't matter anymore." He inched forward, kissed her on the lips and stared into her soulful eyes for a few seconds before they simultaneously closed their eyes.

A burst of machine-gun fire erupted and Gray shuddered, waiting for the darkness of death to snatch away his life, a life he now wished had much more meaning.

But nothing happened.

He opened his eyes. Abby's eyes were closed tightly and a peaceful smile pursed her lips.

"Drop the guns or die," Helmut said, approaching from some trees. He had fired warning shots into the sky. The executioners hurriedly trained their weapons on Helmut but only for a second. Six-foot-five Raul poked his head from the trees and stepped forward, Karen a few steps behind.

The executioners arched eyebrows at the sight of Raul, dropping their weapons instantly and raising arms to the sky. Raul's reign of terror was well-known and justifiably feared in these parts. The would-be murderers knew without a shadow of a doubt to cross him would mean the end of their lives; not to mention the demise of family members and friends. He was the undisputed lord of the criminals.

"Get the hell out of here," Raul ordered as a black SUV pulled into the clearing, stopping a few feet from the men. A passenger window rolled down. A man poked an arm out, pointed a pistol at the executioners, and asked Raul: "Should I kill them? We can put the graves to use."

Raul shook his head. He wasn't here for vengeance. These men hadn't crossed him. They had their own operation exploiting unsuspecting foreigners. It didn't interfere with his drug-smuggling operation. They knew better than to try and enter his market. He was here for two reasons. One, he had a longstanding and loyal relationship with Helmut, a former knight in his army. Two, he had made a deal with Jimmy to protect Gray in exchange for a new partnership that would expand his drug trade into regions of the United States currently controlled by the Columbian drug cartel, his biggest and fiercest competitor.

His dissatisfaction with Rocky and his rag-tag band of followers had been steadily growing. He viewed his new alliance with The Skulls as one with much more potential. Jimmy wasn't a flake like Rocky. He was a man of his word. And better still, a man who had been crossed by The Chosen Ones and had vowed revenge. He had delivered on his promise to kill Rocky. Jimmy's agenda was one that would benefit Raul immensely in the years to come.

As the executioners abandoned their weapons, hopped in the Datsun and sped away, Helmut cut Abby and Gray free. They hugged each other and hugged Helmut, thanking him profusely for saving their lives.

Helmut pointed to Karen and Raul. "I couldn't have done it without them."

"Thanks so much," Abby and Gray said in near-perfect synchronicity, acknowledging Karen and Raul.

Karen hugged Abby and Gray while Raul observed from a distance, allowing himself a token smile and a nod of acknowledgement. He was unwilling to get too close to anyone outside of his immediate sphere of influence. Living cautiously had gotten him this far, and he wasn't about to develop a new modus operandi. Rule by fear and intimidation was what kept him alive and in control.

They climbed in the back of the SUV. A driver expertly spun it around and sped away, blowing up billowing clouds of dust as he navigated the bumpy country road.

Gray studied the drug kingpin sitting silently and calmly in the front seat. His long black hair was tied back in a ponytail, his goatee neatly-trimmed. His carved facial features and high cheekbones reminded Gray of Antonio Banderas, while his intelligent brown eyes harkened back to Al Pacino. He was tall, lean and muscular. There was an air of focused resolve and determination about the man that made it abundantly clear he was not one to be trifled with.

Finally, Gray thought of something to say: "What about Strap?" he asked in Spanish, not wanting to risk offending Raul.

Raul turned his head, acknowledging Gray for the first time. "You don't have to worry about him anymore. He won't be giving you any problems."

# Chapter Thirty-Nine

"If you have any problems, I'm here to help," the shaman said, pouring portions of the thick and hallucinogenic ayahuasca into their respective cups. The orange-red sun had set just outside the small hut, and the rainforest was alive with musical screeching and whistling sounds: frogs, birds, insects, monkeys, whatever manner of living creature—insistently and loudly pronouncing their intention to communicate.

It was music to Gray's ears. *What better way to spend New Year's?* He listened to the shaman explain the ritual and watched the focused faces of Helmut and Abby preparing to be spiritually enlightened.

Deep in the Amazon jungle, they sat cross-legged on foam mattresses in a thatched-roof hut in Puerto Bolivar, a small Siona Indian village along the Cuyabeno River in the Cuyabeno Wildlife Reserve. They were near the Columbian border—Sucumbios Province, Ecuador.

After much of the jungle had been exploited and destroyed by oil and other companies, in 1979, the Ecuadorian government declared 604,000 hectares as protected rainforest, realizing the biodiversity of the region much too precious to be exploited for commercial gain.

After the near-fatal encounter with the Ecuadorian squatters, not to mention the likes of Strap, Gray had decided to make good on his intention to see the shaman. He had his reasons. He wanted to find meaning in his life, wanted to understand why he had been unable to develop a deep and meaningful relationship with a woman, wanted more confidence, and wanted to know why he still had a nagging but pervasive feeling of impending danger.

He had no logical reason for it. Derrick had informed him, as far as Jimmy knew, Strap had been dealt with (he didn't bother asking in what fashion). Jimmy's criminal urges had gotten the better of him. He had left Julie, rejoined The Skulls, and was forging a powerful drug-smuggling alliance with Raul and his organized, efficient underlings.

For his part, Raul had given Gray and Abby two weeks to clear out of Ecuador. He assured them he would see to it officials would allow them to leave the country. Raul had warned Abby in no uncertain terms that, should she decide to renew the fight for her hotel, she would do so at her own peril. He would offer her no protection if she did not heed his advice.

At first she had seemed reluctant to comply. But the news that had broken her will and resolve was a call from her mother-in-law saying her husband Spencer had been killed by a bomb while on a mission in Afghanistan—blown to pieces, his body unrecognizable. Initially planning to return home immediately, Abby had instead decided to visit the shaman first—she wanted to contact Spencer, say her last goodbyes and make some kind of peace. Besides, it would be a while before what was left of his body would be returned to Canada. It had been her preoccupation with the hotel that had led to her kidnapping, which had resulted in missed phone calls from Spencer—phone calls that turned out to be his last. She was overcome with grief and guilt and viewed the ayahuasca healing ceremony as her only hope to come to terms with Spencer's tragic death.

And Helmut had his own reasons for being here; many of which he had already discussed with Gray. Helmut realized just how unhappy he was with Ecuadorian culture, how angry he became when he iterated the formidable cultural differences. And those anger issues were starting to result in conflicts with his son Domingo and his wife Alejandra. To continue on his path would surely mean an end to a marriage he had every intention of preserving. It was one of the very few good things in his life. He lived in Ecuador. If he was going to stay, he would have to find a way to enjoy it. His happiness and wellbeing were on the line. He had to change his perception or leave.

They had prepared for the ceremony for two days, fasting and eating only natural foods prescribed by the shaman. They slept in small barebones cabins in the village, populated by about fifty native Indians.

"I want to be clear about a few things," explained the shaman, who was dressed in traditional bright red regalia with beaded necklaces dangling from his neck. He exuded a powerful inner peace and happiness that was infectious. Either he was higher than a kite or naturally at peace with himself. "Ayahuasca, a concoction of jungle plants, is not to be taken experimentally or without the guidance of a shaman. We don't manufacture it to sell it commercially. It's strictly for medicinal purposes, part of an ancient ritual that can cure any illness, psychological or physical. Some German women experimented with it on their own in a nearby village recently and the results were disastrous. They stripped off clothes, yelled and screamed for most of the night. One ended up in an insane asylum.

"I hope when you told me your reasons for being here you were all being truthful. This is not a place for deception or games. Do you understand?" He sat in front of them, cross-legged, on a small mat, smoking a mapacho: a large cigar that emitted spirit-cleansing smoke. He studied their expectant faces.

In turn, they nodded.

"Ayahuasca will energize you, connect you with the good spirits, and rid your body of the bad spirits," the shaman said. "It will put you in touch with the plants, animals, and nature, and show you another plane of existence. But you have to be open to it. Don't fight it. And don't be afraid. I'm here to help you, as I said. I can sense when bad energy or bad spirits are trying to overpower the good. I will help you rid yourself of these evil influences, should they materialize. Be brave. With my help, the help of ayahuasca, you'll learn to save yourself."

Gray knew a little about ayahuasca, the so-called medicine so many people claimed was responsible for spiritual enlightenment. He'd read reports it also cured everything from cocaine addiction to cancer. He'd heard stories of people taking it and embarking down a path they thought was one of spiritual enlightenment but ended up being nothing more than a prolonged experimentation with all manner of psychotropic drugs available in the jungle—giving up on goals, personal growth and development and choosing instead to live stoned on mind-altering substances with the mistaken belief they were somehow living on a higher plane—a plane that had become disconnected from reality and indeed was nose-diving into a crash-and-burn landing. Often they returned to civilization broke and psychologically scarred, with no interest in pursuing a career, bettering their lives, or helping their fellow man.

He had no idea if he was in store for that kind of experience. He thought it had a lot to do with the individual and intangibles like emotional intelligence. He hoped he was mentally tough enough for ayahuasca. On a gut level, he knew one thing for sure: he would be thrust into a hell in which he would have to confront his demons, real and imagined. He gritted his teeth. *Be brave.*

A man entered with three vomit buckets and three rolls of toilet paper used to wipe their faces after vomiting. He placed them beside the foam mattresses and disappeared.

The shaman smoked, blowing swirling rings that hung in the air, slowly stretching and dispersing.

But for a flickering kerosene lamp, darkness had enveloped the small hut. The resounding calls of the insects and animals grew louder, as if they too were readying for the ancient healing ceremony to commence.

The shaman opened the bottle of ayahuasca, poured it into tiny cups, exhaled smoke over it as a blessing ritual and handed a cup to each patient. He began a ritualistic chant that lasted about ten minutes. Then he instructed them to drink.

Gray drank the thick brown sludge—a taste not unlike a sweet and sour prune juice—and suppressed an immediate urge to vomit into the bucket.

When they finished drinking, the shaman extinguished the kerosene lamp and near-total blackness enveloped the small hut.

******

The shaman shakes his leaf rattle and sings a spirit song, interspersed with a ritualistic chant.

Gray closes his eyes. For twenty minutes nothing happens. Then a bright green hue permeates the blackness behind his eyes. He opens them. The green hue is superimposed over the surroundings, creating a distorted but pleasant reality. Then vibrantly-colored, multi-dimensional geometric shapes dance in front of him, expanding and contracting in a stunningly beautiful symmetry.

He closes his eyes and the brightly-colored shapes continue dancing. He opens them again. They are superimposed over the shaman, the ceiling beams of the hut, Abby and Helmut, lying on their respective mats. Gray is conscious of Abby's rapid breathing while at the same time mesmerized by the brilliant display of color.

Suddenly he understands the calls of the jungle. The animals and insects communicate with him in a way that floods his body with a feeling of harmony with nature. They sing to him—a singular and powerful message of love. He sees through the hut at the trees, stars and moon and the extraordinary beauty of the jungle. He can't explain it but there is oneness with nature he has never felt before. It changes him. He stares at the tree in the distance. It looms larger than life and enters the hut. He touches it, puts his head on it and a powerful wave of love for the tree sweeps through his body. On some level, there is a message to preserve and respect Mother Nature; but it's much more powerful than mere words can describe.

Abby's shrill scream snaps his focus away from the image. Abby is writhing on the mat, uttering some incomprehensible chant like a possessed demon. She is convulsing and the shaman has her pinned down. His words are distant but comprehensible: "I'm here Abby. I see the demon. Release him from your body."

A knot forms in Gray's stomach and he reaches for the bucket. As he vomits he hears Abby's screams, the shaman's reassuring words and Helmut splashing vomit in his bucket. Abby utters a short, shrill scream, grows quiet for a second, then jerks up, reaches for the bucket and vomits a stream of black liquid; although her only food that day was mango juice, water and a fruit salad.

Then the all-consuming blackness comes, first in the form of a black all-encompassing wall. Gray sees it and turns to run. But another wall springs up, darker, thicker and closer than before. He tries to flee but is caught in the power and the fury of the black abyss and sucked down into a fiery black hell where demon-like faces scream and howl, serpents hiss and large, sinister black eyes watch and wait.

He drops onto a dungeon-like cold floor, the screams of terror saturating his being. His heart pounds in his chest. His hands shake, then his legs, then he convulses uncontrollably on the small mat and the pain is so excruciating he wants to die so it will end. Three dark hooded figures are silhouetted in the darkness. A fourth, with eyes of blazing fury, emerges. Gray is sure it's the devil himself. "You'll never leave this dark place."

Gray is writhing and moaning. Now he can feel the hands on him—the shaman, holding him down and chanting to drive the devil away. The pain is unbearable now, like a million tiny needles piercing his skin. Gray is sure he'll explode with the force. He hears his own voice, distant. "I need some help here."

"I'm here. Release the demon," the shaman says, pinning his arms while someone else holds his legs.

The devil speaks—accompanied by fresh stabs of pain—like a knitting needle penetrating his heart: "You'll never leave this dark place."

The devil's face contorts into the face of—no, no, it can't be—The Strap. His long straggly hair is greasy and black, his ugly features grossly misshapen and exaggerated. "You're dead."

Gray fights against the intense physical pain, hundreds of screaming and haunting images and a terrifying feeling of despair, darkness and evil. The Strap steps forward. "It's over."

*It's in your mind. It's not real.* But it feels dreadfully real.

"That's it," the shaman says. "Exorcise the demon." Through the suffocating blackness, Gray suddenly sees a pinhole-sized light far away. The shaman begins chanting, reaches a hand inside Gray's throat, pulls hard and extracts a black hissing serpent.

Gray gasps for breath as the oversized tail slops out of his gaping mouth, snapping around, hissing, poised for another attack. But the shaman waves a hand and the hissing serpent vanishes.

The small pinhole of light grows and the excruciating pain subsides. Suddenly Gray is catapulted out of the black hole, transforms into a large black bird, flaps his wings and soars into the starlit sky toward the glowing moonlight. Floating in the sky before him is a brilliant, glowing white face of a man with a white beard, his features calm and serene. "You are loved," he says. Gray morphs into himself again and walks on a star toward the deity's embrace. Gray hugs him. "You are loved," the unknown deity says again, infusing Gray's body with an overwhelmingly positive energy and love for everybody, everything. As he floats down to the hut, he feels the tears of joy spreading across his cheeks and knows he cannot stop them.

He is on the mat again and the brilliant, dancing geometric hues of color bombard his senses—a kaleidoscope of colorful brilliance beyond imagination. He smiles. Adriana's face appears. She smiles. "I know I'm not the one. Be honest with me."

He frowns and her face becomes one with a geometric orange pattern and fades away.

Karina's face emerges out of a floating array of brilliant red roses. "I want you Gray. Tell me what you want. Be honest." The roses explode into a million tiny red dots and Karina's face vanishes.

Gray feels himself standing as a part of him senses the shaman comforting Helmut, holding him down—chanting as Helmut yells, screams and bucks like a raging bull. Gray glances back. Abby, suffused with a brilliant orange glow, is lying peacefully on the mat. A man in a military uniform floats above her—Spencer. He hears animated voices. They are talking, saying goodbye.

He glances at the shaman pinning Helmut, who has begun frothing at the mouth, hundreds of angry demons swirling around and out of his body. But Gray is far removed from the visions of his friends. They have their paths, he his. Feeling possessed by a benevolent spirit, he leaves the hut, steps into the small clearing, and stares up into the sky. The stars rocket across the darkness, trailed by brilliant beams of color. It's overwhelming to the senses and Gray feels himself kneeling in the grass, crossing his hands and praying.

But it doesn't feel like him praying. He never prays. It feels like he is channeling the energy of some divine entity that he'll never fully comprehend. Divine energy, a deep communion, love and understanding for nature and humankind. An epiphany. True spiritual enlightenment. Who would believe it if he told them? He hears the words, but they are not his anymore. "I know this is the beginning of a new life. Thank you. Amen."

The revelation brings fresh tears to his eyes and he stands up, barely conscious that he can feel no more pain in the tailbone that had been aching ever since the kidnapping in Atacames. He is caught in the moment, in love with the jungle, in love with himself, in love with the whole world. He wants to give back but he has no idea how.

But a voice says: "Don't worry. You'll know when the time comes."

# Chapter Forty

*I'll know when the time comes. Know what?* But as Gray lay on the mattress on the floor of his rustic jungle cabin the next morning, churning the words around in his mind, the meaning finally did become clear. He knew his calling was not about self-serving ends anymore. It was about helping people. The ayahuasca session had made that abundantly clear. And he would know what that calling was when the time came. For now, that would have to be enough.

But one thing was clear. Last night in a dream, after the ceremony had ended, Lola's image had appeared high in the sky, in an eerily glowing moon. But her previous disapproving frown had been replaced by something else—a hopeful smile. And, although most of the details of the dream were sketchy, Gray remembered her words clearly. "You're not dead anymore, Gray. You're finally alive." Then her image had mysteriously morphed into a black, grinning serpent and suddenly vanished. He remembered now why that relationship—that at the time held so much potential—had ended. He had been too selfishly preoccupied with his own life, with little regard for the well-being of family, friends and loved ones.

*But not anymore.*

He pushed away the mosquito netting, leaped up from the mattress with a renewed vigor and energy and went into the bathroom. There was an underlying peace and confidence in his disposition he was also cognizant of. The ayahuasca session had been a life-changing experience, and he was elated that he had followed through with his plans. He couldn't wait to sit down for breakfast with Helmut and Abby and hear about their experiences.

He looked at his image in the mirror. He thought he saw a few gray hairs, but dismissed the thought as soon as it emerged. *Age is just a fucking number. You're as old as you feel.* And he felt like he was twenty-five again. He also noticed his eyes—previously bloodshot and unfocused—now alert and focused. It might have been his imagination, but it seemed the small dark circles under his eyes had all but disappeared. *I'm getting younger by the day.*

He climbed into the shower, relishing the cold, refreshing water washing away the last remnants of sleep. It had been a deep REM sleep, one of the very few he had enjoyed since his arrival.

Later, he sat down for breakfast with Abby and Helmut in a thatched-roof open hut by the river. A few cumulus clouds floated lazily by and the sun shone brilliantly overhead. They sat at a wooden picnic bench while nearby, native children swam in the river. Adults washed clothes in the water while others shampooed their hair. A few roosters cock-a-doodle-dooed in the village, while the insects, birds and frogs commenced a shrill morning dialogue.

Abby positively glowed, while Helmut still had a disturbing darkness deep within his blue eyes. Gray wished them a Happy New Year. They nodded and returned the greeting.

"Do you know it's the year of the snake?" Gray said. "It's going to be a good year."

"The snake?" Abby asked. "That's not a good thing, is it?"

"Actually it is. Snakes shed their skin. They're a symbol of new beginnings, healing, rebirth, transformation. Even magic, among other things."

"What other things?" Helmut asked.

"People seem to conjure up negative images when they think of a snake," Gray said. "They're misunderstood. But the snake is actually one of my favorite reptiles. For a long time, I never understood why. But then I learned they also symbolize fertility, health and healing, protection, and immortality."

"Speaking of immortality, I came to grips with my own mortality and Spencer's mortality last night," Abby said.

"I actually saw him, too," Gray said. "Tell me all the details."

She told the story of brilliant hues of color enveloping her senses before her world suddenly turned dark and horrifying. She felt pain and suffering the likes of which she had never experienced. Her stomach had twisted and turned. She vomited and vomited until there was nothing left to purge. But still, it felt like some dark energy needed to be released. At one point the dark energy overpowered her will, and she thought she was going to die. "But then, all at once, I accepted this. I thought, if it's my time I guess I'll go. And I was okay with it. I was ready. Anyway, after that acceptance, it seemed a gigantic dark weight was lifted off my shoulders, and I experienced this incredible feeling of bliss and inner peace."

"I felt something like that," Gray said. "I think we had similar experiences. Sorry, go on."

"That's when I saw Spencer floating above me. And he was smiling. Told me everything's okay, he's in a good place. We said our goodbyes." Her eyes welled with tears as she relived the experience. "He told me he loves me ... that I should get on with my life, forget about the hotel. It's not his fault, but he apologized for not being there. How could he possibly be there? He was serving our country, pursuing something he perceives as honorable. Protecting us. That's just how he was, though ..."

"But it's okay now?" Gray asked. "You're okay now?"

Abby wiped her eyes. "Sorry. Yeah, I'm okay. I've found peace with it. I've realized in the whole scheme of things, the hotel means nothing. It's just money anyway. I made it, I lost it. I can make it back, if that's what I decide to do."

"You're happy then?" Gray asked.

"Actually, I don't ever remember being this happy," Abby said. "It's about time I did something meaningful with my life."

"That's quite the epiphany," Helmut said, turning to Gray. "What about you? What was your experience like?"

Gray recounted the events of his experience, starting with the green hue, brilliant colors, the dark and evil place where he thought he would die and how the shaman at one point put his hand in his mouth and extracted the serpent, the hissing snake which had released all the black energy. He went over the events of how he had seen the evil face of Strap in the black abyss, and recounted, for Abby's benefit, how Strap had stalked him around Ecuador, trying to kill him. It suddenly dawned on him the snake, an image he had automatically construed as evil, might have rescued him from Strap. "You know, something just occurred to me. Strap changed into the serpent. The shaman removed the serpent. Maybe the serpent possessed Strap and removed his dark energy from my body. I never thought of it that way before. But it's the year of the snake. It all fits."

"I guess you can read a lot into it," Helmut said. "I don't know about you guys, but for my part I'm not done. I went down into a dark pit of hell, saw a glimmer of hope in the form of a needle of white light, but it was snuffed out and darkness prevailed. I don't want to go into a lot of detail. It's hard for me. There were some fleeting images of love or something, some sort of a blissful state, but it seemed a long way off."

"You're staying?" Gray asked.

Helmut nodded. "I need a lot more work. My issues run deep. You only know the beginnings of my story, not the whole thing. Do you know I used to be connected to the Columbian drug cartel? That's how I met Raul. I used to hang around with assassins who would kill you for fifty bucks."

A silence fell over the table for a few moments. The children laughed and played in the river.

"A glimmer of hope may turn into a ray of sunshine," Abby finally said.

"That's why I'm here," Helmut said. "If the ceremony last night did anything, it showed me how fucked-up I really am ... how much shit I need to get out. I need to be like the snake, shed my skin and make a new beginning. What are you guys going to do?"

"I don't have any plans," Abby said. "Not for the next few days, anyway." She looked at Gray.

"I was thinking of hanging around the Guacamayo Ecolodge near here for a few days. Fifty bucks a night includes a room and three meals. I hear the guides are really good. They'll take you to Indian villages, piranha fishing, walks through the jungle, swimming in the lagoon, searching for alligators, fresh water dolphins, all kinds of things. I'm here now ... and I feel a strong connection to the jungle. I love the vibe, love the energy. I think I'll hang around a bit."

"Sounds good to me," Abby said. "Don't mind if I join you?"

"I was hoping you would."

A half hour later, they stood on a small wooden dock on the river, belongings packed. A long motorized canoe glided in, a driver at the back controlling the motor while another man sat starboard, the eyes of the boat.

Abby hugged the shaman, who smiled warmly. His wife and three children stood behind, watching the departure. "Thank you very much," Abby said.

"You're welcome. I hope you find your path."

"I've found it, thanks to you."

She turned to Helmut and hugged him warmly. "Thanks for saving my life. I love you."

A lone tear formed in the big man's left eye. "No problem. Best of luck."

Gray helped Abby into the boat and turned to the shaman. "I don't know what to say. But thanks. You're a miracle worker." He shook the healer's hand.

"Peace be with you," the shaman said, smiling. He turned and left.

Gray turned to Helmut. "Thanks so much, buddy, for everything. If we can, maybe we'll visit."

They shook hands. "I'd like that."

To the waves and smiles of a dozen people who had gathered to bid farewell, the canoe chugged up river, Gray and Abby sitting next to one another contentedly on the cushioned bench-style seats.

Gray was amazed at the thick foliage, the calling of the jungle creatures, the beauty of the river and how adeptly the captain navigated the twenty-foot canoe around the many twists and turns of the life-giving waterway. At one point, in a shallow section of the river, the canoe got stuck on some tangled branches from a downed tree. They were in a narrow section, thick with overhanging trees and vines, a lone canoe in a powerful, awe-inspiring and mysterious jungle.

The driver popped the rotor out of the water and turned to them. "We need more rain. Lack of water makes passage difficult. Could you stand and rock the boat?"

They stood up, moving from side to side. The boat swayed. The man popped the motor in the water, revved it, but it wouldn't move. It had bottomed out. He stepped into shallow water and started pushing. It inched forward slightly and stopped.

Gray heard a scream that he thought was a monkey call before he knew what hit him. By that time it was too late. Strap lunged out of a tree, wielding a combat knife. Gray grimaced as the blade penetrated the top of his shoulder and fell into the water, Strap landing on top of him and flailing the knife wildly.

A man with an assault rifle emerged from the riverbank and pointed it at the three stunned onlookers. "Don't move or you die."

Gray swallowed mouthfuls of water as his head went under—it was do-or-die time. He thrust his hands forward.

Raising the knife, Strap attacked. Gray grabbed at it and felt a stinging pain across the palm of his hand as it sliced through and grazed his chest—a near miss. In a flash, Strap raised the knife again and plunged it down, straight for Gray's throat. Gray turned his head and the momentum drove the knife into the thick, mucky river bottom.

*It's my chance.* While Strap extracted the knife, which snagged on some underwater vines for a split-second—just long enough for Gray to scramble to his feet—Gray stepped forward and kicked him hard in the side of the head.

Strap stumbled back.

As he attacked Strap, he heard the deafening rattle of machine-gun fire, saw Abby fall out of the canoe, her lifeless body splashing into the water.

It enraged him.

He throttled Strap's neck and choked with a surging energy. "You fucking bastard ... you fucking bastard. You're going to die. This time you're going to die."

He felt the knife slice into his bicep and he elbowed the attacking wrist. Strap's hand released the blade, now imbedded in Gray's arm. He continued choking the man, relishing the life draining from his ugly, twisted and psychotic features.

*Thwack, thwack.*

With his remaining energy, Strap had fished out a chunk of wood from the river and clobbered Gray hard over the head. Gray felt his world fading to black as he fell, splashing into the river on his back. Through the muddy, shallow water, he saw the distorted face of Strap crouching above him, the log raised for the final crushing blow.

Gray opened his mouth, swallowed muddy water, blew bubbles, and the world as he knew it faded away. *You're dead. He was right. I'm dead.*

Strap raised the log. Just then, a green Anaconda dropped from an overhanging tree branch, its twenty-five foot mass twisting around Strap's neck—his entire body—swiftly and efficiently. Dropping the log, falling backward, Strap gasped for breath as the boa-constrictor suffocated the life out of him.

The armed man raised the AK-47, but a six-meter alligator slithered rapidly through shallow water and leaped into the air, clamping its massive jaws on the arm holding the weapon. The man screamed, but the beast dragged him into the water. There was furious splashing for a short time, and then a large pool of blood fanned out into the muddy brown water. The river grew quiet.

This afternoon, the jungle predators would be feasting on human flesh.

# EPILOGUE

"It was a flesh wound," Gray said. *Like the other ones, fortunately.* He was responding to a question from his realtor a month later as he put the final initials on a contract for the sale of his suburban bungalow in Calgary. Sitting at the kitchen table that Friday afternoon, snowflakes drifting lazily to the ground outside, Bill Baxter had pointed to the large scar on the palm of Gray's right hand and asked how he got it.

"A flesh wound? From what?" Bill asked, looking all prim and proper in a black suit, crisp white starched shirt, matching black tie. He gathered up the contract, stood and prepared to leave.

Gray walked him to the door. Opening it, he said: "A rumble in the jungle. Maybe I'll tell you about it sometime."

Closing the door, he flipped open his palm and studied the three-inch scar. He had been lucky; it had healed nicely. He felt like a new man after the Ecuadorian trip—more spiritually aware of his path. On reflection, he also realized Ecuadorians at their core were just like everyone else. People were people, the world over. Perhaps many viewed gringos as the great exploiters and harbored some uncertainty about them? In many ways, the Ecuadorian people had their reasons.

*And Look at America,* Gray thought. *Crazy with guns. Everyone is killing everyone else.* And he had recently read an article claiming violent crime in Ecuador was not that common.

Sure, there were dangerous areas, dangerous people, but what country doesn't have its dangers?

If you took the time to get to know Ecuadorians, break down some of their walls, they wanted the same things as everyone else: security, happiness, love, the ability to provide for their families, maybe spiritual enlightenment. He thought North Americans could learn a thing or two about love from these people. Their family bonds—for the most part—were much tighter than North American family ties, at least Canadians.

Entering his office, he scratched his head: *What was I reading the other day? One in three Canadian households is a single-person household. How many of them are single? Is that any way to live your life?*

He cleared paper from his desk. He had work to do. After arriving home miraculously with his life, he had immediately listed his house for sale and sent out resumes—resumes geared to writing for humanitarian reasons. And one of them had panned out. A heroin-addiction center in Vancouver had responded. He had flown to the city and had secured a job as a public relations officer for the government-funded community-service organization. Part of the arrangement was that when he wasn't writing press releases for the center, he would train to become a drug-addiction counselor. At least now, he had a way of giving back to the world. He would be leaving to begin his new life in a month.

*Which reminds me,* he thought. *I have some calls to make.* He picked up the phone and dialed. Three rings later, Ray, still living in Atacames, answered in his husky voice: "How you doing, my friend?"

"I'm good as gold—goes with the territory. You?"

"At least I'm on the wagon now. And, I've seen some qualities in Karen I didn't know existed before. You were right."

"What do you mean?"

"Remember—if you can't be with the one you love, love the one you're with."

"I didn't know what I was talking about then."

"But you made me realize something."

"What's that?"

"That I actually *do* love her. She's an amazing woman, you know."

"Karen saved my life. I'm eternally grateful for that."

"Did your house deal go through?"

"Yes. I get paid in a month. You still plan on opening that convenience store?"

"I'd like to. I'm not doing anything now."

Gray had promised to loan Ray the start-up money, help a friend out of a financial dilemma; give him back some self-worth. "Once I get paid, I'll wire you the ten thousand."

"Thanks, Gray. You have no idea what this means to me. It'll give me a new lease on life."

Gray hung up, smiling. Who else had received a new lease on life? Jimmy had disappeared underground. Two other more members of The Chosen Ones had been murdered. Jimmy had forged a strong alliance with Raul and rumor had it he was leaving for Ecuador in a few days. Gray scratched the stubble on his chin. It would be good to leave all this bad energy behind.

Like Helmut had done. After ten days of ayahuasca sessions, he had emerged a spiritually enlightened person, a new man. His marriage had improved, he was much more adjusted to Ecuadorian culture, and he had brought in a partner and opened a bar in *La Mariscal* in Quito, a cosmopolitan and culturally rich district of the city Gray still had a fondness for. He loved the nightlife and, despite the dangers, was drawn to the vibe. He had enjoyed watching the street life in Plaza Foche, drinking café lattes, chatting with expats and locals, solving all the world's problems.

Gray knew he had a long way to go, but at least he was discarding baggage. Two weeks after his return, he had called Adriana and explained to her that, while he had enjoyed their time immensely, there was no point in filling her head with false expectations. With so many new and interesting places in the world to visit, he had no idea if he would ever return to Ecuador. He hoped they could remain friends, he had said.

Her reaction was unexpected: "I totally understand. And I appreciate your honesty. I had an amazing time with you as well, and I hope we can be friends. I want to be friends. I think you're an amazing person and I can't understand why you're still single."

But it was something he was hoping to change. He checked his Skype contacts. *Good. She's online.* He had maintained a regular communication with Karina. He clicked the call button. After two rings, a face he found strikingly beautiful came into focus. He had told her most of the Ecuadorian ordeal. She was impressed with all the positive changes he was making in his life.

But there was one thing left to say. After a minute of small talk, he got to the point. "Honey, I sold my house."

"That's great."

"It is. There's something I'd like to do, now that it's sold."

There was a moment's pause while her soft features grew serious. "What's that?"

"I have some time before my new job starts. I'd like to come and see you."

Karina smiled warmly. "I was hoping you'd say that."

"I can't wait to see you. I miss you."

"Me too."

They talked about dates and different sightseeing possibilities.

"The only sight I want to see is you," Gray said. He was serious.

A few minutes later, he hung up the phone. A pleasant tingly feeling permeated his body and mind. He scratched his stubble and went into the kitchen, where he refilled his coffee mug. Returning to his office, he marveled at the beauty of the snowflakes creating the blanket of pure white outside. *Funny that. I never liked snow before.*

He noticed an incoming text message: *Call me. Did your house sell?*

He grinned while dialing. It was a message from a friend he hadn't spoken to in a few weeks.

She picked up on the first ring. "Gray, how are you?"

"Very well, Abby. Very well indeed. I sold my house."

"Congratulations."

As it turned out, the bullet from the AK-47 had only grazed Abby's head, a mere flesh wound. She had plunged into the water, faking her own death. She too, had been one of the lucky ones.

They chatted for a few minutes, getting caught up on each other's lives. Gray spoke of his romantic interest in Karina, and said he had a new job with the potential for far more humanitarian endeavors.

"Me too," she said excitedly.

"You too? What're you doing?"

"I'm returning to the jungle—this time to Peru. I got offered a job at an ayahuasca healing center. I'm going to train to become a shaman."

"That's awesome. Congratulations."

Hanging up, he realized for the first time he had been right about the snake. In his ayahuasca vision—and in reality—the snake had ended Strap's life.

And Lola, morphing into the grinning snake, had been right all along. Gray just didn't understand the dream at the time. He *was* dead. But now he was very much alive.

It was finally time to forget The Strap.

The Strap was dead, replaced by The Year of the Snake—*my year of rebirth. No. Our year of rebirth.*

## Also by William Blackwell

*Phantom Rage, Poison Rage, Infected Rage*
*Nightmare's Edge*
*Resurrection Point*
*Brainstorm*
*Rule 14*
*Assaulted Souls*
*Assaulted Souls II*
*Assaulted Souls III*
*Blood Curse*
*Black Dawn*
*The Strap*
*The End is Nigh*
*Orgon Conclusion*
*Freaky Franky*
*The Witch's Tombstone*
*The Dark Menace*
*Tales of Damnation*
*In Your Dreams*
*Macabre Alley*
*A Head for an Eye*

## *Freaky Franky* Preview

"If you're looking for a horror with a slice of religion, I recommend this book. It's one of the greatest horror novels I've ever read and it's not a cliché plot. I rate this book 10/10." Goodreads

When an enigmatic town doctor saves the life of Anisa Worthington's dying son, she abandons Christianity in favor of devotion to the cult of Saint Death. Some believe the mysterious skeleton saint will protect their loved ones; help in matters of the heart; provide abundant happiness, health, wealth and justice.

But others, including the Catholic Church, call it blasphemous, evil and satanic.

Anisa introduces Saint Death to troubled Catholic friend Helen Randon and strange things begin happening. One of Helen's enemies is brutally murdered and residents of Montague, a peaceful little town in Prince Edward Island, begin plotting to rid the Bible belt of apostates.

Anisa suspects Helen is perverting the good tenets of Saint Death but, before she can act, a terrible nightmare propels her to the Dominican Republic in search of Freaky Franky, her long-lost and unstable brother, who mysteriously disappeared without a trace twenty years ago.

To her horror, Anisa learns Freaky Franky is also worshiping Saint Death with evil intentions. As a fanatical and hell-bent lynch mob tightens the noose, mysterious murders begin occurring all around Anisa. Unsure about who's an enemy and who's an ally, she's thrust into a violent battle to save her life as well as the lives of her unpredictable friends and brother.

## About the Author

Canadian dark fiction author William Blackwell studied journalism at Mount Royal University and English literature at The University of British Columbia. He worked as a journalist for many years before pursuing his passion for storytelling. His novels have been characterized as graphic, edgy, and at times terrifying. Currently living on a secluded acreage on Prince Edward Island, Blackwell finds much of his inspiration from Mother Nature, odd people, traveling, and bizarre nightmares.

## Author Comments

Thank you for reading this book. I would be eternally grateful if you would post a book review on your favorite book retailer website. A positive review is the highest compliment a writer can receive. Reviews are crucial to the success of any author. You don't have to say much. A few sentences will suffice.

In other news, I have a gift for you. Complete the signup form contained in the link below with your name and email address and download a FREE copy of *Resurrection Point*, a dark tale about the horrifying consequences of experimenting with death and resurrection. You're only agreeing to be kept up to date on blog posts, new releases, and freebies. I promise I won't spam you and you can unsubscribe at any time.

Thanks again for your support.

http://www.wblackwell.com/free-ebook/